just like february

february

a novel

Deborah Batterman

Published by SparkPress, a BookSparks imprint,
A division of SparkPoint Studio, LLC
Tempe, Arizona, USA, 85281
www.gosparkpress.com

Published 2018

Printed in the United States of America

ISBN: 978-1-943006-48-9 (pbk)
ISBN: 978-1-943006-49-6 (e-bk)
Library of Congress Control Number: 2017960219

Formatting by Katherine Lloyd, The DESK

For Lew and Sara

contents

a spoon and six dolls *1*

a family undivided *37*

postcards 55

postscript *127*

skeletons in the closet. *131*

womanhood *163*

endings. 191

beginnings *217*

epilogue *245*

about the author *247*

a spoon and six dolls

The summer I was born, Neil Armstrong walked on the moon, Ted Kennedy put Chappaquiddick on the map, and my parents, along with my uncle Jake and me, set out on a pilgrimage to Woodstock. Only Jake got there. Midway across the George Washington Bridge, our car began sputtering, losing steam by the second. We made it just to the tollbooth. My father, who'd had reservations from the start, saw this as a sign that maybe the trip just wasn't meant to be. My mother accused him of being smug.

Cars passed by, there were offers of help, but the engine had died. Jake, at my mother's insistence, hitched a ride with a blond girl in a red Corvette. "I want details," she said, kissing him goodbye. It took two hours before a tow truck finally came and carted my parents and me back to Brooklyn. I wailed, my mother was silent, my father and the driver talked. "I could kick myself for not hitching a ride, too," my mother always says when she tells the story of that infamous day. Her voice is like glass: cold, clear, transparent with subtext. *If it wasn't for your father . . .* Eventually she softens; the news reports, she had to admit, gave her second thoughts about being in a sea of mud with a nursing infant. Besides, my father had recently purchased an elaborate new sound system. All weekend long they listened to the crystal-clear voices of their favorite WNEW-FM disc jockeys bring up-to-the-minute coverage right into our living room; it was almost like being there.

A need to rationalize any simple twist of fate colors my father's perspective. "The last time I saw Jimmy Briggs was on a chopper leaving Saigon, and here he turns up driving the tow truck that takes us back home—that's more than just coincidence, even for a cynic like me." All the way back to Brooklyn, they talked about the endless nights and rain-drenched days in Vietnam, the buddies who had died and those still alive. They talked about Woodstock, too, which they agreed was nothing more than one big antiwar demonstration masquerading as a party. Not that my father wouldn't have loved to hear Jimi Hendrix and the Butterfield Blues Band and Santana and the Jefferson Airplane live, on the same stage, within the space of a few days.

The starting point for Jake is a spoon he came across at a small shop in the town of Woodstock. Candy, the girl he drove up with, wanted to go antiquing before heading over to Yasgur's farm. So they browsed antique shops—she bought an old piano stool that barely fit in the trunk of her car—had lunch in a funky café, and stopped in a gift shop, where Jake found the small wooden spoon that he bought as a present for me.

Shaped like a flower petal and inscribed with the words MAKE LOVE, NOT WAR, the spoon ended up being more ornament than utensil. My mother kept it on the windowsill in the kitchen, next to the stained-glass sun that illuminated the window like a bright, smiling orange. Supposedly, it was the source of my first word. Squirming in my high chair, I'd point to the spoon. "Boon," I'd say, refusing to eat until my mother gave me the smooth-as-pearl spoon to hold while she fed me. When it came time for me to start feeding myself, the spoon mysteriously disappeared. My mother accused my father of "accidentally" throwing it away. My grandmother, who had recently bought me a silver spoon from Tiffany, said it was just as well. "Wood splinters," she reminded my mother. The admonishment irked my mother almost as much as did the disappearance of her one and only memento from Woodstock. "And silver tarnishes," she said.

The summer I turned five, I stopped—quite suddenly, it seemed—playing with my dolls. To my mother, a social worker, it was no big deal, just some latent anxiety over my parents' impending marriage. My grandmother, who was less prone to psychoanalyzing my behavior, immediately went out and bought me a new doll. The way she saw it, I was bored with dolls that looked like babies, so she got me a "more mature" one, with a silky black bob for hair and a red satin dress. Instead of putting her in the large basket where I kept my other dolls, I placed her on a green wicker chair in my room. The chair had a flat floral pillow, and, enthroned in it, she took on the aura of a princess.

I told my grandmother I loved the doll, just so she'd stop saying, "I hope you don't think you're too old for dolls already." Giving up dolls, she believed, meant I was growing up too quickly. Like my mother, though, she had totally misjudged the situation. Six tiny dolls, not the kind you could cradle in your arms and squeeze and pretend to feed, had captured my imagination.

"Every night when you go to sleep," said Jake, when he gave me the small painted box that contained the dolls, "you tell these dolls your troubles and they take them away." He had recently returned from a trip to Guatemala, filled with stories about dusty pyramids jutting through lush jungle foliage, and a king known as Great-Jaguar-Paw, and a ten-year-old girl named Carmelita who lived in a village called Chichicastenango. I laughed, tried repeating the tongue twister—Chichi . . . Chichicha . . . Chichicas—and laughed some more. It was Carmelita who, after a dream one night in which she saw herself flying on the back of a bird, had made the cloth purse that Jake gave me along with the dolls. I'd never seen anything like it. Running along the edge was a braid of black cotton that framed the remarkable bird woven into cross-stitches of red, blue, green, and purple. I traced the bird with my finger. Its beak was too large for its body, and its feathers, spread across the purse, reminded me of a king's robe. In short, there was nothing about this image that should have conjured flight. But, like all things that become the sum of their parts, the bird soared.

The name of this rare bird, Jake told me, was quetzal, and once, when he was sitting in the square with Carmelita, he saw one perched in a tree. He was about to take a picture, with Carmelita in the foreground, when, out of nowhere, it seemed, like a small boulder, her grandmother came barreling in front of him. She didn't say a word to Jake, just put her hand over the camera lens, and when he asked her why she did it, she pursed her lips, looked him squarely in the eyes, and said, with all the wisdom and superstition of a culture he later came to understand, "If you take a picture, you take away the soul." She then handed Jake a box of trouble dolls. For a child he loved.

I immediately turned my attention to the dolls, which lay in a jumble on the coffee table. At first glance, there was nothing striking about the six stick figures of paper and wire. Three of them wore woven skirts (one red and blue, one purple, and one blue and white), and three wore pants. Their shirts, each a different color, were made of threads coiled across them like shawls, and they all seemed to have the same face of painted dots and lopsided smiles. In a way, I liked their tininess, though I really did not know what to make of them. I tried standing them up; they fell down. I shook them as if they were dice, then dropped them to see if they would come up face up or face down; five out of six, or all six, always landed face up, which made me pay particular attention to the way their arms, outstretched like the arms of wooden soldiers on the march, were forever poised in a gesture of giving.

I picked up the dolls one by one and lined them up in my hand. They had no weight to them, they were hollow, but lying side by side in my hand they were somehow transformed, right before my eyes, into a flesh-and-blood family. Mother, father, grandmother, grandfather, and two more—maybe a girl and her uncle—became a unit that, if Jake was right, would somehow dissolve my troubles, whatever they might be.

I gently placed the dolls, one by one, in their box, slid the box into my precious new purse, and gave Jake a kiss of thanks. Then I took him by the hand and led him to the door. "Let's go to Chichicastenango," I said.

"Right now?" Jake asked.

"Right now."

"Don't we need to pack first?" No one indulged my whims the way Jake did.

"Nah—it's better to travel light."

Jake let out a hearty laugh, told me I had wisdom beyond my years. I didn't really know what was so funny—I was simply saying what my mother said to me whenever we went away for a weekend and I wanted to take half my toys with me—but I laughed along as we headed out the door. It was a soft summer afternoon, the kind of day that rings with the voices of children and the bells of ice cream trucks, and we made our way to the park, past baseball fields, and deeper into the park, where we sat ourselves on a shaded bench alongside a lake, pretending we were in Chichicastenango. All around us were children with olive eyes and thick, black, shiny hair, Carmelita's the thickest and shiniest of all. It was siesta time, Jake explained, and while the fathers slept and the mothers fed the leftovers from lunch to hungry dogs and cats, the children skipped around the square, singing their favorite songs, and Carmelita sat close by in the shade of a tree, humming along and patiently weaving dreams.

"If you live long enough, you see everything" is an adage that haunted my childhood and that, perhaps more than any other, captures the sum total of my grandmother's wisdom. She, like Jake, had a flair for narrative, and she always began with a phrase that set the tone for the drama that was about to unfold. I might be sitting at the kitchen table, playing tic-tac-toe with her or watching her unscramble the pieces of a jigsaw puzzle while I nibbled on cookies with rainbow sprinkles that she baked for me, when the phone would ring. No matter who called, no matter what the greeting—What's new? How's everything?—Grandma, letting out a deep sigh, would say, "Don't ask," or "You shouldn't know from it," or some equally weighty expression of dismay. She would then unburden herself of the day's or the week's or the month's disaster, leaving me temporarily to my own devices of amusement. My choices, as long as I remained in the kitchen, were to continue scratching out X's and O's by myself; start one of the half dozen or so jigsaw puzzles Grandma kept in her house ostensibly for me, or, as was more often the case, finish one she had already begun to piece together; get my crayons and color in the patterns on paper napkins—an art I learned from Jake; and, of course, to continue to eat cookies.

Each choice had its obvious satisfaction, but sooner or later the urgency in Grandma's voice and the way it registered an absolute command of life's inconsistencies, its rewards and punishments, or its debt to God (inconsistent or unfathomable as He may be) would distract me. Immediately I would become transfixed by this small, powerful woman. I mentally recorded her sighs and commentary, the reflexive way she reached for a cigarette and lit it as soon as she began a phone conversation, the way her forehead wrinkled when she became agitated. There was no telling what valuable insights into the complex web of life I might pick up just from listening to my grandmother and observing her mannerisms as she paced back and forth entangled in phone wire or, tired of pacing, leaned forward on the washing machine, nodding as she listened, smoking as she talked, all the time gazing thoughtfully out the window. The drama invariably centered on relatives or friends who were having problems—Grandpa's bad heart, Aunt Vivian's on again–off again affair with the "married I-talian," the constant fights between Grandma's lifelong friend Sophie and her lazy son Arnold—and the way she told it always left me feeling that struggle was the norm and unfettered happiness the exception.

That's not to say that all was hopeless. With struggle, Grandma implied, comes hope, or at least vindication. And nothing I have ever heard expressed hope more poetically than an eight-word phrase filled with the cadence of the shtetl: "If you live long enough, you see everything." How long, I wondered, did one have to live to live long enough? My father's father died of a stroke at fifty, and I never knew him, and his mother died when I was four, so I barely knew her. Did they live long enough? Did they see everything? I decided one day, when we were playing tic-tac-toe, to ask Grandma Ruth if Grandma Lilly had lived long enough to see everything.

"Who puts these ideas into your head?" My grandmother leaned back in her chair, folded her arms.

I smiled at her. "You. The other day you said to Mommy, 'If you live long enough, you see everything.' You were telling her that Arnold got a job working for an accountant."

My grandmother, about to take her turn, held her pencil in midair. "What else did I say?"

I rattled off everything I'd heard her say about Arnold and Sophie: he's a big boy, she babies him too much, he should be supporting her, not the other way around.

"What are you—five going on twenty?"

I took my grandmother's remark as a compliment.

"Oh—one more thing. You said there are worse problems than a sensitive nose."

Arnold, you see, suffered from hyperosmia. Odors that were mildly offensive to most people were unbearable to him, and fragrant smells were simply overpowering. Consequently, Sophie could never wear perfume (which she insisted was no major sacrifice), and even her cooking had to be tempered. Onions did more than bring tears to Arnold's eyes, and if Sophie cooked cabbage or cauliflower, she had to do it when Arnold was out of the house, which wasn't often, since his condition had turned him into a virtual hermit. Jake, who was six years younger than Arnold, once told me how helpless he felt when the other kids in the neighborhood made fun of Arnold, calling him the Schnoz or Elephant Nose, and when they did nasty things, like deliberately farting in his presence and then laughing while Arnold, stoic as ever, took a handkerchief to cover his nose. If it looked as if he were going to sneeze or blow his nose, one of them would incite the others into running from the monsoon of snot their meager imaginations conjured and Arnold would be left standing, handkerchief over his nose, until he mustered the strength to make his way home.

"I don't suppose you remember everything your mother said, too."

I nodded. My mother said the best thing Sophie could do now was to tell Arnold to find an apartment. Grandma became indignant. You don't send your only child out into the streets the minute he gets a job, she insisted. To which my mother replied, you're missing the point. No, Grandma shot back, *you're* missing the point. Frankly, I didn't know what the point was, much less who was missing it. I knew only that something about Arnold made me sad. And something about his getting a job made Grandma feel good. "I tell you," Grandma said to my mother, her face one big smile of pride, "if you live long enough, you see everything."

"Well," said Grandma, returning to my original question, "I would guess that your grandma Lilly—may she rest in peace—would have liked to see a few more things. After all, she was only fifty-two when she died. But with a granddaughter like you"—she kissed my forehead—"I guess what I'm trying to say is that she knew you, she knew what it was to have a grandchild. What else is there?"

The phone rang. It was Sophie.

"Got a minute, Ruth?" she bellowed. Sophie's voice was loud, and even though the receiver was against Grandma's ear, I could hear everything Sophie said.

"The job is kaput."

"What do you mean, kaput?"

Arnold had apparently gotten into a fight with his boss about the deodorizer in the office bathroom. The scent made him so sick that he couldn't bear to use the bathroom. I imagined Arnold, in the checkered cap he always wore even when he was indoors, eyes cast downward, asking his boss if they could do without the deodorizer.

"His boss says, 'What are you—some kind of nut?' Which was not the thing to say to my Arnold."

"The f-word, Ruth—he said the f-word to his boss." And he was out the door.

"I didn't bring my son up to talk like that," Sophie went on. "I taught him respect—and this is what he does?" Sophie told Arnold to go back to the office, apologize to his boss. "And you know what he said to me?"

"*Oy vey*," sighed Grandma, reaching for a pack of L&Ms, tapping it against the wall, and pulling out a cigarette. "I don't know how else to say this, Sophie, but maybe he needs help." Grandma, who was never one to mince words, uncharacteristically treaded lightly. "Could you maybe get him to go to someone? You know what I mean—a psychiatrist or something?" she suggested.

"There's absolutely nothing wrong with him that a good job wouldn't cure. But it's not easy, with a problem like he's got."

"There you go, babying him again."

"Say that one more time, Ruth, and I'll hang up."

Grandma changed the subject.

"I have a genius for a granddaughter, Sophie. Beats me at tic-tac-toe all the time now. And you should see her do jigsaw puzzles, not to mention the things that come out of her mouth! Not five minutes before you called, the *shaina maideleh* asks me if I think her grandma Lilly lived long enough. Don't tell me—I know what you're thinking. You're thinking, *What kind of question is that from a five-year-old?* And I'm telling you this is no ordinary five-year-old. She reads. Excuse me? You don't believe it? Well, believe me, she's been reading since she was three. That's what I said—reading."

Grandma was stretching the truth a little. At three, I was memorizing, not reading. At five, I was just beginning to read.

"But you know something?" Grandma continued, taking a drag of her cigarette, quickly followed by a sigh and another drag. "It's no big deal to read. I'll tell you what *is* a big deal. The *shaina maideleh* thinks. Who knows, maybe she'll be a doctor one day, although if the doctors around today are any indication, she's heads above them already. I swear, I don't know who she gets her brains from. I'd like to say she inherited them from my daughter, but Susie was no genius. A smart girl, yes, but no Mensa material. And her father . . . well, I shouldn't talk."

Grandma, of course, continued to talk, oblivious to my presence. "You shouldn't know from it, Sophie. A man lives with a woman, then waits five years after they have a baby to marry her. You explain it to me."

"Be thankful they're getting married," I heard Sophie say as I slipped out of the kitchen, leaving behind the puzzle and the cookies and the unwinnable game of tic-tac-toe.

Exactly forty-four days passed between the time my parents announced their plans to get married and the actual day of their wedding. In that month and a half, I contracted chicken pox, my mother called off the wedding two times, my father had a wisdom tooth extracted, Jake took off for Australia, and Grandma became sentimental to the point of tears nearly every time she looked at a picture of her mother. "Susie was her favorite," she would explain, as her face twitched with a measure of loss and expectations unfulfilled, and I don't know how I understood what I understood, but I always said, "Don't worry, Grandma. You'll come to my wedding."

"I should live so long." The tone of Grandma's voice was a mix of despondency and hope—Jewish hyperbole was what my mother called it—that sometimes had the effect of worrying me.

"How does God decide how long people live?" I asked her.

"Well, He's got this very big book, and as soon as you're born, your name goes into it, along with your birth date and the day you're going to die, although it's entirely possible that your name goes in before you're born, since God has to know that, too—why else would He be God?"

The biggest book I'd ever seen was the oversize dictionary my father kept on the bottom shelf of his bookcase. The writing was tiny, and I liked turning to the color plates of birds and butterflies, cats and monkeys. I could not lift the book, but I could manage to pull it from the bookshelf to the floor whenever I wanted to look through it. Now I was being presented with the idea of a tome that would have to be even bigger than the four-inch-thick book of words that I was sure made me smarter each time I opened it. Where did God keep such a monumental and precious record of life and death? Could anyone besides Him see the book? And what would happen if He lost it?

I doubt that Grandma ever thought much about this book except as a metaphor of faith, and the answers she gave me reflected the simple fact that God was an assumption to her, an assumption as unquestioned as air and water are for life.

"God doesn't lose things," she said, "and I can guarantee you that He keeps the book in a very safe place, because the truth is, people are not supposed to know when they're going to die." She was rolling out dough for cookies and became pensive for a moment. "Although I wonder if it would really make a difference, because no one ever believes it's coming, except maybe if you're really, really, really sick. Sure, you always hear stories about people who have cancer or something like that and are told they have six months to live, so they cash in their life savings and take a trip around the world. But most people, if they knew the exact time and day they were going to die, they just wouldn't believe it was coming."

"Why?"

"I wish I had a dime for every time you asked that question; I'd be a very rich lady." She wiped her hands on her apron, started shaping cookies. Stars, crescents, four-leaf clovers began to materialize, along with an answer for me. "Human nature, I guess. Know what that means?"

"Uh-uh." I grabbed some rainbow sprinkles from a bowl, dotted cookies with them.

"It's just the way people are."

My next question made her wince. "Do children die?"

She knew she could get away with telling me about a mythical book of names, but an out-and-out lie did not sit well with her. "They're not supposed to," she said, "but sometimes they do."

She could have stopped right there, because this was one of the few times when I really did not want any more information than I'd been given, but it was early evening and she was staring out the window across the driveway to the gray ranch house, almost identical to hers, where her friend Lena had lived until the thing that was not supposed to happen to children happened to one of hers. It was a car accident, he was twenty, and the impact of going sixty-five miles an hour into a stone wall killed him instantly. Grandma spared me the details, told me only that when God takes a child you try to tell yourself that He must have some good reason. "But the truth is," she said, still staring at the gray house, abandoned before it could even be sold, standing empty like a shrine to the thing that's not supposed to happen, "no mother wants to outlive her child."

Grandma put her hand across her eyes and the way she did it made me think of a night a year earlier when I found her at the kitchen table, head bowed, one hand across her brow, the other covering a nearly empty glass of scotch. I was supposed to be asleep, but I was restless, so I went downstairs. Grandma looked up at me, her lips quivering with the tears she tried to hold back. When I told her that her eyes were very red and she should go to sleep, she smiled, lips still quivering. Then she pulled me close, held me tightly against her soft bosom, and I could feel her body shake with tears. "You shouldn't know from it," she said. "You should never, never know from it." Grandma finished off the glass of scotch, took a deep breath, told me how skinny Lena had gotten and how gorgeous she had once been, with her violet eyes and jet-black hair, and how they had to dope her up just to get her to stand near the grave of her son for the short, simple ceremony in which they unveiled his stone.

I have no memory at all of Lena's son (who was the same age as Jake), and the encounters I had with Lena before she moved to Florida were, thankfully, brief. She had the trembling smile of someone forever in mourning. "You're beautiful. Live your life," she would say, putting her hand to my cheek or my chin. Making me cringe. Like water spots on an exquisite silk dress, pain and loss shaded the violet beauty in her face and turned her pink-white skin a pale gray.

"You're beautiful. Live your life." That's all she could manage to say to me before she retreated into the house that had become her cave. Curtains drawn, afraid of the harsh sunlight, Lena spent her days watching soap operas and popping Valiums into her mouth like lozenges. "Come on over for a cup of coffee," Grandma would call across the driveway, and once in a while she did, though all she could bring herself to talk about were memories of Michael. *Remember the tree house Michael built with Jake when they were boys, and how we couldn't get them down from it? And remember how the girls were always after them both—that's how handsome they were?* Grandma would nod—what else could she do or say?—and that affirmation spoke worlds to me about the secrets mothers share and the things I was not supposed to know from.

"Well, I'm never going to die," I said, with all the assurance of my youth.

"Well, I'm very glad to hear that." Grandma bent down, kissed the top of my head. The cookies were ready to go into the oven.

Forty-four days. How would I ever get through them? I had my very own vision of a wedding, with my mother in a white satin gown studded with pearls and I in something equally extravagant, and my father looking very handsome in a Fred Astaire tuxedo and top hat as he bowed to my mother and asked, "May I have this dance?" I had never been to a wedding, and the fact that my very first was to be my parents' only enhanced the magic. From the moment I woke up until the moment I went to sleep, my head was filled with images of soft white and sugar. A soft white veil and a soft satin train. Sugar roses on each tier of a three-tier cake filled with buttercream and chocolate. A bride and groom framed in a plastic heart crowning the cake, so real to me I could taste the icing on my finger.

My anticipation was overshadowed only by the fear that something terrible would happen to Jake in Australia and he would not make it back for the wedding.

"For the life of me, I don't understand it, Sophie," I overheard Grandma say. "He can't stay in one place. He's got this travel bug. Takes a job for three months, doesn't spend a penny of his earnings, saves it all up for a trip. 'Settle down,' I tell him, but he won't hear of it." Grandma had traced Jake's wanderlust to his time in Vietnam, which, as she saw it, had brought about a very unwelcome transformation in her baby boy.

"You tell me," she went on. "What bright Jewish boy drops out of college in 1971 and lets himself be drafted, *knowing* he's probably going to end up in that jungle? It's unheard of. Something's got to be wrong. You think you have troubles with Arnold and his nose? I'll tell you what trouble is. Trouble is having four grown, seemingly normal children, not one of whom is married. Yes, I know Susie is getting married; you don't have to remind me. But she's not exactly doing it the conventional way."

It was Jake, it seemed, who troubled Grandma most. "Something is just not right with him, and I can't put my finger on it. He's a very bright boy. And very artistic. You should see how he draws! But he's home less than one month from the jungles of Guatemala before he's off to God knows where. I'm telling you, something happened to him in Vietnam. Something he won't talk about." Grandma sometimes bit her lip when she was worried. Like now.

"If I tell him it's time he looked for a serious job, not these fly-by-night ones he takes, he tells me he's going to do that as soon as he gets back from Australia. But he said the same thing after he got back from Guatemala."

Grandma shook her head, let out a deep sigh. "*Oy gut*, Sophie— what are we going to do with these overgrown kids of ours?"

"Speak for yourself."

"Knock it off, Sophie. Your son is a big baby—he's afraid to get a job, afraid to go out and socialize. My son, on the other hand, I just *wish* he were more afraid of things. And I wish he would stay in one place for more than a month. You shouldn't know from it. There are all kinds of bugs in the jungle—bugs you and I never even heard of. Who knows what diseases they carry! And there are crocodiles. If you ask me, this is not a healthy way to live."

It was then that I remembered the calendar I'd found in a box in the attic, and when Grandma finished her conversation with Sophie, I asked her about it. Jake had sent the calendar to her when he was on leave in Australia. He had another five months to go in Vietnam and thought Grandma might worry less if she pictured him in the land of kangaroos and button-nosed koala bears. "I'm a long way from home," he wrote, "but days quickly pass into months, and before you know it I'll be kissing your always comforting cheek." He scrawled, "I love you" and signed off with the suggestion that Grandma mark off the days till his return.

Grandma began doing just that—marking an X each day on the calendar—but stopped on Jake's birthday, February 29. Superstition gets you in the funniest ways, she told me the day I asked her about the calendar, and maybe it was her emotions as well, but she simply could not scratch an X through Jake's birthday. Her explanation was simple and straightforward: days pass much too slowly when you count them, and she was never one for measuring time. She also figured she would know when he was coming home.

"When you're a mother, you feel these things," she said. "Don't ask me how. That's just the way it is. You'll be going about your business, not thinking about anything in particular, when suddenly you'll find yourself drinking a tenth cup of coffee to calm yourself down, knowing that defies all logic, but you just poured salt instead of sugar in the rice pudding, so who cares about logic? Or you'll find yourself yelling at the checkout girl in the supermarket for being too slow, when she's really no slower than usual, and after all how is she supposed to know you're expecting an important phone call any day now and it can only be good news because you will not accept anything but good news?" Grandma gently touched my cheek, pushed a wisp of hair behind my ear. "You shouldn't know from it," she said, "but one day you'll be a mother and you will."

A much more pressing concern to me than what I would one day know when I became a mother was whether I could keep the calendar. This very week, this very month, this very hour, Jake was on the other side of the world. I knew a little something about the planets and how they revolved around the sun and none of it, in truth, made sense. If the earth was always spinning, then we should all be walking around dizzy, and maybe we were but didn't know it because we had gotten so used to it. Equally unfathomable to me was the vastness of the earth. It would take nearly an entire day to get from New York to Australia by plane, Jake told me, showing me on a globe he kept in his room the distance he would be traveling. I followed the arc his finger made, tried hard to understand how a globe that measured two feet around could encompass the world.

When Jake was gone, I took to playing what I believed to be a very clever game. I would go into his room, place my finger on New York, close my eyes, lift my finger, spin the globe, and count. If I counted to ten, my finger always landed on Australia. And while the globe spun around, I tried to imagine a place where animals had names like kookaburra, wallaby, and dingo. A place where people once made paintings right on rock, and if you stood very still, Jake said, you could feel the colors and taste the marsh and smell the kookaburra before you heard it and believe, for a minute or two or three, that you were on the very edge of time. This very week, this very day, this very hour, Jake might be admiring a rock painting or weaving his way through coral in the Great Barrier Reef or boating down a river in search of crocodiles while I, halfway around the world, dreamed of sugar roses and white lace and tried very hard to understand how forty-four days could simultaneously pass so swiftly and so slowly.

Grandma seemed only too glad to relinquish the calendar, and the reminder it was of a time dictated by anxiousness of the worst kind. And when I told her of my plans to X off the days until my parents' wedding, she laughed. "You're in the wrong year."

"Makes no difference," I said. "The same days come every year, don't they?"

Grandma thought that was a very wise answer, and rather than give me a lesson in the passing of days into months, she leafed through the calendar with me. There was a patch of cotton clouds enhancing February's Sydney skyline, and the emus of April danced off the page and it was no small irony (as Grandma pointed out) that May, the month Jake returned, was graced with a kangaroo and her cub tucked safely in her pouch. July, my starting point (coincidentally, the month of my birthday), showed purple starfish bathed in the dreamy blue light of the sea, and August presented a stark view of the outback that seemed to change from day to day once I began my fastidious accounting of time. Some days the landscape was welcoming and I imagined myself right there with Jake, hiking along a dusty road or climbing steep rocks of red or stopping for a picnic lunch near a watering hole that turned out to be a mirage. Other days it was absolutely forbidding and I was sure I saw a crocodile's head jutting from the craggy recesses of a cave. How, I wondered, could the same pictures look so different from day to day?

I looked at myself in the mirror. It was August 1. My face was spotted with pox, my mother had just canceled the wedding for the first time because my father had been out all night—just catching up with friends, he said, losing track of time—and my fear that Jake might be devoured by a crocodile was so strong that I took my copy of *Peter Pan*, ripped it up page by page, and flushed it down the toilet.

Two days later, I received three postcards from Jake.

Dear Rachel:

Right now I'm looking at a pearl-white moon casting shadows on a crocodile's back. When a crocodile is resting, he's so still you can mistake him for a log. But when he's swimming, he looks like he's carrying the river between his jaws—that's how much command he has. Will write again soon.

xxx Jake

Dear Rachel:

I made friends with a kangaroo and saw a koala bear nestled in a tree just like the one on the front of this postcard. It did not seem to me a very comfortable position for sleeping, but the koala didn't seem to mind. Unlike you, koalas seem to cherish sleep. In fact, on a typical day they're asleep more than they're awake.

xxx Jake

Dear Rachel:

Tomorrow I'm off to an island of surprises—birds in every color of the rainbow and luscious flowers and trees with leaves so thick they're like tents. They say here that Dreamtime People created the world, and I don't exactly know who these people were but I can tell you I feel as if I'm going from dream to dream. This is a very special part of the world—I hope you'll visit it one day.

Love and a hug, Jake

I taped the postcards on the wall alongside my bed, where I kept the calendar and a picture of a bride that I had cut from a magazine. I liked looking at the images and touching the gloss of the paper and wondering what Dreamtime People dreamed about and why brides always wore white and whether the moon was full in Australia when it was full here. I knew that if it was midday for me, it was the very wee hours of the next day for Jake, and there was something very exciting about thinking that Jake was in tomorrow. At bedtime I'd pet the sleeping koala bear and study the rock formations on the calendar and, just before I shut off the light, remind the bride, with a kiss and a whisper, that the wedding was one day closer.

In the morning before I got out of bed, my eyes still crusted with sleep, I'd perform my first ritualistic act of the day: marking an *X* on the calendar. I needed to touch each day, to see the calendar fill up with *X*'s as forty-four became forty-three and forty-three became forty-two and thirty-three became thirty-two and thirty-one and thirty.

On August 20, I received a package from Jake. It came wrapped in sturdy brown paper over a layer of soft brown paper that crinkled to the touch. Inside the wrapping was a book filled with pictures of undersea coral, and taped to the back cover was a teardrop stone, also coral, on a gold chain. *I found this at the bottom of the sea,* Jake wrote. *I think it belonged to a mermaid.*

I showed my mother the necklace, asked her to put it on for me. As she fastened it around my neck, all the power of mermaids and witches (good and bad) and little old men who spin straw from gold radiated through me. I closed my eyes, saw blue—waves of blue erratic as the peaks Jake made with my Etch A Sketch—and darting through the blue was Jake. Iridescent Jake. Jake the fish. Jake the red-cloaked pirate in search of undersea treasures and the stories they unlocked. If I had in fact been under the sea, I would suddenly have found myself gasping for air in total blackness when my mother informed me (in her mildly impatient, finish-your-breakfast tone of voice) that the wedding was off. This was the second time the wedding had been called off, and when I asked her why, she looked down, fidgeted, said nothing. And looking down, always down, except for a momentary glance my way, she fidgeted, stammered, stopped one inch short of kicking the wall, then turned to me, eyes up, steely, hard, uncertain whether to cry or to scream.

"Let's go outside," she said. We had the garden apartment of a brownstone in the Park Slope section of Brooklyn, and it was a cloudy day and I was about to burst into tears because just the day before we had bought my dress for the wedding. I had chosen it myself and loved everything about it, particularly the scalloped bottom and violet ribbon running through the hemline. To me, this was more than a dress. Peeking through each and every eyelet that comprised the fabric were intimations of Cinderella and fancy balls and a glass slipper for my delicate foot alone.

We sat down on a stone bench in the garden, and my mother, elbow propped on her knee, chin resting in her palm, began speaking.

"Your father and I . . ." She faltered, took my hand, rubbed her thumb across it. "Your father and I . . ." She was clutching my hand now.

"Ouch," I said. "You're hurting me."

She let go, looked at me apologetically, touched my face lightly. "You have your father's eyes," she said, "and his cheekbones." She was smiling now, almost in a trance. "Did I ever tell you how we met? Or where?"

I shook my head.

"It was in the subway. I remember it was a crowded train—probably rush hour—and the lights went out. Suddenly I felt someone's hand on my behind." My mother laughed, quickly explained it was not my father who grabbed her. (He would enter the picture when the train came to a stop at Grand Central Station.) Not one to be intimidated by a rush-hour subway pervert, my mother rammed her elbow into his ribs.

"I'm telling you, the guy didn't know what hit him. He was wearing an army-green jacket—that's a detail you can't forget—and when he doubled over from the jab I gave him, he looked like a sick turtle. It never occurred to me that I was dealing with a combination pervert-pickpocket until I was off the train and realized my wallet was missing. That's where your father comes in. He had been eyeing me on the train, trying to figure out a way to strike up a conversation or something. Of course I wasn't aware of it, but even if I had been, I probably would have ignored him because I wasn't in the habit of picking up men in the subway. Anyway, your father was a witness to the pickpocketing and had to think fast: Should he follow the pickpocket and try to retrieve my wallet, or should he follow me? He followed the pickpocket, told him he was an undercover cop, and easily retrieved my wallet. Now, Grand Central Station is pretty big, but I guess your father and I were destined to meet that day, because he found me near one of the ticket booths, frantically fishing through my knapsack for my wallet. I admit I was a little suspicious when he handed it to me and asked, 'Is this what you're looking for?' I mean, how did I know he wasn't in cahoots with the pickpocket-pervert? But he had a very convincing and clean way about him. And he had the sexi . . ." Her cheeks flushed. "He had the most beautiful blue eyes I'd ever seen."

My mother stopped talking and looked up at the sky intently, as if she were watching a movie, which in a way she was. Clouds were moving in a montage that I would piece together, scene by scene, over the years, but today, as she thought about marriage and tried to make sense of love, the images belonged to my mother and would run together something like this: A man and a woman are boating on a lake in Central Park. It is early summer 1967, and he (first lieutenant Robert Schneider) rows; then she (undergraduate Susan Cohen) takes her turn; then he rows and she drifts, he wanting to rest his head in her lap, she fixing her gaze on his eyes, crystal blue and glistening in the sun. The scene shifts, and they are under a tree, he (first lieutenant Robert Schneider) caught up in the smile and voice and long, beautiful legs of this woman who he does not know whether he'll ever see again, she (undergraduate Susan Cohen) seduced by this strong, handsome man who makes no assumptions, a perfect gentleman in a time that seems to value imperfection. Holding hands now, they talk about her preference for vanilla and his for chocolate and the cuts they like on the Beatles' latest album, and their palms are sweaty now on this early-summer day, but still they hold hands, talking about anything and everything, it seems, but his imminent departure for Vietnam and her opposition to the war.

Now they are on her doorstep, kissing good night, a long, passionate kiss that will hold her through all the letters filled with lines from Simon and Garfunkel and the Beatles and Leonard Cohen and my father's own strains of corny love. He writes very little of the gritty side of life as a soldier in Vietnam, and she writes nothing of her opposition to the war. She is in love with the love letters, and, politics aside, she is in love with a soldier. He returns, wants to marry; she does not. Three months later she wants to marry; he does not. They separate for two months; then he calls. And in a smoke-filled Greenwich Village bar they meet for a drink, she telling herself this really is love, he swearing never to let her get away again.

I tugged at my mother's dress to bring her back to Earth. "Where was I?"

"You weren't born yet."

This simply made no sense to me. "Was I dead before I was born?"

"No—you just weren't born yet."

This was my very first moment of truth. I had been told (hard as it was for me to believe) that babies start out inside their mothers and keep growing until they're ready to be born. The part about pushing their way through the birth canal was even less plausible, and I'd sooner have believed it took a magician's hand to spirit baby from womb. But that was all in the abstract. Now, for the very first time, I was face-to-face with an unsettling reality. Beneath her white, Indian-cotton summer dress, almost transparent in sunlight, was a tan, athletic woman with strong, beautiful legs and marshmallow breasts that I liked to touch with my very small hands, sometimes even pretending I could still drink from them. And now this tan, athletic woman who was my mother was telling me about a time before Rachel at a time when I needed to believe, more than ever, that there was nothing before Rachel.

My mother stood up, started pacing. "Rachel, I'm a little upset. I don't know what I'm doing anymore. Should I get married? Shouldn't I get married? What's the point of it all? We've been living together happily for five years now—what's the point of getting married? What I'm trying to say is that this is not a good time for me to tell you about the birds and the bees."

"I'm not asking about birds and bees!" I screamed. *"I want to know how I got born!"*

"Didn't anyone ever tell you about the stork?" I turned to see my father coming into the backyard. His face was swollen (he'd just had a wisdom tooth pulled), and he looked sad. I ran over to him—"Daddy! Daddy!"—and he scooped me up in a game we liked to play, he the trapeze, I the daring young girl who flew through the air with the greatest of ease, he singing, me flying—"Higher, Daddy! Higher!" It was a game we loved to play, only today, not knowing how I got born, not even knowing whether this woman who was my mother and this man who was my father would be there to catch me when the trapeze snapped, as it seemed about to right now, I threw my arms around my father, clinging, Daddy, clinging. Then, uncontrollably, I began to cry.

"This is a very interesting way to wash a shirt," my father teased me, as he carried me over to a chair, where I sat in his lap, my face still buried in his shoulder.

"Are you and Mommy going to live together?" I sobbed.

"As far as I know, we are." He did not sound convincing, and I hit him. Delirious with anger and disappointment, fists closed tight and hard, I hit him with all the force I could muster. I punched him in the chest and I hit his neck, and with what must have looked like the deliberateness of a boxer, I landed a punch on his jaw. I was not aiming for his jaw, mind you, and when I saw the blood trickle out of the side of his mouth, I gasped. My mother scrambled inside for a towel and some ice, and the bleeding stopped, and there was no reproach at all, not even a wince of pain. So I hit him again. Only this time he blocked my punch by grabbing my wrists.

"I hate you!" I screamed. "I hate you both! I don't care if you never get married anyway, because I'm gonna live with Jake when he gets back." This seemed to upset my father more than being punched.

"Over my dead body," he said, spitting out the words, still holding the towel to his cheek. "Even if your mother and I never get married, even if we stop living together, you will not live with Jake."

I had hit a very sore spot, and I plowed right in. "Yes, I will," I sang. "I'm five years old now, and I can do whatever I want, and if I want to live with Jake, I will."

My father's eyes, a deep crystal blue, flared red, and in them I saw dragons. One. Two. Three. Ten dragons breathing fire, blue fire, red fire, yellow fire streaked with green. His cheek swollen, eyes flaring, he had become as large as a dragon right before my eyes, and when his arm reached out to grab me or hit me, I don't know what, my body shook. I had never been hit by either of my parents, though there were times when my grating whine ("oh please oh please oh please let me have gum") or my shrieks of insistence about absolutely hating the very same chicken I had loved yesterday (and the day before and the day before) were provocation enough. But everything happened so fast—my father's fingers had just brushed my arm when my mother deflected him—that only for an instant was I really terrified of being physically hurt. Much more frightening to me was something I could not identify in my father, something that changed his very countenance and that I would one day understand as the desperation of a man who believed himself on the verge of losing everything that he loved.

The realization that he had come so close to hurting me embarrassed my father, and without saying a word he left, deliberately slamming first the back door, then the front door, then, loudest of all, the car door. I cringed. There was a large oak tree in our backyard, and when we had first moved here I had been intimidated by its thick trunk, which reminded me of the nasty trees in *The Wizard of Oz*, and its network of bulging roots. Fear turned to awe one day as I watched ants make their way along the trails carved by the roots and disappear into a hole. Just a little larger, I thought, sitting there in the hum of a silence left by slamming doors, and this would be a perfect hole for Alice and her White Rabbit and me.

"Is Daddy coming back?" I asked my mother. She bit her lips, brushed some dead leaves on the ground with her foot, picked up the wrapper of a straw that I had probably dropped, and finally, when there was nothing more within easy reach to distract her, pulled me close and started to sob.

"I'm all mixed up, Bunny," she cried to me. "Sometimes I want to get married, sometimes I don't. We're happy, right? So why change things? Why not just leave things the way they are?" Then she said it was "hippo"-something to get married after five years of living together, and at last I had a clue. Somehow, in some odd way, a hippopotamus had interfered with their wedding plans.

"It's totally hypocritical," she said again, letting go of me.

I started to feel cold, though the sun was still shining strong, and I went inside, to my room. I threw myself on my bed but could not stay still. I jumped up to tear the picture of the bride from the wall. Pulled my dress from the closet door, slipped it on, refusing to take it off for dinner, which I insisted on having in my room by myself, refusing to take it off even at bedtime.

"Do you want to talk about this?" my mother asked. I shook my head. She kissed me good night and left the room. Sleep did not come easily. Running through my head were visions of wedding cakes, and in the shadows across the ceiling was the hippopotamus, a massive, unattractive animal that, in the part of my soul forever keyed to childhood, will always represent an enormous obstacle to love or, at the least, something that can crush it with the weight of one leg.

Just when sleep seemed to take hold, I was awakened by voices in the living room. I got out of bed, opened the door, stopped short before heading down the foyer. The TV was on, and the voices sounded breathy, and I could not really hear what they were saying or doing, and not being able to hear what they were saying or doing made my heartbeat accelerate with a peculiar, unknown feeling. The sounds were becoming more breathy, and my heart was beating along as if I were a part of whatever they were saying or doing. I could no longer stand it, being alone in my room with wedding cakes that looked like hippopotamuses, and my heart was beating so fast I knew I was not supposed to walk into the living room right then, but I did. And when I saw my mother half-undressed on top of my father, I felt only mildly embarrassed. I had been told a little something about how mothers and fathers kiss and hug in a way they don't kiss and hug children, but my first glimpse (and a glimpse was all it was) into the lovemaking acrobatics of adults was particularly painful. I felt excluded, and it seemed to me selfish—even a little cruel—for my parents to keep me from their reunion.

My mouth was dry and I needed a drink, so I asked for a glass of water, and the way I asked it, or just the mere asking, made my parents laugh.

"That's not funny!" I blasted them, gulping down the water very quickly and running back to bed, where, as soon as I lay down, I was overcome with a terrible stomachache that could be soothed only by my mother, then my father, then my mother, then my father lying next to me and rubbing my belly. As a child I was not particularly prone to bellyaches, but I had my share, and the timing of this one gave me great satisfaction. Maybe spite had turned my stomach acid, or simple jealousy, or maybe, as my mother suggested, bologna was not a good thing to eat under any circumstances, particularly not when you have chicken pox. "That's baloney!" said my father, bringing a smile to my mother's face while she rubbed my belly and he put a cold towel to my head, which was once again filled with thoughts of sugar-laced cakes. Maybe spite had turned my stomach sour, or simple jealousy, or maybe just some bad bologna, but in those tender moments when my mother's hands were on my belly and my father's on my head, I grasped the power of sickness. I could have stopped right there, I suppose—I had what I wanted. But the sour taste in my mouth grew stronger and the pain in my belly more intense, and maybe it was spite that came up, or jealousy, but my father would insist he saw pieces of bologna in the pool of vomit on the floor. Throwing up is disgusting to write about, even more unpleasant to experience, but when I threw up on my father's pants and my mother's dress I was not aware of spite, or jealousy, or even bologna, only that maybe the wedding was going to take place and maybe it wasn't, but my parents, for better or for worse, would have no reunion that night.

～

At the bottom of my grandmother's large mahogany armoire is a drawer she calls her junk drawer, and rummaging through it was a favorite pastime of mine. There was always some new treasure to unearth: scarves screened with flowers or abstract designs or the names of celebrated cities, wallets in all sizes and shapes, bobby pins still in their cardboard, hairnets, batteries, rubber bands, packs of writing pads and pens.

The night before my parents' wedding, while Grandma took a bath, I sat myself on the floor in front of the drawer and began combing through it to see if any new knickknack had been thrown in. Like the magician who pulls out the endless scarf from his sleeve and somehow comes up with a rabbit, I reached deep into the drawer. At the very bottom—under the red-and-gold scarf that had coins hanging from its fringes and turned me into a gypsy making my way through the Black Forest—was a rectangular black box, plain except for the red letters spelling an unfamiliar word—s-c-r-a-t-c-h-o-m-a-t-i-c—and a drawing of a woman holding something against her back.

I opened the box to find a plastic hand attached to a thin metal rod. The fingers, about the size of a baby's, were curled, and the tips looked like tiny fake fingernails. Also in the box was a cylinder that looked like the body of a flashlight. I picked up the cylinder, put it next to the rod with the hand, and quickly figured out how to attach them. Then I turned on a switch and was jolted by a vibration in my palm. Imitating the woman on the box, I reached behind me, placed the plastic hand under my shirt, started to laugh at the sensation of plastic fingers vibrating against my back. The lower part of my back started to itch. I repositioned the Scratch-O-Matic. The spot beneath my shoulder blade cried out for scratching. I slid the plastic hand along my back. Relief was never so much fun.

I was very much in a gypsy mood, so I put the red-and-gold scarf on my head, enjoying the jingling of the coins as they hit against each other, and tiptoed into the bathroom, back scratcher in hand. Grandma was in a sea of bubbles, wet cotton balls on her eyes, beads of sweat on her forehead, and I could never have anticipated that I would end up drenched and in tears as Grandma jumped from the bathtub, screaming from shock more imagined than real. All I did was put the back scratcher to her neck. She opened her eyes and let out a howl, and I dropped the Scratch-O-Matic into the bathtub. That made Grandma howl even more and scream at me for trying to kill her.

"Help!" she cried out. "I'm being electrocuted. Help!" Grandma quickly hopped out of the tub, splashing me in the process, and reached for a towel. "Don't you put so much as one finger in that water," she warned me. "There's electricity in there."

"Shouldn't we drain the water from the tub?" I asked.

"No!" she snapped. "Just hand me my bathrobe—and let's get out of here." Grandma was in a frenzy and had me believing that sparks of electricity were about to burst from the water the way popcorn explodes in a pan. Under the assumption that electrocution can come in stages, she believed herself to be in the first stage of acute electrocution, a condition marked by dizziness and tingling, and headed for her bed, where she collapsed.

At the sight of her lying there, and the thought that I might have accidentally been responsible for her death by battery, I burst into tears. No one was home—Jake and Grandpa had gone out on a mysterious mission whose purpose would unfold the next day at the wedding—and I panicked. The phone on Grandma's night table caught my eye. I picked up the receiver, started to dial my phone number, 241-9848, got only as far as the first 4. I dropped the receiver back in the cradle. My parents were not home; they were at a hotel in the city. *What am I going to do?*

Dial 911, I thought. *That's what my mother said to do in an emergency.*

Terrified, I dialed the three digits. A woman answered, identified herself, asked me what was wrong.

"My grandmother . . ." I stammered. "My grandmother. . ." No other words came out. How could I possibly say, or even believe, that I had killed my grandmother? I tried again. "My grandmother . . . I think my grandmother . . ." I felt as if a ten-pound drum were inside me, beating, beating, beating. *I think my grandmother is dead, I think my grandmother is dead, I think my grandmother is dead.* I began sobbing pitifully. "My grandmother . . ."

The woman on the other end of the receiver remained calm. "Can you tell me where your grandmother lives?" she asked.

"She lives here," I answered.

"The address, I mean. Can you tell me the address?"

"I don't know it," I cried.

"Do you know the street?"

With each question, an eternity seemed to be passing.

Yes. Yes. Yes. I knew the street. "Avenue Z!" I blurted out. "Near Sheepshead Bay."

"What's your grandmother's name?"

"Grandma Ruth."

"That's very good. Now, what about her last name?"

"Cohen—Grandma Ruth Cohen."

The next question put me over the edge. "Can you spell that?"

"Cohen! Cohen! Cohen!" I shouted into the receiver. "I'm five years old. I can read, but I can't spell names. My grandmother is . . . she needs help. Can you *please* send someone over here?"

"I'll tell you what," said the woman, who I imagined wearing a police cap and a short-sleeved blue police shirt. "If you can read the telephone number on the phone, we'll be there very quickly." I did as I was told.

I don't know how long it took the police to arrive. But in the time between the call and their arrival, I seemed to have covered a lot of ground. I was afraid to go near my grandmother or to touch her or to even look at her. And I was equally afraid to leave the room. So I stood against the bedroom door, waiting for the police, thinking what I would say to them.

My grandmother was taking a bath. I wanted to play. It was an accident. I glanced at Grandma, who still had not budged. *This is nothing more than a bad dream*, I told myself. She couldn't be dead. It was just not possible. I loved her too much.

I closed my eyes, hoping that the suggestion of a dream—bad or good—would shatter the reality. Sounds took over. The dripping bathtub faucet. The hum of the air conditioner. The excruciating tick of Grandpa's alarm clock. I covered my ears, trying to drive away the sounds, but they became only more pronounced, bringing with them visions more and more terrifying. Red Riding Hood's wolf was circling the bed and Captain Hook's crocodile was ticking along after me and all I could do was run out of the room, out of breath, up the stairs to the guest room that, by all appearances, had become my room. Toys, dolls, books, games, and puzzles that Grandma kept neatly in baskets between visits from me were all over the floor. And in the middle of the mess I saw the reason for the terror that had driven me upstairs. Without wasting a moment, I opened the purse Jake had given me, pulled out the box of trouble dolls, dashed downstairs to Grandma's room, and laid them out, one by one, on her dresser.

You have to help me, I told each and every one of them. *I did something awful, and I need your help very badly.* I picked up the one wearing a blue-and-white woven skirt. *Bring Grandma back*, I pleaded. *Please bring her back.*

Something told me to take the tiny doll and place her on the bed next to Grandma, which I did, not pausing long enough to realize that Grandma was breathing and of course had not died. When I was older and better able to reflect on why I hadn't done the obvious—that is, put my ear against her heart—I could not come up with a satisfactory answer. I was five years old. I panicked. Case dismissed.

In the process, of course, I learned the overwhelming power of guilt. To believe, even for a minute, that you've killed someone you love is unbearable. My body went cold, hot. Cold again, hot again. I couldn't stand still. I couldn't move. My legs buckled under me. My arms went limp. My hands became clammy. I cried, told myself this was a bad dream, laughed to will it away. Grandma was not dead, could not be dead; it was simply not possible. Not on the eve of the day my parents were to be married.

My thoughts went from the ridiculous to the sublime. I had to run away, get away, go someplace very far. The airport, I thought. I had to get to the airport. Jake had a friend who was a pilot, and once, when we took a ride to the airport, his friend let us sit in the cockpit of a parked plane, pretending we were flying to the moon. "Maybe you'll be the first woman astronaut," Jake had said. He loved to fly and wanted to be an astronaut himself, but only a certain kind of man became an astronaut, he told me, and he wasn't that kind of man.

The airport, I thought. *Somehow I have to get to the airport.*

I heard sirens, then a commotion as the front door opened. Jake and Grandpa had arrived at the same time as the police. It sounded like troops were marching through the house. Grandma lifted her head from the pillow, and at the sight of her—alive—I could feel the blood draining from me. I ran to Jake, collapsed in his arms, heard Grandpa's starchy voice above everything.

"What the H is going on?" he asked.

The two police officers went over to Grandma. One of them, husky, knelt at the side of the bed, took her pulse.

"Easy," he said, helping her sit up. "Looks like you passed out. Your granddaughter over here called us."

Everybody looked at me. "I thought . . ." I burst out crying. "Grandma was taking a bath and I wanted to scratch her back and the back scratcher fell in the bathtub and she thought I electrocuted her." Nobody knew what I was talking about until Grandpa, who had gone to the bathroom to investigate, returned with a broad smile on his face and the soaking-wet, battery-operated back scratcher in his hand.

Grandma was not pleased that Grandpa was laughing. "Sure, it's funny," she said sarcastically. "Remind me to laugh the next time you burn your hand taking a potato from the oven."

Grandpa turned to Jake. "Sonny Boy, will you please tell your mother that batteries don't electrocute people?"

Jake carried me over the bed, propped me against a pillow right next to Grandma. I reached out to touch her arm, to see if *this* was now the dream, and was overcome by the feel of warm flesh. I opened my mouth to say something, *anything*—I'm sorry, I'll never scare you again—but not a word came out. Even when Jake, cupping Grandma's hand, repeated that batteries don't electrocute people, not a peep came out of me. I had crossed a very fine line between reality and imagination, a line so fine that nothing seemed real to me and nothing—not Jake's words, not my grandmother's soft, spongy flesh—could reassure me of my innocence.

"I don't care what you say," Grandma insisted. "I felt a shock."

"Bet it felt good," teased Grandpa, as he placed the instrument of imagined doom on the bed. Jake dried it off, inside and out, and turned on the switch.

"Still works, Mom. Want to give it a try?" The back scratcher had been a present from Jake to Grandma before he had gone off to Vietnam. "If ever you get blue thinking about me when I'm away," he had written in a note accompanying the present, "take this out and tickle your back."

Ignoring Jake, Grandma turned to me. "Look at her in that babushka," she smiled. "Is that a face!" She kissed me, and my cheeks burned with dry tears. Whatever had left me speechless had also taken away my tears. I wanted to run out of the room, far away, where I would not have to hear another word about the bath that Grandma said took ten years from her life, or see the smirk of the skinny police officer who said this was one for the books, or hear the voice of the husky one telling me I did a good thing by calling. Clutching my box of trouble dolls tightly, I squeezed my eyes shut, imagining I *was* out of the room, when suddenly I felt the beginning of a warm trickle between my legs. I quickly jumped up, embarrassed but at the same time relieved that my escape was within reach.

No sooner was I off the bed than Grandpa, camera in hand, yelled, "Hold it!" To admit that I couldn't hold it would only have furthered my embarrassment, so I stood stock-still—and held it—while Grandpa, who treasured candid moments and had made a hobby of chronicling them with the Polaroid camera that Jake, Susie, and Vivian had given to him after his heart attack—snapped a picture. Jake tried to divert him, and Grandma threatened to rip up the photo, but Grandpa had learned to be quick.

"Look at this." In the palm of his hand, which seemed forever coated with sawdust from his years as a carpenter, was a photo in the making. Before my very eyes, a blank piece of paper turned iridescent with images. First I saw the head of a girl who I thought was Carmelita, and in the background her grandmother, but very quickly the images sharpened and there was Grandma, despite her professed annoyance with Grandpa, grinning broadly; and the two police officers, also smiling; and Jake, not smiling, holding up the back scratcher; and me, looking very twisted and not very happy. When Jake told me that the Indians in Guatemala wouldn't let him take their picture because they thought the camera would somehow suck up their souls, I did not understand what they were afraid of. Now I think I do. To someone who was not there on that peculiar night, the photo would be very funny, but how would anyone know that Jake was holding up his hand not to show off the present he had given Grandma, but to stop Grandpa from taking away my soul?

The police finally left, and after graciously thanking them for their help, Grandma turned on Grandpa, once again threatening to rip up the photo. Grandpa was not intimidated. He knew as well as she did that one day in the not-very-distant future she would look for the photo, not to rip it up but as an embellishment to her telling of the crazy night she thought she had been electrocuted by a gypsy in a babushka (the night before Susie's wedding, no less), and how two very handsome policemen saved her life.

For me, on the other hand, there would always be hidden images shadowing the anguished face of a five-year-old in a babushka, images of my grandmother as she jumped up from a peaceful bath, soaking wet and naked and shrieking, and of me calling the police, thinking she was dead and waiting waiting waiting until they arrived and to my surprise and joy resurrected her, though in time I would laugh, too, at the funniest images, the ones never photographed: those of Jake when we were alone upstairs, huddled in a tent made of blankets, and he ceremoniously untied the scarf jingling with coins, which I had forgotten I was still wearing, and put it on himself. He looked silly in the scarf, and I told him so, and that only made him do sillier things, especially when I pretended to take his picture as he made a giant, drooping bow tie out of the scarf, then coiled it like a turban and shook his head so the coins would sing. The turban fell apart from the shaking and became a veil, and I pronounced Jake queen of the gypsies and myself the king, which made him laugh so hard that his sides hurt, and his laughter made me laugh, though of course I would not get the joke for many years. And even when I did come to understand how much a part timing and innocence play in humor, I would never laugh at the idea of Jake as a queen, only at the image of him in a gypsy scarf, the most heartwarming image from that peculiar night (and the funniest), the photo never taken, the one that Jake said was "up here" (pointing to his head), as if to remind me that things all too often are not what they seem to be.

a family
undivided

"Flowers for the flower girl," said Jake, bowing as he handed me a small arrangement of pink tea roses. I was sitting on Grandma's bed, picture-perfect in my white eyelet party dress, waiting for Grandma to finish putting on her makeup. Unlike my mother, whose entire selection of makeup consisted of three shades of lipstick, matching eye shadow, and blush-on the color of summer peach, Grandma had an entire vanity drawer filled with eyeliners, eye pencils, lip pencils, lipsticks, mascara, foundation, rouge, and an assortment of night creams, day creams, eye creams, throat creams, and creams with strange names that hardened on her face. "The throat is always the first to go," she said to me earlier that morning as she emerged from the bathroom, her face and throat covered in what looked like clay. I should have been terrified to see her cheeks, ordinarily smooth and pink, flattened to a featureless gray. But Grandpa, who had just walked into the bedroom, let out a funny shriek and told Grandma she looked as beautiful as she had on their wedding day. I had no choice but to laugh.

"This is no ordinary arrangement," Jake went on. "Hold it like this"—he held the flowers up by the stem—"and it's a bouquet.

But turn it around like this, and voila! You have a wrist corsage." He fitted the corsage on my wrist, and I twisted my hand back and forth, admiring my bracelet of flowers, feeling almost dizzy from the fragrance of fresh rose. I touched the flowers very gently. Blue sparkles, spread across the petals like pixie dust, adhered to my finger.

Jake had also brought a wrist corsage for Grandma—an orchid—and she thanked him, but without so much as a smile. She was seated at her vanity, wearing a full-length white satin slip. She always put on her makeup before her dress.

"Lighten up, Mom," said Jake. "This *is* your daughter's wedding day."

Grandma shook her head, let out a big sigh, got up from her chair. Launched into a tirade about the cockamamie world her children lived in. The blame, as she saw it, rested largely with Ed Sullivan. If he hadn't put Elvis Presley and the Beatles on his show, the brouhaha over them would have died as quickly as it had flamed and all the malarkey about a sexual revolution, which, according to Grandma, wasn't much of a revolution at all, would have been put to rest.

"There's nothing revolutionary about sex." She looked at Jake. "You kids think you're doing something new? You're not doing anything new. You're just a lot less discreet about it." I didn't know who Ed Sullivan was, but I knew who Elvis Presley and the Beatles were because my father played their records a lot. He usually sang along, and I could always tell his mood by the music I heard blasting from the living room. *Sgt. Pepper's Lonely Hearts Club Band* was his favorite album and became mine, too, for a time, partly because the cover made me think of a circus but mostly because at the first note of the first cut my father would put on a funny hat and pull out his army jacket and start singing to his plants and to me. He was convinced that his plants thrived on *Sgt. Pepper's*.

"I'm *telling* you, the world changed the day the Beatles appeared on Ed Sullivan. And not for the better. Boys started looking like girls. Girls stopped shaving their armpits and legs. And for what? To prove that everybody could be slobs together?" Grandma had gotten worked up over things before, but I'd never heard her sound so bitter. "Is it too much to ask for one of my children—just one of them—to do things the normal way? Believe me, I was no angel in my time. I went dancing, stayed out late, screeched along with all the other girls at the sight of Frank Sinatra onstage. And I fought with my mother the way Susie and Vivian fight with me. But one day—overnight, it seemed—I became a wife and a mother. And suddenly I saw there was an order to things. It's all well and good to talk about how there's more to life than baking biscuits, washing floors, and going to PTA meetings. Fine. I agree. But you cannot— and you can quote me on this—you cannot in one fell swoop wipe out all remnants of tradition. There's something to be said for tra- dition and for the order it gives to life. You can try to modify it, but try to wipe it, and mark my word, you'll end up with nothing short of chaos. Which is exactly what the world is like right now. Chaotic."

Jake tried to distract Grandma by kissing her shoulder and making a joke about wanting a girl just like the girl who married dear old Dad, but he only got her more worked up.

"Go ahead—make all the fun you want," she said. "But mark my word. One day you kids are going to wake up with a tremen- dous headache from this dream about an ideal world where there are no wars and everybody loves everybody and nobody has to get married and children are born with smiles on their faces."

Grandma looked away from Jake and me, began brushing her hair, talking to her reflection in the mirror. "It's a funny thing," she said, "but if I could take a ride in one of those time machines, I'd zero in on Sunday nights with Jake and Susie and Vivian and

George. Why Sunday night? First of all, it was the only night of the week that I didn't have to break up fights or listen to complaints. No fights between Susie and Vivian over the blouse Susie said she borrowed but Vivian said she stole, or whose turn it was to play a record on the stereo Harry had, with all good intention, bought for them to share. No complaints from George about having meat loaf for dinner. No complaints from Susie about *not* having macaroni. No complaints from Vivian about everything on her plate and in her life, particularly Susie. On Sunday nights, there were simply no complaints. We always ate Chinese food or deli, and we always ordered the same thing: shrimp with lobster sauce for Harry, George, and Vivian. Chow mein, fried rice, egg rolls for everyone. And an extra bag of fried noodles for Jake so he could dip them in duck sauce. That's all he seemed to eat—that and fortune cookies. If we had deli, it was french fries and a hot dog for Jake, corned beef for Harry, pastrami for George and Vivian, roast beef for Susie and me.

"Now, George, who during the week always rushed through his dinner and holed himself up in his room, reading just about anything but mostly about the ocean, was like a different person on Sunday. Sunday, it seemed, was the night for George to *interact*—that's the word my daughter the social worker would use—with his family." She swiveled around in her chair, looked at me. "He'd take a bite out of a shrimp and suddenly start telling us everything he had learned about life under the sea that week. That's all he ever talked about. Whales. Dolphins. Sharks. Swordfish. Man-o'-wars. Crabs. Oysters. You name it. He'd even tell us about the sunken treasures that to this day have not been found.

"Vivian, who was impatient or jealous or simply bored with George's intelligence, was always the first to leave the table. 'Gotta make a phone call,' she'd say, excusing herself and dashing off to her room, where she'd spend a solid hour with her ear glued to the receiver of her pink princess phone. Harry was next. 'I'm going to the library,' he'd wink, and with the Sunday paper folded under his arm, he'd disappear into the bathroom. That left George, the ocean-ographer-to-be, with a captive audience of Jake and Susie and me.

"From George, we'd turn our attention to Walt Disney. Now, *there* was a man who knew how to make a movie, though I must say I preferred his cartoons. George, of course, took himself too seriously to enjoy cartoons, and Vivian, my on-the-sly-cigarette-smoking high school cheerleader, would not be caught dead indulging in the escapades of Mickey Mouse or Dumbo. But I could always count on Jake and Susie to watch Walt Disney with me. Jake loved cartoons, like I did, and Susie loved doing anything with her baby brother.

"Then Lassie would come on and capture us with her devotion and brilliance, not to mention her beauty, and by now Harry would be in his recliner with a newspaper in front of his face, pretending not to watch but as in love with Lassie as Jake and Susie and I were.

"And when it was time for *The Ed Sullivan Show*, we'd all be sitting around the TV, watching poodles climb ladders and waiting for the big stars, like Jackie Mason or Robert Goulet. It was a really great show—and I looked forward to watching it every week—until the Beatles appeared. I'm telling you, as long as I live I will never forget seeing those four mopheads on TV. George, who had just returned from a trip to California, was sitting on the couch next to me. Harry was in his recliner. And Susie, Vivian, and Jake were cross-legged on the living room floor, all three of them fidgety with anticipation. Finally, the moment arrived for Ed to introduce the Beatles, and an absolute hush overtook my household. Not a whis-per. Not a sigh. Don't ask me what they sang. Don't ask me what their music sounded like. Just ask me about the fight that broke out when George remarked that they had about as much talent as Topo Gigio and I, certainly without intending to, made matters worse by saying they weren't nearly as cute."

"I think you're getting a little carried away, Ruth," said Jake. He removed Grandma's new, blue silk dress from the closet door and handed it to her. "You can't hold the Beatles or Ed Sullivan responsible for what happened that night. It was pretty awful, but it was no one's fault. George and Vivian never got along."

She took the dress from Jake, threw it on the bed. "They never got along—but they never said the ugly things they said to each other that night. And they never fought on Sunday. Kind of makes you wonder how many other families across the country were fractured that Sunday night in 1964."

"This is all very fascinating"—Jake pointed to the clock on the nightstand—"but I think it's time you got dressed."

Grandma was not about to be rushed. "They waited this long to get married," she snapped. "They can wait a little longer." I looked at Jake for a word, a gesture, something to save me from the wicked queen my beautiful grandmother had suddenly become. He did not disappoint me.

"Let's go outside while your grandmother finishes dressing," he whispered, but Grandma stopped us.

"I'm sorry," she said, pulling me onto her lap and kissing my head. "I shouldn't be talking like this, but I'm a little on edge. Do you know what that means?" She was squeezing me tightly now and rocking me. "You know, when your mother was a little girl, she would sit on my lap just like this while I dried her off after a bath or brushed her hair, and we would talk about what she did in school that day or she would tell me about a new toy or book she wanted. And my mind sometimes would jump into the future to this very day—her wedding day—and I would see myself still fixing her hair, or I might be straightening the veil on her head or a crease in her gown." Grandma sighed. "Things don't always work out the way you expect, do they, cookie?" She pulled a piece of lint from my dress, and while she daydreamed about walking down a carpeted aisle arm in arm with the bride she was being deprived of giving away, I put my hand on her powdery cheek.

"You look beautiful, Grandma," I said, studying the shades of blue and violet and copper that transformed my very pretty grandmother into the most glamorous woman I'd ever seen.

Grandma planted a kiss, wet with lipstick, on my cheek. "Lipstick doesn't belong *there*," she said, rubbing off her kiss. She got up, took some light pink lipstick from her drawer, and dabbed it on my lips. "There!" she said. "Not that you weren't absolutely stunning without it. Am I right, Jake?"

"You're never wrong, Ruth." He winked at me, said if I were a little older and if uncles could marry their nieces, he'd marry me. I blushed.

"Zipper me, please," said Grandma. Jake helped her with her dress. I hoped he would not look my way again until the warm flush left my cheeks.

"Let's get this show on the road," Grandpa called out from the living room. Jake bowed and took my hand, and I thought he wanted to smell the flowers on my wrist, but instead he kissed my knuckles. No one had ever kissed my knuckles, and Jake's kiss was soft and warm and brought another rush of warm blood to my face.

Grandma checked herself in the mirror once more and freshened her lipstick, and we all scurried to the car. It was 11:00 a.m., the Sunday before Labor Day in the year 1974, and in exactly one hour I would witness my parents take their marriage vows. My heart was fluttering. I wanted everything to be perfect, so I sat perfectly still, continually smoothing out my white eyelet dress with its starchy freshness and pushing back the wisps of hair that kept falling into my face. We were racing along the parkway and Grandpa and Jake were singing about love and marriage and Grandma was telling them to be quiet and the wind was blowing in my face but I didn't mind a bit. On my wrist was a bouquet of roses, trimmed in lace, and in my lap was my quetzal bag (filled with six tiny dolls and a wooden spoon), and next to me was my very favorite uncle. The wind, soft and summery, tickled my eyes and Grandma's Paris perfume tickled my nose and filling my ears were off-key harmonies about the horse and carriage of love. Clouds in the distance threatened rain, which Grandma said was good luck on a wedding day, and I asked if the sun meant bad luck. Of course not, Grandma reassured me, but for one fleeting instant, as I looked at the radiant sun above, my heart sank with the possibility of disappointment. What if my mother once again changed her mind? The only complaint my father seemed to have had in the past forty-three days was my mother's insistence on keeping her last name. It was bad enough, he argued, that my birth certificate said Rachel Cohen (minus Schneider)—his fault, mostly, since he didn't arrive at the hospital until after I was born and the nurse had already recorded my name. What if he gave my mother a last-minute ultimatum: marry me, take my name?

A phrase from a picture book I had read with Jake popped into my head. "Rain makes applesauce," I said, hearing the surprise in my voice, the awareness drawn from leaps of nonsense. I repeated the words, chant-like: "rain makes applesauce rain makes applesauce." And when the first drops hit the car as we crossed the Brooklyn Bridge, my heart soared. Sitting next to me was my favorite uncle, and on my hand was a kiss, and it had been only the previous night that my grandmother, because of a back scratcher and me, had lain in a faint on her bed, and in a very short while I would eat the sugar flowers of a wedding cake or something equally sweet. Grandpa was now singing about the little girl he carried and Grandma was adjusting her hat and rain was making applesauce against the hood of the car and I was sure, on that September day in 1974, that I was the happiest person on Earth.

"Where are they, already? According to my watch, it's twenty-five minutes after twelve and they were supposed to be here at twelve. Can't they be on time for anything?" Grandma was pacing back and forth in front of the synagogue where we were supposed to meet my parents. It was an old building made of stone the color of mud. "I'm not even going to ask where Vivian is. Couldn't she get another plane last night? It's not like she's flying in from Kathmandu. She's coming from Florida. There must be planes every hour. Why did she have to wait till the last minute? Never mind—look who I'm talking about."

Unbeknownst to Grandma, Vivian had flown up the night before. So had George, whom Grandma did not expect to see at all today. It was all part of a grand surprise that Jake and my mother had orchestrated.

"I knew we should have picked them up." Grandma folded her arms. Unfolded them. Folded them again. "Who takes a taxi on their wedding day? I realize my daughter likes to do things her own way, but what's so terrible about a limousine—or at least having someone from your family pick you up—on your wedding day? I know Susie would like to treat this like any other day in her life, but it isn't any other day. Why can't she just accept that?"

"This has a very familiar ring, Ruth," said Jake.

Grandma continued walking. Back and forth. Back and forth. "I have no idea what you're talking about."

"Sure you do. It was a day just like this."

"I felt a raindrop," said Grandma, looking up. Hesitating. Thinking. "It was not a day like this at all. It was a monsoon. In all my life I never saw such rain. And where was my daughter with her three-day-old baby? Having a pastrami sandwich."

I'd heard this story before, in bits and pieces. Streets were flooded, traffic moved at a snail's pace, and my mother, on her way home from the hospital three days after giving birth to me, had a terrible craving for a pastrami sandwich. So my father, with the skill (if not the speed) of Bobby Unser, maneuvered his way down Flatbush Avenue, parked the car in front of Junior's Restaurant, and indulged the mother of his seven-pound, ten-ounce bundle of joy.

"Your grandmother was a wreck," Jake told me. "We were all waiting in your apartment. Your grandfather was reading a newspaper, I was reading a magazine, and she kept walking from room to room, peering out of every window. 'Where are they, already? It should take twenty minutes—a half hour at most—to get here from the hospital. What if?—I should bite my tongue just at the thought of it—but in rain like this, anything is possible.'"

I laughed. Jake did a good imitation of her.

"When your mother and father finally walked through the door with you, she broke down and cried."

Grandma listened. Cleared her throat. Pretended not to listen. "Has anyone spoken to the bride or groom this morning?" she asked. "I mean, do we know for a fact that they haven't changed their minds again?" Not knowing which direction they would be coming from, she continued to pace, craning her neck whenever she saw people headed toward us, as if the very act of looking could make my parents appear.

Suddenly her face turned white. "Oh my God!" She was staring down the block where she saw two figures walking toward us, arm in arm.

Even before Vivian got close, I recognized the *clip-clop* of her high heels. Unlike my mother, Vivian always wore high heels (at least whenever I saw her) and lots of makeup and clothes that hugged her body. Maybe it was a certain fascination with my distant, glamorous aunt that made me look forward to her visits: her hair was frosted, her lipstick was red or pink, and she wore silk dresses or tight-fitting sweaters and pants that accentuated her tiny waist and round hips. She always smelled pretty, too. She could rattle off the names and prices of expensive fragrances from around the world. And she was the only person I knew who dabbed perfume on her ankles and heels.

This was only the second time I'd ever seen George, whose round, rimless glasses and full beard camouflaged any resemblance to his siblings. He was the oldest of Grandma's children and the only one to have earned a degree that gave him the right to be addressed as "Doctor" (George was a doctor of biological oceanography). Grandma often talked about him as if he were on the verge of some major discovery about life under the sea.

"I don't believe it!" she exclaimed, hugging George first, then Vivian. "I just don't believe it!" She was absolutely beaming. Grandma did not see George very much (he lived in San Diego and spent most of his time traveling the oceans of the world), so his presence today—on the arm of Vivian—nearly sent her into a state of cardiac arrest. "You were supposed to be on a ship somewhere in the Pacific. That's what you said in your letter to me." She was trying to put all the pieces together. "When did you get in? Why didn't you call?"

"Then it wouldn't have been a surprise, Mom," answered Vivian, who went on to explain that she had arrived at the airport at six thirty the previous night and George had arrived at seven thirty and they had stayed up most of the night at my house, making up for years of virtually not talking. It didn't take long for Grandma to figure out why Jake and Grandpa seemed a little evasive about where they had disappeared to (while she was nearly electrocuted by a gypsy in a babushka), and she was absolutely beaming. Then my mother and father finally showed up, and there was more hugging, only now there were some tears, too. Grandma was crying and Vivian was crying and my mother, in a Victorian lace dress and broad-rimmed straw hat, was fighting her tears.

It was up to my father, who looked so handsome in his white

dinner jacket and white linen pants, to shepherd the wedding party into the synagogue, where the rabbi was waiting in her chambers. Each day for the past forty-three, I had fastidiously marked an *X* on my calendar to remind me of something I was waiting for, and now the thing I was waiting for was about to happen and I felt almost numb with happiness. We walked through a hallway, past glass cases filled with scrolls and mezuzahs, and into a small room lined with bookcases, where I would find myself standing next to my father, with Jake next to me, and Grandma, Grandpa, Vivian, and George behind us. There were some prayers in Hebrew, and then the rabbi spoke in English and my parents drank from the same glass of wine, and before I knew it, the ceremony was over. I was charged with holding the rings and did not realize how tightly I had been clutching them until I saw the two concentric circles in my palm after I relinquished the rings to the rabbi. My parents, who had seemed so serious to me all during the ceremony, finally smiled when they said their vows, and I cried only when my father smashed his heel on a glass covered with a cloth napkin.

"It's good luck," he explained, as he wiped my tears, and that may very well be so, but to me it was as unexpected as it was frightening.

Jake was the first to kiss the bride after the ceremony; then he lifted me in the air and announced he wanted to be the first to kiss the daughter of the bride, and Grandpa took pictures of everyone kissing everyone. Vivian said we needed a picture of Grandpa, too, so she made Grandma and Grandpa pose with my mother, my father, and me. I started to feel dizzy with the smell of perfume and flowers, and it was a relief when we were outside again, heading down Central Park West. The air was humid but cool, and the park was filled with people bicycling, walking, jogging, and I was filled with such happy thoughts that all I needed was Tinkerbell to sprinkle me with pixie dust and I'd be soaring. Powdery clouds were moving across the sky, and I did not know what it meant for two people to be married, but everybody (not just Grandma) seemed to be beaming now. Grandma thought it was very peculiar (so did I) that we had to go through the lobby of an apartment building to get to the restaurant where we were having lunch, but Vivian said it was chic. Grandpa suggested that maybe the building was once a hotel and this was the coffee shop before it became a fancy French restaurant.

We sat at a cozy corner table. On the walls surrounding us were paintings of naked women. The waiter brought a bottle of champagne, compliments of Vivian's boyfriend, Tony, who was supposed to join us at the restaurant if he could discreetly pull himself away from a family barbecue. "His wife's family," Vivian snorted. My mother let me take a sip, and I started to giggle from the tickling sensation of the champagne, and I giggled even more as I stared at the paintings on the wall.

"Don't give her any more," said Grandma. "She's drunk." And in a sense I was, but not from the champagne.

Grandpa, who was not used to fancy French restaurants, joked about wanting shrimp with lobster sauce, which started George off on a tangent about the different varieties of shrimp around the world.

"Here we go again," groaned Vivian, who then said she had to make a phone call, only instead of getting up she turned to George and kissed him. Everyone (except me) laughed, and Grandma said this was the best Sunday she'd had in a long time. Then Grandpa made a toast to my mother and father, and my father toasted Vivian's and George's reconciliation, and that started Grandma reminiscing about the Sunday nights of *Ed Sullivan*. In the middle of the reminiscing, George said he had a funny story to tell about four stranded harbor seals that he helped save in 1967.

"It's not funny in the ha-ha sense," he began, fidgeting with his tie, which was imprinted with whales. "I mean, if you've ever seen a beached seal, you would not laugh. He's kind of lost his bearings, and all he wants is to be with the rest of the herd, but by the time he's beached, he's rather disoriented. And if he's been stuck in the sand for some time, he's rather hungry, too—"

"Get to the punch line, George," Vivian interrupted.

"The punch line is this: these four seals were visibly distressed when they were not in each other's presence, so we named them John, George, Ringo, and Paul—and it was my idea. I was joking, of course, and someone else suggested we name them after the Beach Boys, since they were indigenous to the Pacific, but another colleague said they looked more like the Beatles. 'I was joking,' I said. 'Really! We can't name seals after a rock group.' While we were in the middle of arguing about what to name the seals, one of the secretaries at the lab came running in. She had tears in her eyes, and she told us about a woman who had just burned herself to death as a protest against the Vietnam War. After we heard that, nobody cared what we named the seals, but somehow John, Paul, Ringo, and George stuck."

"Nice light lunchtime conversation," said my father. Then he filled up George's champagne glass. "Drink up, George. You need it."

Grandpa ordered another bottle of champagne, and my mother—over Grandma's protests—let me have another sip.

"It's not every day that my daughter gets married," Grandpa told the waiter, who as he poured the champagne assured Grandma that yes, the salmon was fresh, and yes, she could have the hollandaise sauce on the side. Grandpa ordered shrimp (without lobster sauce), my mother and Vivian went for crab cakes, my father and George ordered steak *frites*, and Jake asked for an *omborgeur* to share with me. Grandma, a little giddy from the champagne, recounted the previous night's episode in the bath (and after), detail for detail, while we waited for the food, and everyone (except me) laughed.

When we finished lunch, Vivian really did have to make a phone call. "Tony's taking me to Sicily tonight," she said. When Tony was in New York, he was hard to pin down (Vivian would certainly never have called him at home), but he told her where to call him at exactly 3:00 p.m. if he didn't make it to the restaurant.

"He's got friends in Sicily," explained Vivian, "and they've arranged everything. We'll have a villa to ourselves, and a car and driver at our disposal, although Tony really likes to do his own driving."

"I'll bet he's also arranged for a special dispensation from the Pope for a divorce," said Grandma.

"Why can't you just let it go, Mom?" said Vivian. "I love the guy; he loves me; I have a pool, a car, a year-round tan—what more do I need?"

I'm sure Grandma had an answer for Vivian, but she was distracted by the three-tier dessert cart the waiter brought over to the table. "There goes my diet," she said, playing a game of Eeny, Meeny, Miny, Moe between the chocolate mousse cake and the apple tart. I wanted something that looked more like wedding cake.

There were eight of us at the table, and we ordered five different desserts (none of which looked like wedding cake). I shared a chocolate mousse cake with Jake, Grandma shared hers with Grandpa, Vivian took one forkful of my mother's apple tart, my mother had one spoonful of my father's profiteroles, and we all tasted George's crème brûlée.

After lunch, my parents were off to the Plaza Hotel for another honeymoon night, Vivian and George drove back to my house, and Grandpa once again started singing about the little girl he carried.

"Stop with the singing, already," said Grandma, which only instigated more singing, this time with Jake.

I stared out the window, at nothing and everything. The wind, cooler than it had been that morning, tickled my eyes, and the flowers of my corsage tickled my nose, and off-key melodies about the horse and carriage of love filled my ears. The motion of the car, coupled with my lack of sleep the night before, made me drowsy, and I laid my head in Jake's lap. It may have taken just minutes to fall asleep, but in that short time I seemed to compress every moment of the day into Morse code–like messages that imprinted themselves in a substratum of my consciousness. Sometimes if I'm riding in a car on the parkway and there's a distinct feel of late summer or early autumn in the air, I'll close my eyes to the breeze and for the briefest moment I'll smell the flowers of the corsage I wore that first Sunday in September 1974, or I'll see my parents poised in a ceremonial kiss, or I'll wipe the lingering traces of chocolate mousse cake from my lips. Invariably the breeze will shift or a voice in the car or from the radio will break the trance with a cruelty akin to having a bucket of ice water poured on my head. It might be something as innocuous as my mother's telling me about her day or asking about mine, or it might be the fifth radio commercial in a row, no more strident than the other four but irritating in its cacophonous insistence, that prevents the messages or images from running in sequence up and down my body the way they seemed to as I drifted off in the warmth of Jake's lap that Sunday in September 1974.

The word "harmony" comes to mind. My father taught me all about the subtleties of harmony and the ways it can be manipulated (musically speaking). There is tempered harmony and pure harmony, open harmony, even false harmony, and it irked him that the term had become a catchall metaphor for states of personal bliss. Whenever he said this, my mother accused him of being too much of a purist, to which my father would reply that one can never be too much of a purist. In any case, I took to heart his purism, added my acquired sensitivity to the subtleties of harmony, and concluded, when I tried to give a name to the feeling I had as I lay in Jake's lap, filled with images of a perfect day, that it was nothing short of harmony.

The essence of harmony (musically speaking) is a combination of specific notes or chords. Take just one component away, and every bit of the sweetness is gone. I can't say it's sweetness, per se, that I'm seeking now (though I wouldn't mind some)—just a chance to feel the full, rich harmony of the happiest day of my young life. It was the first Sunday in September 1974, and we were all so happy, and never never in my wildest dreams could I have imagined that ten years and eight months later my parents would separate, and never never in my darkest dreams could I imagine I would one day be driving along the parkway, windows open to a cruel breeze that would take me from the edge of harmony to a cold, flat reality. "Jake is gone," I hear myself say. Jake is gone.

postcards

It's a known fact that if you were to drop a penny from the top of a tall building, the force of its motion would dent the hood of a car. It's also a known fact that the effect of gravity will cause a feather and a ball to fall at the same speed. Jerry Goldberg, who's a real brain, told me these are important things to keep in mind when you're cruising at an altitude of thirty-five thousand feet and there's a movie playing that's not really for children and you can't sleep or read because (a) you're too restless and (b) some baby is howling. So what you do, said Jerry, is imagine that you're dropping pennies (or feathers and balls) from the airplane. Or you pretend the world below is one big Lionel train set and it's up to you to keep things in motion. If none of these suggestions works, said Jerry, start writing postcards. That's what his mother does. First she orders a Bloody Mary, then she starts writing to the twenty-some people she promised she would send postcards to.

This was her way of "getting them out of the way," Jerry explained to me. "People don't care when you wrote the postcard. They just want to see that proof-of-presence picture on the front of the postcard and a couple of nice words on the back to let them know you remembered to write. So she calls the hotel they're staying at ahead of time and asks for a dozen assorted postcards to get her started. What does she write? 'We're off and flying. The weather promises to be good. I'm already feeling relaxed. See you when we get back.'"

I stared out the window, waiting for the plane to take off. Vanessa, my personal stewardess, came over to me and gave me a plastic pin in the shape of an airplane. Wisps of white-blond hair fell from her otherwise perfect French braid.

"First time on a plane?" she asked. I nodded. "You're not nervous, are you?" I nodded again, and we both laughed. I wanted to tell her that I was going to visit my favorite uncle, who had an apartment overlooking the San Francisco Bay, and I was the only one of my friends who had gone anywhere by herself and I was really more excited than nervous and did she know there was a very small earthquake in the Bay Area last week—they call it a tremor? But my mouth suddenly felt the way it feels at the dentist's office when he puts in that tube that sucks up saliva, and all I could say was, "I'm very thirsty—can I please have a drink?"

She brought me a plastic cup filled with club soda, pulled a pillow and blanket from the overhead bin for me, then left me to my own devices of comfort, which included a copy of *Black Beauty* and my ever-growing collection of postcards. Each and every one of the postcards I had received from Jake over the years (my collection thus far spanned four continents) was imbued with the mystery of something unknown to me. There were times when the picture was enough to capture me, times when the words, short and sweet as they may have been, were filled with a suggestion of place that transported me to the very corner of the earth Jake happened to be. In a sense, the postcards also framed my life, grounding me in time.

Dear Rachel:

I spent the night at a small inn on the top of Machu Picchu, an old Inca site nestled high in the Andes. The air is thin up here and the mountains remind me of thick green carpets. If you look carefully at the postcard picture, you'll see a large stone (supposedly a sun dial) known as the Intihuana, *or "place where the sun is tied." I stood next to it this morning as the sun came up. And for a moment time seemed to stand still. It's believed that "chosen women," devoted to rituals of sun worship, lived here. Theirs was a religious life (not to be confused with Vivian's brand of sun worship).*

Love, Jake

"What's with the raspberries, Ma?" asked Vivian. There were three large glass bowls on the table, filled to the brim. I was helping Grandma make fresh whipped cream.

"Rachel loves raspberries," said Grandma. She winked at me. I winked back, relishing my newfound role as co-conspirator in my grandmother's "plot."

"So do I—but isn't this a little overkill?" Vivian dipped a long, pointed fingernail into one of the bowls, scooping out a single berry. Her nail polish, gypsy red, seemed to sparkle in raspberry juice.

"Between you and Susie—and Rachel—I've never had a problem getting rid of raspberries." Grandma handed me the bowl. It was my turn to whip. I took the eggbeater in my hand, began making swirls in the thickening cream. *Maybe it will finally happen*, I kept thinking.

It was a simple plan, one that began simmering not long after my parents' wedding. *So?* Grandma would say to my mother once a month on average. So *what?* my mother would respond. To which Grandma would respond, *You know*, throwing a glance my way. My one simple question—*What's she supposed to know?*—would always bring the conversation to an abrupt halt. *Don't ask so many questions, Rachel.*

Month after month passed, and the dialogue was always the same, though the bite in my mother's response would get sharper and Grandma's exasperation would deepen, until one night, shortly after my parents' first wedding anniversary, it reached a pitch. *Rachel needs a brother*, she said, slamming her hand on the table. *Or a sister.* My mother's response was curt. *This is not about Rachel*, she said. *It's about you.*

Vivian continued picking at the raspberries. "There's nothing like raspberries picked fresh from a bush." She licked her finger. "We got one in our backyard. Hard to eat these mushy ones after you've tasted a *real* raspberry." She was wearing a blue silk kimono that slipped off her shoulder whenever she moved. Cream and coffee were what I thought of, glimpsing the skinny strap of her nightgown against her bronze shoulder. Wrapped in sky.

The telephone rang. Vivian ran to answer it, thinking it might be Tony. Whenever they came to New York, she stayed with my grandparents while Tony spent time with his children. His wife, according to Vivian, would sooner let him sleep on the sofa bed than divorce him. *She's a bigger fool than you are*, Grandma would say.

"That was your mother," said Vivian. "She'll be here in twenty minutes." Vivian reached into her pocket for a box of Chiclets, offered me some. The smell of mint mingled with the residue of Joy (her favorite perfume) on her kimono. It was a smell I loved.

By the time my mother arrived, the raspberries and cream—not to mention raspberry strudel that Grandma had baked earlier that morning—were laid out on the table.

"You look thin," Vivian said to my mother.

"And pale, I might add." Grandma sat down at the table, lit a cigarette. It wasn't often that they were together, just the three of them, and it brought a noticeable change to her face. She seemed younger for a moment, her eyes softened by the reverie of having been here at this very table before, just the three of them, eating, arguing, laughing. It was only a flash, maybe a second or two, a suspension of time and place. As quickly as the moment came, it passed; Grandma turned to Vivian, then my mother, and took a deep drag of her cigarette, savoring, as long as she could, the illusion that everything her daughters would do, all that they would become, was still far in the future. She snuffed her cigarette in the ashtray, turned again to my mother. "Don't tell me it has nothing to do with that juice fast you were on. If people were meant to live on juice, God would not have given us chicken. Here—have a rugelach. I made them for you."

Grandma winked at me again as she slid the plate of rugelach closer to my mother. I tried to will her to pick one up and eat it. *Go ahead*, I thought, *take one. Or two. Or a piece of strudel. Or some juicy red raspberries.* She reached into her knapsack, pulled out a bottle of green powder, mixed some in a glass of water, and drank it down. *Go ahead*, I thought, *take one, to wash down the taste of that putrid spiru-something-or-other.* That's what Grandma called it. She'd been thumbing through a copy of *Vegetarian Times* that my mother had left on the table one morning when she'd dropped me off. *This is food for rabbits*, she said, riffling through the pages, muttering to herself about that *putrid spiru-something-or-other* that had become a staple in my mother's diet. An article on herbs caught her eye. Red raspberry jumped out at her. *Good for "female" things,* she said to me. That was all she needed to know.

My role was simple: Say nothing to my mother. Just sit back and watch her sip Grandma's raspberry tea concoction or nibble on a piece of strudel à la raspberry. *Good for "female" things*, Grandma said to me over and over again. When I asked what that meant, she explained that raspberries contain something that would help a baby grow inside my mother. What more did I need to know?

I moved over to my mother's lap, kissed her cheek. "Want a raspberry?" She shook her head, said she was feeling a little queasy.

"Stop drinking that putrid spiru-something-or-other, and you won't feel queasy," said Grandma.

"It has nothing to do with that." My mother began combing her fingers through my hair. She asked Grandma for a cup of "that tea" she had given her the last time we'd been here.

"You do look a little thin," Vivian said again.

My mother shot her an angry look. "Maybe it's because I've been throwing up for the past three mornings."

Vivian was the first to catch on. "Well, whaddaya know!" She leaned across the table to kiss my mother. "Congratulations—you didn't tell me you were trying for number two."

"I wasn't trying."

Vivian pinched my cheek. "So, how does it feel to know you're going to have a little brother or sister?"

I turned to my grandmother, whose face took on a glow that I'd never seen before and have not seen since. All these months, all those raspberries, all that power.

I had power, too. I could stop my mother from crying, which she did a lot in the first weeks of her pregnancy. My grandmother said they were tears of happiness, Vivian said it was hormones, my mother said nothing, just cried and cried. If my father bought her flowers, she cried. If he went out at midnight to get her a hot fudge sundae, she cried. Only I could stop the crying. All I had to do was put my ear to her belly, tell her I could hear the ocean in there, with a tiny baby swimming around. *I think it's a boy*, I would say, desperately wanting a brother. Or I would start singing lullabies into her belly button. She always stopped crying.

The morning she got out of bed without a trace of tears on her face, I was heady with that sense of power until she said, "Something's wrong." She didn't tell me any more than that, just said to get dressed and call Grandma to say we'd be over soon. My father, working as an account executive in training for a public relations firm, was out of town. Within minutes, we were in the car on the way to my grandmother's house. Not a word was said during that short ride. Afraid I'd upset my mother by asking what was wrong, I stared out the window, counting red cars. It was a game I usually played with her (she chose the color, I looked for the cars) whenever we went on long drives. I counted three red cars between our house and my grandmother's.

After a phone conversation with her doctor, my mother went to lie down in Jake's room, the only bedroom other than my grand-parents' that still had a bed. She asked me to bring her a cup of tea (chamomile with raspberry). Between sips of tea, she told me about the cramps and the spotting. "There might be a problem with the pregnancy," she said.

"Maybe he [I was sure it was a he] just wants to come out already." Fourteen weeks seemed long enough to me.

"It's too soon." She took my hand and kissed it. Grandma called me into the kitchen. "Your mother needs to sleep."

The cramping got worse, the spotting heavier. My mother called out from the bathroom. She needed a plastic bag. When I brought her a large white plastic trash bag that Grandma had given me, she burst out laughing. "Do you think it's big enough?" she asked, showing me the small red blob of life in her hand. I ran back to the kitchen. Grandma tried to keep me there—*You shouldn't know from these things*, she said—but I pulled away from her, opened the drawer where she kept baggies, brought one to my mother, watched with awe as she slipped the tiny blob of life into the transparent plastic. The doctor would need to take a look at it, she explained. She kissed my forehead, said she was proud of me, didn't want me to be scared. All the while, Grandma kept her distance, calling out from the kitchen, *Is everything okay? Is everything okay?* When I went running to her, dangling the bag, she gasped, grabbing it from me and putting it inside a brown paper bag. *You shouldn't know from these things*, she said.

The phone rang. It was Sophie. Grandma said she couldn't talk, my mother had just lost the baby. "The baby's not lost!" I yelled. He was right there, on the table, no fingers or toes yet, no eyes or nose, but not lost. I reached for the bag, wanting to take another look. My mother scooped me up in her arms, said I'd seen enough for one day. We spent the rest of the afternoon on the couch in Grandma's den, watching cartoons. Grandma kept walking in and out of the room—*How about some cookies and milk? Or a cup of tea?*—stifling tears and muttering, *It wasn't meant to be. It wasn't meant to be.* My mother, in contrast, was a cushion of calm. *At least she's not crying*, I kept thinking. *At least she's not crying.*

～

Dear Rachel:

Florence may be the most beautiful city I've ever seen. I spend afternoons walking along the river, when the sun seems to wash the city in gold. Took a trip to Rome last weekend—you've never seen so many cats in one place! Every nook and cranny of the Colosseum is filled with them. I thought about you when I saw newspaper photos of the tall ships on the Hudson. What a birthday party you must have had! We (i.e., Americans in Rome) lit sparklers on the Spanish Steps (pictured here). I bet your father pulled out his army fatigues for the occasion.

xxx Jake

"Just be your charming self," my mother said to my father. We were stopped at a traffic light on Riverside Drive, on our way to Renata's. Renata was my mother's best friend, and she lived with Paco in a large rent-controlled apartment overlooking the Hudson River. Paco moved in not long after Renata's husband moved out. She needed the rent; he needed the room. It was an arrangement that made my father uncomfortable. Whenever they came to us for dinner, he never said much, just sat back in his chair, observing, listening, picking at food, his eyes glazed with scrutiny. Once, he laughed. Loud and hard. We were eating dessert—Renata's apple tart. Paco smacked his lips, joking about the joys of living with a fag hag who was a patisserie chef extraordinaire. There was release in my father's laugh. *You're pretty funny for a fa—.* Looking at me, looking at my mother, he stopped himself. Language, he would say, is all in the context.

My father's jaw tightened. Twitched. He looked straight ahead. Another car, turning from a side street, cut him off just as the light changed.

"Motherfucker!" he screamed, ramming the horn. I was beginning to wish he'd stayed home, the way he wanted to. Or at least take off the stupid hat and camouflage vest he wore open to display his dog tags. *Even if I gave a flying fuck about this bicentennial,* he said before we left, *even if my body were not a minefield of cynic's scars, I would much rather watch the fireworks from the comfort of my living room couch.*

"You're taking this much too seriously," said my mother. "It's just a party—a chance to eat, drink, mingle. Chill and be charming."

Charming? I thought. *How does a person be charming?* Charm was something measured in gold and pearls on my aunt Vivian's wrist, small mementos that she said told the story of her life. The first charm to go on the bracelet, a boxy phone, was still her favorite. Mine was the baton wrapped in a fine twist of gold and topped with a pearl on each end. Or it was something for good luck, something singular and magical, like the small heart-shaped locket Grandpa had unceremoniously given me a few months back. Or it was candy.

It was not a person, certainly not my father.

"Exactly my point," he said. "Just a party. A big blowout to wipe the blood under the rug. Pretend the last ten years were nothing more than an out-of-control family argument." He shook his head.

"Come on, Susie—six years ago you would have been protesting. Today you're gonna drink champagne."

"It's called healing, Robert."

"It's called bullshit, Susie."

I fingered the locket around my neck, the one with the tiny picture of Jake's face that I'd cut from a family snapshot. He'd left for Florence three weeks earlier, to study art. Grandma was not happy. *Don't come back thinking you're going to paint my ceiling.* She wanted him to settle down already, someplace close to home. So did I.

I stuck my head out the window. Sounds drifted by—radio voices traveling like disembodied spirits, notes from the guitars of street musicians waving like kite tails. People were headed toward the river, arms stuffed with blankets and towels, beach chairs and picnic baskets. Red-white-and-blue kites danced in the sky.

"Get your head back inside, Rachel." My mother reached over the backseat and pulled at my shirt.

"We're moving at minus five miles an hour, but your mother is worried that some Mack truck is gonna come speeding by and decapitate you." My father winked at me in the rearview mirror.

"Of course, if we'd done what *I* wanted to do, we would not be creeping along in traffic like this." My father knew how to make a point. Sprawled across the backseat were maps. He'd wanted to get out of the city for the weekend, go someplace where the word "bicentennial" might be banned. Amish country had caught his fancy. He'd never been there, thought it would be *the* place to at least pretend to forget what the rest of America was spending so much energy making a show of remembering.

"If we'd done what *you* wanted to do, we'd be sitting in traffic on the George Washington Bridge. That's if that car didn't break down."

Some spooky—and stupid—song about Alice in Wonderland started playing on the radio. Almost instantly, the tension in the car eased. It was as though a spell had been cast, or a charm with the power of recasting memories, shuffling them from spades to aces, had made its way into the car.

God must be in radios, I thought. My father turned up the volume, started singing along. His head moved with the music. My mother joined in.

God, I thought, *must* really *be in radios*.

Renata greeted us with a large white platter of red salsa and blue chips when we walked into her apartment. I had never seen blue chips before. She was wearing stars-and-stripes boxer shorts with a white tank top. Paco, also in a white tank top, trailed behind her. His shoulders erupted from his shirt like sunbursts.

"*Bienvenue*," said Renata. "It's one of the few French words I know." In her four-inch red platform shoes, she was almost as tall as Paco, whose legs seemed carved into his combat boots. She was always saying that she wanted legs like Paco's.

My father made his way to the terrace, where he stationed himself in a white plastic chair, beer bottle in hand. Glen, a lawyer who worked for the same agency where Paco, Renata, and my mother worked, was half-hidden by a large spider plant that hung from one of the living room windows. He came over to my mother and kissed her cheek. His arm seemed to linger around her waist. I was glad my father didn't see.

I sat myself down on Renata's wine-colored velvet divan, which looked out of place without the two brocade chairs that used to surround it like ladies-in-waiting. Renata had inherited the divan from her grandmother. The chairs were the only pieces of furniture Paul wanted when he left. He'd gotten them dirt cheap at an auction upstate. Renata tried to talk him out of taking them, they were so perfect in her living room. This was one investment he was not going to lose on, he said.

On the end table next to the divan was a lamp with a milky glass globe painted with roses. I liked the changing levels of light the globe gave off when I turned the switch, a brass key attached to the neck of the lamp. If I turned it once, the light was dim, almost gold. Twice, it took on the softness of clouds. Three times, the red roses popped.

"Pretty lamp, isn't it?" A woman sat down next to me. She had hair so black it looked almost blue, and skin as dull as baby powder. *Snow White*, I thought. She asked me how old I was now, said she had a niece my age. Her family rented a bungalow on a lake in the Catskills. She usually managed to visit once or twice a summer.

"What are you doing this summer?" She had a fistful of peanuts. She popped some into her mouth. I counted seven rings on her fingers.

"Things." I shrugged.

"Not too talkative, are you?"

The light of the lamp suddenly seemed harsh. I reached to turn it off. I could have told her that my birthday was yesterday and my grandmother had baked a chocolate cake for me and I'd gotten the new bicycle I'd wanted.

Or I could have told her what I'd learned last night—that my mother went into a panic when July 3 rolled around and I was a week overdue. It wasn't being overdue that bothered her; it was the dread of fireworks and sparklers announcing my birth. So she walked aimlessly through the neighborhood, stopping here for an ice cream cone, there for potato chips, through the park, all the way to my grandmother's house. *You have this backwards*, said Grandma. *Movement puts a baby to sleep.* My mother stretched out on the couch. I began to move. It was six o'clock in the evening. An hour later, she went into labor. I was born at 11:58.

But who was she, this strange woman sitting down next to me, taking up half the divan that I wanted for myself?

She touched my hair, told me how pretty I was and how she hadn't seen me since I was a baby.

Who was she?

"I went to school with your mother."

Who was she?

"We marched together—almost got arrested once." She leaned close to me. Her breath smelled like peanuts and beer. "I think it's what your mother secretly wanted—to be arrested, once, for protesting the war. I talked the cop out of it." She popped more peanuts into her mouth. Her bracelets, halfway up her arm, jingled. "Seems like a lifetime ago."

Again, she touched my hair. "Want something to drink?" I shook my head. Hard. I hated when people touched my hair. Like I was a dog.

Through the window, I glimpsed sparklers being lit. My father had bought a box. For me, he said. I ran out to him, reached for the box of sparklers in his vest pocket. He put his hand on mine. "No point in lighting them till it gets dark."

"But . . ." I looked at the woman holding the sparkler. She started waving it like she was conducting an orchestra. There was glitter on her cheeks. She caught my eye, bent toward me, and offered me the sparkler. Her bell-bottoms were painted with flowers and peace signs. "Make a wish," she said. "A good one."

My father watched closely as I clutched the sparkler at arm's length. It was a mystery to me, the way you could light a stick and watch it turn into bits of shooting stars. I started waving it the way the woman had. The sparks danced. I wanted to touch one, crush it between my fingers before it disappeared like dandelion fuzz. It was harder than trying to catch a butterfly.

"Did you make your wish?" The woman was lighting another sparkler. "Better make it before the sparkler fizzles out."

I turned to my father, who had his eyes on the sparkler in my hand.

No point in lighting them before dark.

He knew that I knew not to touch the hot spot. But he would not take his eyes off my hand. Just in case.

The sparks were down to a sputter. I'd made my wish yesterday, a secret wish, blowing out the candles on my birthday cake. There was nothing else I wanted.

Except . . .

I looked at my father, still keeping a watchful eye on the lit sparkler. I looked for my mother, who was someplace inside. Talking. Drinking. Chilling out.

I made my wish—a silly one, I thought. A waste of wishing power. But it was all I could think of at that moment.

I wish for my parents to be in the same room. For more than thirty minutes. Since my mother's miscarriage, they didn't seem to talk much, except at dinner, which lasted an average of thirty minutes, sometimes less if the subject of *the lost baby* came up. My father wanted to *try again.* My mother said *trying took the joy from love.* The miscarriage, she said, was a sign. When her agency placed her at a home for pregnant teens not long after the miscarriage, she saw it as another sign. She was not meant to *have* babies, just to help other women take care of them. *Doesn't mean I don't love your father,* she said. *Just no more babies.* The only time they seemed to spend more than thirty minutes in the same room together was at night. In bed. Sleeping. Watching TV. Making love. Without trying.

The smell of charcoal burning wafted up from the terrace below. Right about now, I thought, my best friend, Laura, would be squeezing ketchup on half a hot dog bun and mustard on the other half, a combination she said brought a sweet tang to her mouth. She'd wanted me to come to a barbecue at her house. "I need you," she'd said. "Just a bunch of babies gonna be there. Stupid little cousins and the Brat." She never called her one-year-old sister, Ricki, by her name, just complained a lot about how much better life was before the Brat. She hated the baby drool and the baby talk, made fun of the way her parents clucked at the Brat all the time when she was an infant. "You don't want a baby in your house, Rachel, believe me. They turn your parents into chickens, clicking their tongues, making strange noises all the time. And when they're not clicking or clucking, they're oohing and aahing at every stupid little thing she does." She pinched her nose. "The Brat can stink up a room like nobody else, then smile, like she's proud of what she's doing. If you had a younger brother or sister— and believe me, you don't know how lucky you are not to—you would understand." I told her I did have a "brother," but he died. Of pneumonia.

When she asked me his name, all I could think was, *Baby Baby Baby*. "Bobby," I blurted out. "His name was Bobby."

"So you know what I mean." She begged me to come for the Fourth of July, to help babysit the stupid cousins and the Brat, who she said was crazy about me. Whenever I visited their house, Ricki would take my hand and lead me in circles around the backyard. I loved the way she turned my name into a lazy sneeze. *Ay*-chel.

I need you, Rachel. When I told her what I was doing, she begged me to take her. My mother said it would be fine. Her mother would not let her go, said she had to be with her family.

You don't know how lucky you are, Rachel. No babies, no brats.

Renata came out with a platter of tiny hot dogs. A joint the size of a cigar dangled from the platter. My father picked it up. He inhaled, passed the joint to a man whose curly brown hair moved like springs when he flung his head back to take a long hit. A canvas belt patterned with peace signs held up his fatigues.

"There's a word for guys like him," said my father when the man handed him the joint and walked back inside, "but I'm too polite to say it."

Charming? I thought. Was this what it meant to be charming?

He took another hit. "*This*"—he pointed to his vest—"is *real* army issue. Don't you forget it."

Keep smoking, I thought, *and in just a matter of minutes you'll turn from Grumpy to Dopey*. I wandered into the kitchen for a drink. Huddled over the counter was Paco, chipping away at a tiny piece of white rock with a razor. Huddled around him were the man with the hair like springs and a woman with short streaked-blond hair. They took turns bending their heads close to the counter, like they were looking for a lost contact lens. I couldn't see exactly what they were doing, but I could hear the strong sniffling. They reminded me of the three little pigs. Huffing and puffing.

Just outside the kitchen, on Renata's dining table, was a sandwich the length of the table and a strange assortment of snacks—rainbow-colored cheese, something called grape leaves that had no grapes. Some birthday party, I thought, wanting a piece of that sixty-foot cherry pie I'd seen on TV. I walked over to my mother, who was telling Glen about one of the girls at the home where she worked.

"Lucinda, she calls herself. *Lady of the Light*. All of fifteen, thrown out by her parents, ditched by her boyfriend, and about to become a mother. Anyway, she's been having nightmares ever since she saw that TV movie with John Travolta—*The Boy in the Plastic Bubble*." I'd seen the movie with Grandma, who'd told me, during commercials and between tears, about the "real" boy in the bubble.

"First time John Travolta shows up in her dream, she thinks it's a good sign—you know, handsome baby, maybe rich and famous one day, too." My mother put her hands on my shoulders. "Next night, she starts to worry. His face is not attached to his body. It's in a bubble." My mother shakes her head, squeezes my shoulders. "By the third night, she's totally freaked out. 'It's a sign,' she cries to me. 'I just know it. My baby's gonna die.'"

My mother shook her head. "I keep telling her this immune disorder is an aberration, a one-in-a-million kind of thing—"

Paco danced over to my mother, kissed her cheek. "Did you say 'one in a million'? Were you talking about me?" He was whispering to her now. I caught a few words: *Downtown all night. Pretty horny boys from all over the world.* He licked his lips.

My father came inside, began stuffing chips and cheese into his mouth. He picked up a paper plate, loaded it with a wedge of the giant sandwich and some grape leaves. And more chips. Just as he was about to bite into the sandwich, someone turned up the music. Ray Charles was singing.

O beautiful for spacious skies
For amber waves of grain

I could see my father's face turn red. I thought he was choking. He came running over to mother.

"I'm leaving, Susie." His mouth was tight, like it was tied in a knot. Glen asked what was wrong.

"It's the farce of it all, the bullshit. I can't handle the bullshit." His voice grew louder.

"It's just a party, Robert." My mother's hands dug into my shoulders.

"It's *not* just a party—it's a mind game. A stupid fucking mind game. I mean, what planet are we on here? Two days ago—just two days ago—North and South Vietnam were officially reunited. Does anyone in this room even know that? Does anyone even care?" Everyone was looking at him. Ray Charles was still singing.

"You want to know how to celebrate the 'bicentennial'? I'll tell you how. You"—he looked straight at my mother—"and all your social worker friends should go down to the East Village, find some strung-out vets, and start a support group. Today. Figure out how to free them of their nightmares. Now, *that* would be healing."

"You're being such a party pooper, Robert." Paco poked him in the arm.

My father snarled—*the queen has spoken*—then stormed out.

America, America
God shed His Grace on thee

My mother tried picking up the threads of her conversation with Glen, whose arm was around her waist again.

"'Lucinda'—don't you love the sound of her name?—'Lucinda,' I said, 'you're going to have a beautiful, healthy baby, with dimpled cheeks just like yours.'"

She said nothing about my father.

And crown Thy good
With brotherhood

I ran to the terrace. Nobody was there. I looked down, over the stone ledge, just in time to see my father crossing the street. The farther he got, the smaller he looked. He reminded me of a chicken, weaving his way through the crowds lining Riverside Drive. A riddle I learned from Grandpa popped into my head: Why did the chicken cross the road?

I thought it was a stupid riddle. It made no sense.

Why *did* the chicken cross the road?

To see well, to find the answer, I knelt below the ledge and peeked through the steel railings. I looked up, following the voices of people on the terrace above. I looked out, saw faces pressed against windows, legs dangling from fire escapes.

Why *did* the chicken cross the road?

My father was disappearing before my very eyes.

I moved to the corner of the terrace, climbed onto the ledge. It was wider than the high beam at my gymnastics studio. Balancing myself, I stood on the ledge, one foot in front of the other, looking down. All I really wanted was a better view—no bars squeezing my cheeks, no ledge scraping against my forehead. For a second, one split second, I believed I could fly.

"Rachel!" My mother's scream threw me off-balance, made me totter. I don't know where he came from, he was so quick, but there he was, lifting me from the ledge.

"The ships are coming!" I was giddy now. Paco put me down. *On safe ground*, he said.

Everyone converged on the terrace. *Are you okay? Are you okay?*

"The ships are coming!" I pointed toward the river. The woman who reminded me of Snow White, and the man with hair like springs, and the woman who had given me a sparkler surrounded me. *Are you okay? Are you okay?*

"All I wanted was a better view," I said to my mother, who was shaking. Her face was the color of sand. She would not let me move, said nothing, just stood behind me, her long cotton skirt enveloping me like a sail. Paco stooped next to me. "Are you okay? You scared the life out of your mother."

I was not really listening to him. Through the bars pressing against my cheeks, I glimpsed a regatta of tall ships coming up the Hudson. It was like nothing I'd ever seen before.

"Wanna hear a riddle?" I asked. "Grandpa told it to me. Okay, here it is: Why did the chicken cross the road?"

Paco pretended to be thinking hard of an answer. "To get to the other side?"

I shook my head. *No no no no no no.*

"Well?"

I pressed my head against the cool stone ledge. Against a backdrop of pink-and-purple tie-dyed sky, the ships came closer. People started cheering. Firecrackers popped. Roman candles sailed through the air. And somewhere, down in the streets, a chicken was weaving its way through a thick crowd. "Why?" I asked. "Why did the chicken cross the road?"

I turned to Paco, who was still kneeling, in suspense, waiting for the answer to my riddle.

"Because it didn't know how to fly," I said. "The chicken crossed the road because it didn't know how to fly."

~

My mother never forgave my father for almost getting me killed. She reminded me, over and over again, about the bicentennial minute she said took years from her life. What she failed to grasp was that not for a moment did I ever envision myself, the way she did, splattered across the front page of the *Daily News*. I knew the art of falling. *Balance is precarious*, my father had told me when he'd taught me how to ride a two-wheeler. *It's a head trip. The trick is to keep your mind from getting in the way, to trust the thrill of being on the edge. If you fall, kick the bike away so it doesn't land on you*, he'd said. *And don't fight the fall. You'll hurt yourself more.* When I was balancing myself on the ledge of Renata's terrace, seventeen stories above ground, I felt, simultaneously, the pure lightness of moving in the wind on a two-wheeler for the first time and the steadying power that comes with putting one foot in front of another on the high beam. And when my mother's voice came snapping through the wind, my body directed itself gracefully into Paco's arms. In a flash, just before Paco lifted me from the ledge, I saw myself tottering on a seesaw, my mother at one end, up in the air, my father at the other, on the ground. What I got was a lesson I would never forget about the precariousness of love.

It all boiled down to one word: *if* . . .

If you had not run off like that, she said.
If you had kept a better eye on her, he said.
If you had not acted like a baby having a tantrum, she said.
If you had acted more like a——
Don't say it, Robert.

One word. One breathless syllable, as steady, as fragile, as a hinge. Try to say it softly.

If . . .

The sound lingers, the weight of the word hovers.

If you had not run off like that. If you had kept a better eye on her. If you had not acted. If you had acted . . .

If I were seventeen, instead of seven, I could hop on a jet plane, fly across the ocean, be with Jake, find out what it meant to be in love "with a certain way of living." That's what he had written in his last postcard.

> *Dear Rachel:*
>
> *I'm in love—with a certain way of living. I know Ruth is upset about my decision to stay in Italy longer than I had planned. But I can't leave—not yet. Everywhere I go—Milan, Rome, Florence, Venice—I feel a sense of timeless beauty. Everything that matters is built in stone, carved in marble, painted on canvas. There is a riddle here, I think, though it may take years to figure out.*
>
> *Love, Jake*

On the front of the card was a reproduction of a painting by an artist with a funny name. Titian. I asked my mother for help pronouncing the title of the painting.

"Think of the sound a sheep makes," she said, "and the *ch* in 'chorus.'"

I sounded it out. *Baa-chus. Bacchus and Ariadne.* There were two leopards in the picture, and a dog and a little boy. And a man jumping from a chariot with a wild look on his face. In a corner of the sky were eight stars. Under them was a woman whose hand seemed to be touching the clouds. How could there be stars in the sky when it was daylight? Was that the riddle? Stars in the sky in the day.

"Also known as Dionysus," said my mother. "God of wine."

"And Ariadne—who was she?"

"I think Bacchus fell in love with her—turned her wedding crown into a constellation after she died."

The stars in the picture were elliptical. Crown-like. A daytime constellation, from what my mother had just told me. What was the riddle, then?

If . . .

"I'm sure there's more to the myth—I just don't remember it. I *do* remember my classics teacher—the way she'd walk into the room, put down her book bag, and launch into a discussion of gods and heroes without ever taking off her coat. It was a ploy, I think. Watching her pace back and forth—too deep in thought to even take off her coat—made you hang on her every word. Minotaur. Cyclops. Jason and the Golden Fleece. Persephone and Demeter. She rattled off their stories like she was living them."

My mother took the postcard from me, examined it. "It's all coming back to me. Bacchus—Dionysus—god of wine. 'God of excesses,' she called him. 'God of undue adulation. A misrepresented god.'"

If my mother would just give me a simple answer . . .

"Finally she'd get very solemn—still with her coat on. You have to remember, this was the sixties. The meaning of everything—I mean *everything*—was being challenged, turned upside-down. 'You know,' she would begin, 'to really understand the myth of Dionysus, you have to grapple with death and rebirth. And love immortal.' She always said it in that stilted way: *love immortal.* I think it was her not-so-subtle put-down of the sex-drugs—rock 'n' roll scene. "

If I were seventeen, instead of seven . . .

"'This cultish poppycock degrades the myth,' she would say."

I could hop on a jet plane, fly across the ocean, be with Jake.

My mother handed me back the postcard, went into her bedroom. It was the morning of Christmas Eve. Grandma and Grandpa were in Tucson, celebrating the fiftieth wedding anniversary of Neil and Eleanor Hirsch. Neil had been in the same carpenters' union local as Grandpa before he and Eleanor had decided to retire in Tucson. The wedding anniversary was a surprise, orchestrated by their children. Grandpa saw it as a good excuse to visit a place he'd always wanted to go to. Grandma saw it as putting one foot in the door of an overheated old-age community surrounded by *alter kockers* with brown alligator skin. *One visit*, said Grandpa, *does not mean we're living there.* Grandma knew better.

If they were here, I'd be at their house, eating latkes. Grandma always made latkes on Christmas, even when it didn't coincide with Chanukah.

Or if Jake were here, he'd take me to Rockefeller Center to look at the big tree, maybe even go ice-skating. Or we'd watch old movies.

I turned on the TV. Jimmy Stewart, distraught, was leaning over the railing of a bridge. Clarence the angel jumped in, started screaming for help.

From my mother's bedroom, I heard the chanting.

Nam myoho renge kyo.

It was such a strange sound—

Nam myoho renge kyo.

But if you listened hard, it pulled at you, like overtones on a piano.

I didn't think I was the chanting type, she'd said when she'd begun going to the meetings. *But there was something about the way that woman approached me.* She'd been sitting on the stoop of the townhouse where she worked, having lunch, when a young woman in a cornflower granny dress handed her a flyer that said, "Come chant." The woman said not a word, according to my mother, just handed her the flyer, then seemed to float away behind a curtain of wavy blond hair. The weekly meetings in a dark Chelsea apartment reeking with incense quickly lost their luster, but not the chanting. It was the perfect antidote for her guilt.

My father hated the sound, said my mother was one step away

from standing on a street corner like those Hare Krishna weirdos. *You ought to try it, Robert. It has a peculiarly settling effect on the psyche.* My father said his psyche needed something more dynamic.

If you had not run off like that.
If you had kept a better eye on her.
If you had not acted like——
If you had acted more like——
Don't say it, Robert.

Just keep running, she would say when he put on his jogging sweats. *Never sit still. Run. Run. Run. How will you ever find out what you're running from?*

Jimmy Stewart was in the icy water now, with Clarence.

Nam myoho renge kyo.

My father was out jogging. I looked over at the large window that faced the street. Spider plants, ficus, dracaena, dieffenbachia, lady palm, and the one I called pepperoni (peperomia). These were my father's passion. No flowering plants. Just green, in all its shades and textures. Only he watered them. Only he fed or pruned them. He sang to them, too. He could hear them cry, he said, when he played "Layla."

The front door opened. My father was breathless.

"Cold out there." He pulled off his stocking cap. His face was ruddy, his hair slick with sweat. He had a small paper bag in his hand.

The chanting had stopped.

Jimmy Stewart was on the ground, in the snow. It must feel like a bad dream, I thought. To be thrown out of someplace you know so well, someplace you have been to so many times you can smell it with your eyes closed. To be followed around by a man who says he's an angel, a man who's turning your whole world upside down for the sole purpose of teaching you not to make bad wishes.

I wish my parents . . .

I followed my father into the kitchen. My mother was already there, making coffee. My father opened a paper bag he'd been carrying, pulled out packets of raspberries, began mixing batter. A weekend chef, my mother called him. Pancakes filled with fruit were his specialty.

My mother picked through the raspberries, rinsed off the good ones. She was always in a good mood after she chanted. "Must have jogged to Florida to get *these*." I was relieved that she didn't launch into a lecture on unseasonal fruit.

I looked up at the large neon clock over the kitchen sink. At the center of the clock was an electric guitar. A circle of letters spelling out the names of dead rock stars framed the guitar: Jimi, Janis, Jim.

I don't know why, but suddenly I began spilling out stories about raspberry tea and raspberry rugelach. And raspberry strudel. And just plain old raspberries—lots and lots of them—with whipped cream. My mother started laughing, for the first time in months. *That's so like Ruth.* And my father started joking—*Wanna try again?*—and I held my breath.

If Grandma and Grandpa were here . . .
If Jake had come home . . .

The clock was ticking.

If I were seventeen, instead of seven . . .
If I had never hopped onto that ledge . . .

My father was singing as he flipped pancakes. My mother was caught in a web of reflection. *All those months, all those raspberries, I should have known Ruth—and you—were up to something.*

I looked up at the clock humming the songs of dead rock stars.

By now Jimmy Stewart had figured out what he had to do.

The pancakes were in a platter on the table. My mother put some on my plate, took two for herself. "Winter raspberries," she said. "Now, *there's* a delicacy." I started to worry that the lecture was coming, the one about how we were supposed to eat only fruits and vegetables that were in season and preferably locally grown. "You don't really believe they had anything to do with my pregnancy, do you, Rachel?"

I shrugged my shoulders, unsure.

"I mean, you do know it was just a coincidence—nothing more?"

I nodded to appease her. Coincidence? Maybe the raspberry tea and the raspberry strudel and just plain old raspberries had something to do with my mother's short-lived pregnancy, and maybe they didn't. I couldn't be sure. What I did know, at that moment, was that on the table were pancakes filled with raspberries. My mother was enjoying every last bit of them. My father was whistling Christmas tunes. The clock was ticking.

More than thirty minutes had passed.

~

Dear Rachel:

I'm sitting in a little café on a street called Haight, sipping cappuccino. I come here a lot on weekends. No one rushes me away, and I can sketch cartoons to my heart's content. Sometimes when I look out on the street I feel like it's 1969 again and I'm in Greenwich Village and Vietnam never happened. Ruth says good things happen when you're in the right place at the right time. Right now I know she'd rather I be there, but if you think about it, it's all because of her that I'm here.

xxx Jake

"Don't remind me," Grandma said when I showed her the post-card. Jake had finally returned from Italy in January. But he was different, she said. Restless. *Out all night, never says a word about where he's going.* She thought he needed a job. *It's very nice that he almost makes a living with his cartoons, but he needs a* real *job, a place to go during the day. And a girlfriend.* So she scoured the want ads, made him go on an interview for a job as art director for an advertising agency. Jake would always joke about how she got him the job but not the girlfriend. It was little consolation that his relocation after just six months meant more money and a chance to shape the artistic direction of the ad agency. She wanted Jake closer to home. "Vivian gives me the impression that Miami's undergoing a kind of business revival," she said. "Couldn't they open an office there?" Aside from being so far away, San Francisco, in her view, was not a safe place to live.

She became a fanatic earthquake watcher as a way of offsetting her fears. Convinced that earthquakes were occurring with greater frequency than ever, she came up with a less-than-scientific hypothesis for this global upheaval. *They're sending people up to the moon and they're drilling deep down into the ocean and if you don't think that causes more frequent earthquakes and volcanoes and what have you, you have another thing coming.* She would have loved nothing more than for Jake to move back East, where, at least in her perception, the dangers were more palpable and could be mitigated by the safety zone of family.

"Every day," she told me, "every single day, there are tremors all around the world." She knew where all the major faults were (and even some minor ones, like the Croton fault just north of New York City) and would tell you, once you got her started, about the 1962 earthquake in Denver that was caused by waste deposited in deep wells in the earth. "There had never been an earthquake in

Denver before that." Her voice hushed, she sounded like she was telling a ghost story. "The point," she explained, "is that no place in the world is really safe—but *San Francisco? Los Angeles?* You couldn't get me within a hundred miles of the San Andreas Fault for all the money in the world." By giving a $50 donation to an organization known as Earthquake Watch, she was entitled to call a phone number once a week for an update on seismic activity throughout the world.

"There's got to be a pattern in this—there *has* to be some way to predict earthquakes." If she could do that, if she could just figure out something all the seismologists in the world could not grasp, then maybe, just maybe, she could get Jake home before the Big One came. She had her very own crystal ball (better known as instinct), and over and over it told her that the Big One was coming. Maybe (she hoped) what she was reading in her crystal ball was nothing more than her own fear of things unknown. And maybe it would swallow her up and maybe it wouldn't. But too many times when she thought about Jake in San Francisco she got a reading in her crystal ball that the Big One was coming.

When she wasn't analyzing the seismic data of the week, she was pumping up the volume of her RCA stereo system, the speakers of which were housed in two matching end tables. As pieces of furniture, they had no real design to them—just two oversize light-wood boxes with woven facades to disguise their purpose. One of them had a lid that opened. Like a jack-in-a-box, the turntable rose from it. Grandma had shown me how to lift the needle from its rest—very carefully—and place it on whatever LP she had chosen: the Andrew Sisters singing Jewish songs. Rosemary Clooney singing love songs. Mario Lanza singing arias. These days it was mostly Sinatra and Chopin, at full throttle. She'd never played music that loud before, but the house was *so* quiet now. Too quiet. She knew Jake would go one day—children *always* leave—and it wasn't as if he'd been around very much for the past five years. But there were always remnants of him: the extra pair of jeans he'd decided not to pack at the last minute, the wire basket on his dresser where he kept loose change, the heavy blue wool sweater she'd argued with him to take. Each thing he left behind, like bread crumbs in a fairy tale, was a way back that filled her with expectation. This time, he'd taken the remnants. He'd taken the expectation.

Children *always* leave.

It's *so* quiet.

If I walked in after school and caught her crying, she could blame it on Sinatra tugging at her heartstrings with "Here's That Rainy Day" or Horowitz taking her breath away with one phrase from the "Fantasie-Impromptu in C-Sharp Minor," making her stop whatever she was doing to hum along: *I'm always chasing rainbows.* Sometimes, in the middle of listening to Chopin, she called Sophie.

"I was right, wasn't I?" Sophie took great pride in having "hooked" Grandma with *Chopin's Greatest Hits.* "You wouldn't believe how many famous pieces he wrote—and how soothing they can be. Arnold plays them all." She had recently inherited a piano from the brother of her dead husband, Sidney—a piano she said was fifteen years too late and almost refused. She'd wanted it when Arnold was young and taking piano lessons. She believed he was gifted. He needed a piano. His uncle (Sidney's brother) had a piano that no one played, except Arnold. The once-or-twice-a-week visits to practice on his uncle's piano were not enough to sustain Arnold's talent. He stopped visiting his uncle. And he stopped playing piano. Until now.

"Don't you just love that Revolutionary piece?" Sophie liked drama. She liked open chords dominating the keyboard.

"The Raindrop suits me more." It was the subtlety of the prelude my grandmother liked, the way you could hear the rain dropping through the notes. Almost like tears. The piece they both loved equally was the "Nocturne in E-Flat Major." It was like a lullaby, they agreed. No one played it the way Horowitz did. Not even Liberace. Whenever the Funeral March came on, Grandma asked me to change the record. There was always a Frank Sinatra LP near the turntable to choose from.

When I told my mother how Grandma had been acting, she called it a classic case of separation anxiety. *Her baby's grown up and gone. She can't control the little things about his life anymore. So she fixates on the big ones.* My mother wasn't concerned. I was.

One night Grandma had me really worried. It wasn't just what she said, it was the way she said it. "Close your windows—there's something coming from Jersey." The anxiety in her voice was not about separation.

"What are you talking about?" I tried to sound calm, but an undercurrent of panic swept through me. I understood, for the first time, what "the domino effect" meant. Worry begets worry.

"It was just on the news." Apparently, a cloud of sulfuric fumes, accidentally released from a plant in New Jersey, was moving toward New York.

I hung up quickly and ran around the apartment, closing windows. It was a hot summer night. My mother had just left to go on a retreat upstate with Glen, Paco, Renata, and some other friends from the agency—to kick around strategies, she said. I wondered if what they were doing was anything like soccer. My mother especially needed this time away. Lucinda had recently given birth, and her parents had said she could come back home if she gave the baby up for adoption. She begged my mother to adopt the baby. A healthy baby boy.

My father was finishing up watering his plants, getting ready to watch a ball game. It was the thing that occupied him most, besides writing (a new vocation he had taken to since he'd become a bookstore manager) and jogging. Sunday afternoon and Monday night football in the fall and winter. Any night of the week in the winter and spring, basketball. Baseball in the spring and summer. I had come to understand the changing of seasons in a new way. Basketball was the sport he liked watching most. It was not unusual, especially during Knicks games, to hear my father in an animated dialogue with the TV. *Bench the chucker! Get him outta there!* he'd scream if a player, not passing the ball, hit the rim of the basket on risky, wild long shots.

"What are you doing, Rachel?" In the pause between whispering to his lady palm and settling down on the couch, my father noticed the frenzy of activity around him. I told him what Grandma had told me.

He laughed. "Your grandmother tends to see danger lurking everywhere."

"She didn't make this up—it was on the news."

"Okay, let's say it's true that this mysterious cloud is heading our way." My father was calm, I thought. Not reassuring, but calm. "That doesn't mean we're all gonna get poisoned by it. Besides, all you need is a sudden shift in wind . . ."

One by one, like dominoes, the lamps started flickering. Within seconds, all the lights had dimmed.

My father looked at me. Not reassuring, a little less calm, he tried to place the mysterious cloud somewhere between New Jersey and Brooklyn. He turned on the TV. No sound. No picture. He went to the nearest window, opened it, stuck his head out. No sulfuric smell. No cloud. It was pitch black now. I told him to close the window.

They're sending people up to the moon and they're drilling deep down in the ocean and if you don't think that causes more frequent earthquakes and volcanoes and what have you, you have another thing coming.

I clung to his arm. Reassuringly, he led me to the couch while he went to the kitchen for a flashlight and some candles. "Must be a power outage."

"I knew it! Grandma was right!"

"Not necessarily." He lit the candles.

Didn't he know *anything* about dominoes?

"Stay put," he said. "I gotta find something." I closed my eyes, started counting. *Five ten fifteen twenty, twenty-five thirty, thirty-five forty . . .*

Ready or not . . . I got up from the couch, though not because I was especially afraid of sitting alone in the dark. If anything, I felt safe inside. The windows were closed. Outside some mysterious sulfuric cloud was hovering nearby. If the cloud didn't bring on the darkness, maybe the darkness would somehow keep it away. I made my way to my parents' bedroom, where I found my father sitting on his bed, putting some batteries into a small transistor radio.

"This was a gift from your mother before I left for Vietnam." It got him through the nights, he said. That and her letters. He never talked about the war before. I figured it was the darkness.

He played with the tuning dial for a while, finally got a clear station. Disc jockeys and newscasters were telling everyone to stay home, pull out flashlights, light some candles. Power was out everywhere in the city. People were stranded in subways. In a few hours, they hoped, the power would be back.

It *was* the darkness that made him start talking.

"I was all ears at night," he said, "until I fell asleep. Never had a dream in all the time I was there. Sometimes thought I was too afraid to dream."

Ears. Fear.

"That's what the night did to me. Made me listen in a way I had never listened before. To the rain pounding the trees when I was in the interior. To the sound of the tide when I was stationed near the beach. To the static cutting through the music on the radio. To the way the silence seemed to come so suddenly at nightfall. To the click of insects, the brush of animals. To anything that moved outside the barracks." He had an office job, never saw combat, only its effects, personal and otherwise. "Night was also the time I wrote letters, or reread the ones I'd gotten from your mother. She down-played the whole antiwar thing. And she gave it a face." He kissed me on the head. "It's a lot like your face." Her letters, he said, kept him going. And love, the anticipation of it, kept him from writing what he really thought she should know.

"Language is all in the context," he said. "You take simple words—'love,' 'war,' 'power,' 'winning,' 'losing'—and put them together the way you think they should be heard. The way you *want* them to be heard."

Love is war, I said to myself, just for the sound of the words so mixed up.

"Winning is losing," he said. "Losing is winning. If I had told your mother what was really going on, how the words she read in the newspapers about who was winning, who was losing, were nothing more than word and number games, she probably would have written me off in a minute. She would have accused me of playing with words, playing with her heart."

War is power. The power is out. My father is in the dark.

If nighttime made him all ears, daytime turned him into an eagle, all eyes. "What you could see, you couldn't trust; what you couldn't see, you feared. Or you smelled it—the rankness, the burning, it was everywhere." He scratched his head. "Why am I telling you all this? I swore to myself I would never talk to you about the war."

My father was in the dark.

"Except if you started asking."

I didn't say a word. He kept talking. About language and con-text. About how hard it was to keep up morale when you knew about the antiwar thing back home. About heroes—real, unrecog-nized heroes—thrown into a journey that was beyond redemption.

I let him go on and on, though it would take years for me to understand what he was talking about. It was his voice in the darkness, the graininess of it, that made me listen. All ears, I listened for sounds around his voice, so on the edge of memory. The silence, palpable—no refrigerator humming, no clocks ticking—became a sound all its own. Like snow falling.

There was a knock on the front door.

"Any extra candles?" Our upstairs neighbor was holding a large camping flashlight. My father rounded up some spare candles for him. "It's like a parade of flashlights outside, almost spooky. You should check it out. Gonna be a long night."

All ears, all eyes, I looked for things the darkness had brought. Like stars. Without streetlights, without traffic lights, without the dim yellow light of apartment windows, the stars seemed brighter than ever. We took a walk down the street, where people sat on stoops or ledges, their faces hit by light bouncing from flashlights or shadowed by cigarette smoke. Car headlights took us by surprise.

Grandma!

"She's all by herself," I said to my father. "Grandpa's in the city, having dinner with some old union friends."

It seemed to take forever to get to her house. Whatever cars there were on the streets moved slowly. Recon, my father said. Everybody's on a reconnaissance mission, surveying the situation. Patrol cars were out in full force, policemen were stationed at major intersections, directing traffic, telling people to go home.

When we got to Grandma's house, we found her in the kitchen, lighting candles. Everything from her cabinets had been dumped on the kitchen table.

"Looks like an earthquake hit, doesn't it?" Grandma laughed.

"More like search and destroy," said my father.

Grandma pulled me close to her, kissed my forehead, told me not to look so worried.

"I was trying to find something," she explained. "Remember that wooden spoon Jake bought you when you were a baby? And how it mysteriously disappeared?" I nodded. "It didn't really 'disappear.' I hid it—for two reasons. The first was splinters. You used to like to hold it when your mother was feeding you, and naturally I thought she was trying to teach you to eat with it, so I told her to stop. I don't think I have to tell you what she said to me. So when she began working again and you were with me all day, I fed you with the little silver spoon I bought from Tiffany's. By the time you started feeding yourself, I made sure you had a set of Mickey Mouse utensils and a set of *Sesame Street* utensils.

"The second reason I hid it had something to do with sentimentality and history. I knew Jake had gotten it at Woodstock, so I thought you might want to have it as a keepsake one day. Of course, I forgot where I hid it, but I thought it was somewhere in the kitchen. So I started looking. And as I began scouring cabinets, I had this thought: *I want to change everything around. I want the aluminum foil and wax paper someplace else. I want to open my cabinets and drawers and surprise myself by finding things in unexpected places.* I can't explain what came over me . . ." She looked at my father. "Nothing is the way it used to be. I sit on the couch at night, watching the TV news, waiting for *Johnny Carson* to come on, and the thing that interests me most is the map they show on the screen when they give the weather. *There's Jake*, I say to myself, looking at the left edge of the screen. *And there's Vivian, at the bottom right. And there's George, totally off the map.*"

She shook her head. "Nothing's the way it used to be."

"Time moves on, Ruth. Things change."

"Not always for the better. Did you know, for example, that even with all this highfalutin technology in the world, the best predictors of earthquakes are still animals? I mean, it *is* common knowledge that dogs, cats, horses—even fish, if you can believe it—start acting a little strange before an earthquake hits. In fact, there's a direct correlation between lost pets and earthquakes."

I could see the wrinkles in my father's forehead getting deeper by the second.

"Someone in California—a very intelligent man, I might add—has proven that there's a definite, marked rise in the number of dogs and cats that disappear up to two weeks before an earthquake. What do you think of that?"

It was so quiet. Too quiet.

"It's a little like dominoes. One foreshock leads to another fore-shock. Which leads to another foreshock—then *boom*!" She clapped her hands. "*Some*body, some creature, has to be feeling that . . . that . . . *crescendo*. And just before the big shock, you know what happens? Stillness, utter stillness in the air. Complete silence." She raised her eyebrows. "A little like this—don't you think?"

She was really scaring me.

Did the cloud bring on the darkness? Or will the darkness somehow keep the cloud away?

"The cloud . . . Is the cloud still coming—that one that's gonna poison us?"

Grandma shrugged. "Who knows? Who cares now? It's just another diversion."

My father asked if she'd heard from Grandpa.

She shook her head. "Phone circuits are jammed. There's no subway service—either he'll get a taxi or one of his cronies to take him back to Brooklyn or he'll spend a night at a hotel. I'm not worried about him."

My father said she should come and spend the night with us. "They keep changing their predictions about how long this is gonna last. An overload at the Con Ed plant or something."

"Overload, my eye. Tomorrow they're gonna try to get off the hook by calling it an 'act of God.'" Grandma scanned the jumble spread across the table. "For the life of me, I don't know where I put that spoon." She scratched her head. "Don't worry about me. I'll be fine. I'll have a glass of scotch and go to sleep, and when I wake up, everything will be okay. Of course, I'll have to finish what I began here." She waved her hand like a magic wand. "But once I get things back in order—rather, in a new order—I'm going to give Jake a call, tell him he's got to get a pet." Personally, she liked dogs. But she didn't care what he got. Dog, cat, rabbit—any pet would do, as long as it was keen, especially to the silence.

Dear Rachel:

A friend of mine owns a vintage postcard shop where I came across this image of the China Clipper *leaving San Francisco Bay. I think my fascination with model airplanes gave me an eye for detail (not a bad thing to have in my line of work). It also has helped me exorcise many a ghost. Don't tell this to Ruth, please. She'll think I've gone bonkers.*

xxx Jake

"This," I explained to Jerry and Laura, "is the *China Clipper*." I held up the model airplane Jake had made when he was eleven. "It was the first plane to fly mail across the Pacific." We were sitting in Laura's basement for the first of what would become weekly club meetings. The club was Jerry's idea. He had just moved to our neighborhood with his mother, who wore nothing but tentlike black dresses and kept mostly to herself. She liked to sing, usually around dinnertime or when the sun was going down, and if our living room window was open, I could hear her clear across the street. Her voice was husky but pretty, and her songs—torch songs, my mother called them—seemed to come from a place deep inside her, a place so deep I sometimes got goose bumps listening to her. The day Jerry approached Laura and me to start a club, he told us his father had died of cancer and his mother couldn't stand living in the same apartment anymore.

We liked the idea of a club. Laura, who'd become a *Star Wars* fan since she'd seen the movie the previous year, wanted to call it the Force. Jerry said we needed some sort of initiation. So we agreed to bring something unusual and special to our first meeting. Jerry brought a fossil he had gotten on a trip to New Mexico with his mother. It looked like nothing more than a small piece of rock, until you examined it closely and saw the tiny lines that Jerry convinced us was the foot of a prehistoric bird. Laura brought her mother's Revlon doll, with its entire wardrobe in a small pink metal trunk. "Looks like a Barbie doll," said Jerry.

"But it *isn't* a Barbie doll," Laura sneered. "Revlon dolls have class—that's what my mother told me." She proceeded to show us articles of clothing, one by one: the red satin dress and fur-trimmed sweater; the "mink" stole and pink voile gown. "You have to admit she's prettier than any Barbie you've seen."

When I held up the model airplane to show it off, I told them there was a story behind it. "Look carefully under the wings," I said. Underneath one wing of the airplane, in small calligraphic numbers, was the date Jake completed the model (November 22, 1963), and under the other wing was the date the *Clipper* inaugurated mail service across the Pacific (November 22, 1935). Jake had been sitting at his desk, getting ready to dot the final bit of glue on the sea wing of his model airplane, when his hand had suddenly been unable to move.

We interrupt this program to bring you the following news: President Kennedy has been shot. We repeat: the President has been shot. Stay tuned for further details.

He had been listening to the radio, humming along to Smokey Robinson as he meticulously glued tiny pieces of plastic and wood together, when, for however long it took the announcer to say what he said, time simply stood still.

"The *China Clipper*," I explained to Laura and Jerry, "was my uncle's favorite plane. He gave me this just before he left for San Francisco. And if you look closely, you'll notice there's a rivet missing from one side. He did that on purpose. Well, not exactly on purpose. He was about to glue on the rivet when he heard that President Kennedy was shot. And the rivet fell from his hand, so he decided not to put it on." I wished Jake were with us right now, telling the story the way he told it to me. I could almost hear his voice. "How could this happen?" he said. "This was *the President*. How could anyone shoot the President? Meanwhile, the rivet slipped from my hand and rolled under my bed. I was about to retrieve it when Ruth came rushing upstairs—'Did you hear? Did you hear?' She had flour in her hair and on her apron, and for a minute there I thought she had really lost it. She could not stay still. 'Nobody's safe if a president can be shot,' she kept saying as she paced my room, straightening a book, closing a window, refolding shirts that had already been folded, praying—in the short time there was to pray—that the bullets were not fatal.

"Then she took me by the hand and said let's go downstairs and turn on the TV, and I think she was hoping this was some sadistic radio announcer's idea of a bad practical joke and the television would give us the truth. Which it did.

"And all I wanted to do was go back upstairs to that moment just before I dropped the rivet. I wanted to be alone in my room, at my desk, placing a tiny rivet on a model airplane. No interruptions. No bad news. Just the peculiar reassurance that seemed to go with being at my desk, bent over a model airline. Instead I remained downstairs, with Ruth and Harry and your mother, watching the same images over and over again. The motorcade in Dallas. The confusion. Jackie Kennedy making a blanket of her body. The shock on her face. The bloodstained pink suit—"

"It's sick," said Jerry, as though reading my thoughts. "This obsession with a day in the life of a dead president. I mean, it's not as if Kennedy was the only president ever assassinated."

My mouth dropped. I must have looked hurt.

"Don't misunderstand me," he went on. "I like building model planes myself, and the coincidence here is fascinating. But I'll bet you a hundred dollars that if you ask your parents about John F. Kennedy, they'll tell you, to the last detail, where they were when he was killed. But they won't tell you a thing about him as president. In fact, this was a president who did not win the popular vote by a very large margin and almost brought us to the brink of a nuclear war." Jerry adjusted his glasses as he spoke, black square frames that made his eyes seem smaller. I understood, at that moment, what Grandma meant when she said I was "too smart for my own good." I wasn't. Jerry was. Within a month after he came to our school, he made enemies when he called Philip Kamin a Neanderthal after Philip called him a four-eyed bookworm. Nobody in third grade knew what "Neanderthal" meant, but it sounded like an insult, so Philip punched Jerry. A month later, the principal wanted to move him from third grade to fourth. According to Mr. Roscoe, Jerry needed more challenging schoolwork. His mother wouldn't allow it. He'd been through enough changes lately, she told the principal. "If he's too smart for third grade," she said, "so be it." She'd give him things to read at home. "Better to be a super-smart third grader than a socially maladjusted fourth grader."

At Jerry's suggestion, between our first and second club meetings we conducted a poll of our parents (and some of our neighbors), asking what they remembered most about JFK. Almost without exception, they told us where they were when they got the news of his assassination. My mother was in gym class when the news was announced, and some of the girls started crying, but most of them just sat on the floor very quietly, listening to the radio their teacher had gotten from her office. Jerry's mother (who was the same age as my mother and *should* have been in school) was at home, taking a bubble bath and, she reluctantly admitted, sneaking a cigarette. Laura's mother, who went to Catholic school, said they spent the afternoon in the chapel, praying. My father was driving with his father down Flatbush Avenue when they got the news, and, just to be sure it wasn't some sort of gag, he rolled down his window and called out to the driver in the car next to theirs. "Did you hear?" he asked. "Is it true?" The potential for accidents at that moment was very high, said my father.

"See?" said Jerry. "I was right." We were on our way to an abandoned townhouse we thought might be a good place for meetings. Neutral turf, Jerry called it. A place where we could hide out, no interruptions from mothers, et cetera. The townhouse had belonged to a cat-loving old woman who stipulated in her will that she was leaving it to an animal shelter. She died wealthy, and her children, fighting over the hundreds of thousands of dollars in stocks and bonds she left behind (not to mention the cold cash they were sure she had hidden away), were not about to let stray cats (or dogs) muscle in on what they believed was rightfully theirs. It was Jerry who had found the townhouse, a little off the beaten path that led us to and from school. And it was Jerry who filled us in on its lore.

"So they just let it sit and rot," he said, as he led us through a vacant lot that extended to the weedy backyard of the townhouse. A back door, hanging from its hinges, opened into the kitchen. There was a broken window over the sink. Good thing, I thought. Had it been locked and shut, airtight, the faint smell of old cat food and burned drippings on the stove and the mustiness accumulated from things forgotten and left behind might have knocked us out.

"This place gives me the creeps," said Laura, as we tiptoed through the kitchen into a dining room stripped of everything but the vine-and-buttercup wallpaper. She rubbed her arms. "I don't think I want to do this."

"Oh, come on, Laura." Jerry nudged her along. "Don't tell me *you're* afraid of ghosts."

"I don't believe in ghosts—it's the other things, you know, the creepy things, jumping out of nowhere."

"You mean dead people? Skeletons falling from loose railings?"

We were in the main hallway, which was empty except for a broken chair lying on its side. A dusty banister, coiled and chipped at the bottom of the landing, led to what we figured were bedrooms. Jerry wanted to go upstairs. Slowly, we climbed the creaking stairs. At the top of the landing were two boards nailed together in an X that formed a barrier. Jerry was about to climb over it. Laura noticed the hole in the floor first.

"No wonder you wear glasses," she said, pulling Jerry back.

"That's nothing." He was determined to explore the bedrooms, even if it meant crawling across the loose floorboards.

"Maybe it's not such a good idea," I said. Balance wasn't my concern. Jerry was a little chubby. And the more closely I looked, the flimsier the floorboards appeared.

"Don't tell me you think this place is haunted, too?"

"Not haunted, Jerry. Just falling apart."

"Well, how do you know it isn't haunted?" said Laura. She suddenly "remembered" having heard about a witch who lived by herself in a big house. This had to be it.

"Right," said Jerry. "And there really is a tooth fairy."

Suddenly, we heard footsteps. Laura wanted to make a run for it. Jerry told her to be quiet. "Stop breathing so hard," he said. "You'll wake up the witch's spirit." Afraid to move, afraid not to move, we stood, impaled, against the wall at the top of the landing. Until he found us.

"Well, well, well—if it isn't the fat faggot and his female friends." Peter Kamin, Philip's older brother, looked up at us. "Come on down," he said, "into my parlor." Still not moving, our hands clinging to the wall behind us, we looked at each other.

"Don't be so shy—it's not every day that I get visitors." He beckoned us. What choice did we have?

Slowly, very slowly, we descended the stairs, each of us thinking the same thing. What was Peter Kamin doing here? We knew he'd been suspended from school for carrying a pocketknife. *He only uses it for camping trips—he would never hurt anybody*, his father had argued with the principal, to no avail. Why was he here, in this dusty, abandoned den of witches? Did anyone besides us know?

"Have a seat," said Peter. There was a mattress on the floor of the living room. And a peeling, lime-green beanbag chair. "The furnishings are spare, but hell—what do you expect? The Salvation Army helps those in need, not those who sleep in cushy beds in cushy homes." Like three pop-it beads that could not be pulled apart, we sat upright on the mattress. Peter sprawled himself on the beanbag. He reached into his pocket.

The knife! I thought. *He's going for the knife.*

He pulled out a joint, lit it, looking straight at Jerry. "Listen, you—you fat faggot. Ever get my brother in trouble again, you'll live to regret it."

Jerry swallowed. Hard. I could breathe and taste and hear his fear.

"You shouldn't smoke," said Laura. "You'll get cancer."

"Not from this shit, you stupid little twat." He inhaled, made like he was passing the joint to Laura, who froze. Absolutely froze. "This shit is *good* for cancer. Mar-i-ju-a-na. Sweet Mary Jane. Didn't get that nickname for nothing." He leaned toward Laura. "Come on—just one hit. I promise it'll change your life. You'll never see the world the same." He touched her hair. "You're gonna be a very pretty girl when you grow up—I can tell these things."

Tears started rolling down Laura's face. She started coughing, from the smoke, and I thought, for a minute, that she was playing it up. It was a cough of nerves, a sputter—*breathe out breathe out breathe out*—that almost brought her to choking. I put my hand on her back. The coughing eased. Peter pulled back. "Pissy-ass kids. What the fuck are you doin' here? Will you tell me what the fuck you're doin' here?"

Nobody said a word.

"I mean, do you have any idea what kind of trouble you could get into being here?"

"We just . . ." Laura's chin jutted forward, and her eyes narrowed, giving her face an unfamiliar toughness. I had to blink, almost believed I'd seen the tears roll backward into her eyes, taking bits of fear the way the tide pulls debris from the shore.

"You just *what?*" Peter stabbed the joint into the ashtray. I wished I had some cookies with me. My parents always laughed a lot and ate cookies when they smoked pot. The effect on Peter was different. Looking at his face—the sinister smile, the angry eyes—made me wonder if he was smoking the same thing my parents smoked. It smelled the same. Why, then, was he acting so different? *Cookies*, I thought. *Cookies would really help.* I looked around at the dull gray-white walls of the living room, marked by the edges of paintings or mirrors long gone. Ugly faces and dark landscapes started jumping out at me.

"We just wanted to see if the house was really haunted."

Peter laughed. And laughed. He held his stomach.

Cookies, I thought. *What I would give for just one Famous Amos chocolate chip cookie.*

"Damn straight, it's haunted." He pulled a tiny bottle from his pocket. "Ever see this?" He opened the bottle, which was filled with white powder. In it was the tiniest spoon I'd ever seen. "Friend of mine—a coke dealer—used to take up residence here on occasion."

"So what," said Laura. "Everybody drinks Coke."

Jerry cleared his throat. "It's a drug he's talking about, not the stuff you drink."

"Bingo—the fat faggot wins *Jeopardy*." Peter put the spoon to his nose, inhaled so hard I thought the spoon would get sucked up into his nostrils.

"So, as I was saying before I was so rudely interrupted, this friend of mine used to hide out here from time to time. A little haven, you might call it, smack in the middle of middle-class Brooklyn. Nobody bothered him, it was quiet, he could do his deals and slip away. Sometimes slipped me a little for staking things out. Well, one night I'm supposed to meet him here. He doesn't show up. Days pass, and he still doesn't show up. I finally track down a mutual acquaintance." Peter was up now. Pacing. Shaking his head. Talking. "They cut him up into little bitty pieces. Threw him into a garbage bag. Never to be seen again." He looked straight at Laura, his voice a pitch higher now. "And you're worried about a stupid fucking haunted house."

The three of us were like one heartbeat now, one triple racing heartbeat.

"You want something to worry about, *I'll* give you something to worry about." He leaned his elbow on the fireplace mantel. "Does the name Son of Sam ring a bell?"

We nodded. One triple rushing heartbeat. Just the sound of the name brought to life last summer's reign of terror. Everybody knew he wasn't after kids, but until he was caught, there was little nighttime play on the streets.

"Well I wouldn't be resting too easy about David Berkowitz behind bars . . ."

We were all eyes, all ears.

"Because he ain't the one. Gotta big crime, gotta find a scapegoat. And that's all he is—believe me. This buddy of mine, he wasn't chopped up because he owed drug money. He was shut up because he knew who the real Son of Sam is."

Laura dug her hand into my thigh. Jerry pushed his shoulder against mine. One triple racing heartbeat. Three pop-its stuck together. About to burst.

"You should go back to school," I blurted out. It was a stupid thing to say; it made no sense, telling a delinquent to go back to school. Or was it the very thing that needed saying, the fire that would fight the fire in a power play of age and words? Sense, the deep adrenaline kind, rushed through me, gave me the strength I needed to see what so obvious: Peter was the one in hiding.

"What do *you* know?" He squinted at me. His hair, which looked like it hadn't been washed in days, fell against his forehead like pieces of tar.

I gulped. The only thing I really knew was that Peter—all words, no pocketknife, no sticks and stones—did not want to be found. "I know that if you go back to school, everything will blow over." I had no idea what I was talking about, only that I needed to keep talking. "And that everyone thinks you stole money to go to California. And that your brother—"

"Shut up," he said. "Shut up and get out of here." We jumped up, popped apart.

"But if you tell anybody you saw me, you know what will happen to you, don't you?"

We stood frozen, didn't say a word.

"Son of Sam—the *real* one—will get you."

~~~

In the months following the "initiation" that Jerry said really made us a club, we avoided that street like the plague. Out of sight, never really out of mind, the townhouse (forever and always haunted) became a presence, glue-like in the way it stuck to us, binding us in the way only secrets can. No longer interested in neutral turf, we retreated to the safety of Laura's basement for our once-a-week meetings, where, initially, we were consumed with Son of Sam and whether he really was still lurking on our sticky-in-the-summer, slippery-in-the-winter Brooklyn streets. He had made his mark on our lives, just as Peter had, and for all we knew they were one and the same. That was Laura's theory. Why else would Peter know so much? She confessed to having nightmares from time to time, was afraid that talking would make them real. The things that scared her most—the pot, the cocaine—were the things we talked about least. Potheads, to me, were grown-ups who sat around a kitchen table, starry-eyed, giggling, reduced to human vacuum cleaners sucking up every potato chip, pretzel, pistachio nut, cookie, chocolate bar, or donut in sight. Or they were sprawled on the living room couch, drenching themselves in sound, deep subwoofer bass, screeching guitar, heavy-as-mud or mellow-as-meringue sound. To Laura they were all variations of Peter Kamin, high school dropouts ready to rob you, or worse, for a fix. Jerry said it wasn't the drug that was the problem, just the way it was used. There were places in the Southwest, he told us, where people (Indians mostly) ritualistically ate strange mushrooms that made their heads spin, gave them visions. And on the island of Jamaica, smoking something called ganja was like saying hello. "This is too crazy," said Laura, shaking her head. It was the most emphatic, quietly resounding no I'd ever experienced. "This is too crazy." That was all she said, her head shaking itself into words—*shut up shut up shut up I don't want to hear any more*—making me dizzy just watching her. "This is too crazy." Which was just as well. To talk more about the habits of my parents (and Jerry's mother, I suspected) would have been an act of revelation I was not quite ready for. Some things, even in a club bound by secrets, are better left unsaid.

"What if he's right?" Laura's finger was in her mouth, her teeth like pincers around the nail. Sometimes it was the forefinger, sometimes the pinky. She never really bit, just ground her teeth back and forth across the nail. "I mean, what if the real Son of Sam is still roaming? And why does *he* know so much?"

"Peter didn't really know anything. He was just trying to scare us." All talk, I said, a boy in hiding, trying to act like a man. At least, that's what I hoped. Jerry, who'd been scanning the newspaper, said there was nothing—not one word—about someone else being Son of Sam. As far as he was concerned, Peter was too wild, too obviously crazy, to be a serial killer. "It's always the quiet ones—the next-door neighbors who you wouldn't think could hurt a fly—that end up committing crazy crimes." At least, that's what we hoped.

Membership in the club, which still had no name, consumed us almost as much as the phantom Son of Sam in those early days. It was always Laura who brought up the name of someone she thought we should invite in. "Three people do not a club make," she would say. "Why not?" Jerry argued. Laura really had no answer, admitted that she just thought it would be more lively with more members. Just one boy, "to round things out." Whatever name she mentioned— Harold Rosen, Freddy Becker, Marc Friedman—was voted down on some pretext or other, and Laura never took it personally. Some people need to hear themselves think, and Laura was doing just that: thinking out loud, testing herself, pushing Jerry and me to the limits of our commitment. Denial became a pact, more powerful in its silence than any promises we could have made to each other. Three people *do* a club make. Any other mix would strain the intimacy of our trio, an intimacy coaxed out of us as we sat, week after week, like points of a constellation, in a dark, wood-paneled room.

More mundane concerns would soon take the edge off the fear that had galvanized us. Teachers and parents were very big topics of discussion, followed by classmates we didn't like, the merits of a brand-new game called Space Invaders that Jerry predicted would spawn a generation of video idiots, and current events, which could be anything from unsubstantiated reports of pet abuse—Robert Harris was said to have flushed his sister's hamster down the toilet—to whatever world crisis had gotten Jerry all in a dither. Sometime around our two-year anniversary, he came running down the stairs of the basement, a copy of the *New York Times* folded under his arm, shouting, "You gotta hear this! You just gotta hear this!" Then, throwing himself down on the old plaid foam-filled couch, he began reading: "At 5:15 p.m. today on Main Street here, the only living thing in sight was a brown-and-white dog, wandering aimlessly, oblivious to the radiation that was leaking from the crippled nuclear power plant just across the muddy Susquehanna."

"Jerry, take a minute to catch your breath," I said. He was the only ten-year-old I knew who read the *Times*.

"Don't you get it?" He scratched his forehead, smudging it with newsprint from his sweaty fingers. "We're all in danger. Make no mistake about it. If not Three-Mile Island, then some other nuclear reactor. And if not a nuclear reactor, then possibly—just possibly—a nuclear war. And then it's all over. I mean *over*."

Laura's concerns were always more tangible. "Ever see anything like this?" She held up a black G-string smuggled from her mother's lingerie drawer. One by one, we examined this peculiar configuration of elastic anchored by a lace-trimmed silk triangle.

"Which way do you wear it?" I asked.

"This way, dummy." Laura held it up, triangle forward, and I tried to imagine sitting with a ribbon of elastic cutting into my butt. "That's worse than a wedgie," I said. It was annoying enough (not to mention uncomfortable) when underpants crept into the crack of your behind. Why would anyone choose to wear something designed for obvious discomfort?

"They can't be all that uncomfortable," insisted Laura. "My mother has five of them." The closest my mother's underwear came to scantiness was a few pairs of string bikinis (all cotton). Jerry said his mother was too fat to wear anything like that at all, but she did have a black negligee that you could see right through. Jerry, of course, had never seen it on her, but he knew she wore it because he sometimes found it lying on her bed.

"How come fathers don't wear sexy underwear?" Laura asked.

"They don't know how." Jerry pulled the G-string across his forehead. His glasses got in the way. He took them off, positioned the patch of silk over his right eye. Laura and I burst out laughing; then, in a panic, Laura yanked her mother's underwear (along with some of Jerry's hair) from his head.

"I just hope to God you didn't stretch it," she said, carefully pulling off some of the hairs that had attached themselves to the elastic.

"You could have asked me for it," Jerry scowled. "You didn't have to scalp me." He picked up his glasses from the floor, discovered the temple had snapped from the pressure of Laura's knee when she reached over to grab the G-string. "You broke my glasses!" he screamed at Laura. "You broke my glasses!" Laura apologized profusely, reminding Jerry that her father was an optician and she was sure he could fix them, which was some consolation. She then got some masking tape as a temporary measure so that Jerry could wear his glasses.

From sexy underwear and broken glasses, we segued to the biggest news in the neighborhood: the fire that completely gutted the townhouse. Curiosity, with its perverse gravitational pull, had drawn us back to *that street* one afternoon about a year earlier, when we learned that the house had been cleaned up and rented to a group of airline pilots. The will, finally settled by then, left money to a local animal shelter and the house (along with the stocks and bonds) to the warring children. Jerry wanted to ring the bell, pretend we were selling something, just for a glimpse of what it looked like inside. Laura said just being on that street still gave her the creeps and no amount of cleaning-up could change that. From the outside, it all looked good—smooth new windows, glazed, glistening in the sun, no longer a puzzle of cracked glass with their coded message of no entry. Bamboo shades half-drawn like sleepy eyelids tempted me to walk up the steps and peek in. "This is crazy," said Laura, standing back. "Plumb crazy." Jerry followed me. "This is crazy," she said again, and again, until titillation (or the fear of standing guard by herself at the bottom of the steps) got the best of her and she followed behind Jerry.

At this point, it was more than curiosity for me. I wanted—*needed*—to see if the ghosts were gone or just hiding under a thin coat of fresh paint. I wanted—*needed*—just a peek inside to see the veneered floors and spackled walls that would reassure me of time's power to alter memory. It was a peek I never got. Laura's scream—she swore she saw a shadow at the window—made the three of us run. And run. And run.

Only one of the pilots was at home the night of the fire, and, the story goes, he was dead by the time the firefighters got there. "Smoking in bed" was the first hypothesis. Peter Kamin—who in the two years since our confrontation with him had returned to school, gotten suspended again, returned again, only to drop out four months before graduation—just happened to be driving by that night. He swore he heard a gunshot. "A lovers' quarrel made to look like an accident," he said. "What else would you expect from queers?" "Drug Vendetta," read the headline in the *Daily News*. An ounce of marijuana had been found in the house, along with some coke and poppers. Not enough, according to my father, to make this a drug-related crime. "Although you never know," he said. "An airline pilot living in a pretty low-key family neighborhood would be an ideal courier."

Jerry's theory intrigued me the most. "Insurance," he said. "The owner is having a hard time selling his house, so he torches it."

"Where do you get these weird ideas?" asked Laura.

"My father was an insurance salesman," he answered. "And my mother consumes detective novels the way I consume ice cream— though, I have to admit, it hasn't helped her figure out why my father left."

"What do you mean, he 'left'?" I asked.

"Left. Disappeared. Gone, without a trace."

"That explains everything." Laura tried to be funny.

"Well, it *is* the reason we moved here," said Jerry. "My mother couldn't handle all the busybody questions when he disappeared. And the assumption that something must have been wrong—with *her*. She didn't talk much, just sang and cried a lot, and I was getting very worried. Finally, one night over dinner, she started singing to me—the Animals' 'We Gotta Get Out of This Place'—and I was about to suggest a psychiatrist, when she said, 'That's it. We're moving. And if anyone asks about your father, tell them he died. Of cancer. It gets all the right responses—'I'm sorry for you *and* your son,' et cetera, et cetera—and very few questions.'"

With his sloppily mended glasses resting tilted on his nose, Jerry suddenly reminded me of the haunted house. A few days after the fire, I biked down the street. It was a whim, a charm, maybe, drawing me back, by myself, in an act of personal exorcism. I parked myself in front of the townhouse, stood for a long time staring up at the windows, all broken and boarded now. I imagined mice scurrying around, no cats taunting them, and a man smoking himself to sleep, and in one room a puddle of plastic, once a beanbag chair, thrown onto a dilapidated mattress. Wallpaper peeling, walls stained with leaks from pipes that had burst, the house seemed to groan right through its stone facade. I could hear it groan, see it swell with stories, so many stories: of cats and greed, of secrets and hauntings that owed as much to the living, breathing pulse of a Brooklyn street circa 1979 as to the ghosts of another time. Was that what kept it standing—the groaning, the stories—when everything inside must have been falling apart?

Dear Rachel:

Anyone who knows anything about flying has heard of The Spirit of St. Louis *(remember the card I sent you with a picture of Charles Lindbergh and his famous plane?), but here's one for the trivia books:* Tingmissartoq, *navigated by the very same Lindbergh with his wife, Anne. What does it mean? "The one who flies like a big bird."*

xxx Jake

PS: When are you coming to visit?

I fanned the postcards in my hand like they were a deck of cards ready to be dealt. The images blended into one another, like in those little books that show you how still cartoons are framed to bring the illusion of movement. With the illusion, through the movement, came two distinct images of Jake superimposed on the cards in my hand. One Jake made me think of the photographs in *National Geographic*, a magazine I liked so much that I had asked Grandma to get me a subscription for my birthday. Even when the stories were about tragedies, like floods or earthquakes or wars, the photos themselves, the rich color and the gloss, left me feeling that there was nothing the human spirit could not endure. The cover of one of my favorite issues showed a woman standing, her cheek against the snout of a camel. She made a 1,700-mile trek across the outback of Australia, alone except for four camels and a dog. I wanted to be that woman. I still had that issue and a few select others, reminders of a time in my life when I could travel all around the world. I sat in my room, fingering the thick, shiny pages of *National*

Geographic or the picture postcards I received from Jake. In time, the sitting would no longer satisfy me and I would come to see the images as bits of invented truth, but I would never get too cynical to forget, as Jake once told me, that invention begins and ends with discovery.

He sent black-and-white postcards, too, and one, more than any other, seemed to capture the essence of the other Jake. A man, wearing baggy pants and a white shirt with a tie, was sitting on the wheel of a small propeller plane in a large field. Shirtsleeves rolled up, his bare arms, resting on his legs, asked to be touched. His face, which resembled Jake's so much that I thought some trick photography was at hand, glinted like the face of a movie star in a magazine. I imagined a photographer telling him to smile; instead, he kept his mouth poised in a secret. The effect was of anything but withholding; what I saw, looking at this image, was a man who knew exactly who he was.

I tied a ribbon around the postcards, slipped them back in my knapsack, stared out the airplane window at a sky so blue it was almost white. A boy, eight or nine, tapped me on the shoulder, said nothing, just covered his mouth and giggled before taking off down the aisle. He did this three times, until a woman across the aisle from me, reading a magazine and drinking a Bloody Mary, complained to the stewardess, who sent him back to his seat. *Just like school*, I thought.

I dozed off. It was the crying that woke me. I turned around, saw a young child at the back of the plane, squirming in his father's lap. Howling. His brother, no longer running up and down, just standing in the aisle, kept calling him a crybaby.

I rubbed my eyes, suddenly recalling a dream I'd had the previous night: I was on a stage in a magic show, and the magician, whose face I could not make out, put me in a trunk with my head sticking out. There were lights shining in my eyes, and I couldn't see any faces in the audience, and all I kept thinking was that I was going to learn the secret of swords that cut straight through a trunk without touching the person inside. But just as the magician was beginning to put swords in the trunk, I found myself in the audience, watching the show. The dream turned into a nightmare. David Berkowitz (who, my mother had reassured me, was definitely Son of Sam) had escaped from prison. Grandma was running frantically around her house, closing windows, muttering, "Nobody's safe anymore. No place is safe."

I saw the flowers before I saw Jake. Violet and yellow. Pink and white. Their colors popped, like a fresh, selective assortment of Crayola crayons.

"Welcome to San Francisco." Jake smiled, handed me the flowers, brushed my cheek with a kiss. I noticed a ring on his left hand. Two bands of gold twisted together.

I put the flowers to my nose, started to say thank you. Was overcome by a yawn.

"I didn't sleep a wink on the plane." I took Jake's arm, held it tight. "The last hour and a half was pretty bumpy."

Turbulence, the pilot had said. I did not like the sound of the word.

"It was really neat, though—I could see lightning out the window. There would be this flash all the way at the other end of the sky. Then a couple of minutes would pass and I'd see another streak of lightning, a little closer." *If I tell anyone I'm scared*, I kept thinking, *they'll never let me do this again.* "It was the most amazing thing—to be eye level with lightning. It looked like the sky was cracking in half."

I found myself clutching Jake, holding his arm the way a monkey attaches itself to the branch of a tree. The airline terminal felt cold, the lights harsh white. A poster of the Golden Gate Bridge, hanging over the corridor entrance to the baggage claim area, caught my eye. *I'm here*, I said to myself, rubbing my eyes. *I'm really here.*

"There was a boy on the plane who cried a lot," I said. We were standing next to a baggage carousel, watching for my large green duffel bag. "His brother called him a crybaby. It was the only English word he said: 'Craba*bee*. Craba*bee*.'"

I heard whining, looked around to see where it was coming from. The crybaby was fast asleep on a chair. The big brother was tugging at his father's shirt. And whining. *Pick me up pick me up.* His father peeled the boy's hand from his shirt, told him to be quiet, he'd wake the baby. He pulled at the shirt again. Whined some more. Became distracted by the commotion at the carousel.

"I think some baggage is stuck," said Jake. The carousel had stopped moving. There were sighs. And whines.

In a flash, the boy was on the carousel. Climbing over luggage. Laughing. His mother screamed. His brother woke up, immediately started crying.

"Craba*bee*!"

His father reached for his arm to pull him from the carousel, but he quickly maneuvered his way up the conveyor belt, dancing over luggage, around it, until he disappeared behind an opening in the wall. Above the opening was a sign that said CAUTION. I thought I saw a skull and crossbones, too, and imagined, on the other side of the wall, ghosts and eerie sounds and the incandescent darkness of an amusement-park horror ride.

The carousel started up again. Abruptly stopped. There were sighs again. And whines. The boy's mother was frantic. His father had disappeared to summon help, came running back with a team of airport personnel.

"Stand back," said a burly man in blue, who was about to leap on the carousel, when it started up again. Everyone looked toward the opening in the wall, where, like a boat descending over a waterfall, my oversize green duffel bag came tumbling out.

"Ride 'em, bronco!" shouted the boy, sitting on my duffel bag. Everyone seemed to find this very funny.

Except me.

"That's my bag!" I moved closer to the carousel with Jake.

"I once had a duffel bag just like that." Jake winked. He had left it behind when he'd moved to San Francisco, and I had claimed it for myself.

"They should hire this kid to run the airport," someone joked.

The "kid," cheered as his father whisked him from the carousel, was planted right next to me. For the first time, our eyes met.

"Katerina!" The mother's voice was a mix of anger and relief as she hugged her child.

Katerina? I scrutinized the pug face, the freckled nose, the coffee-brown hair cropped close to her neck. The lizard-like tongue she stuck out at me for staring.

Katerina? I turned to Jake. "Does that look like a girl to you?" I knew girls who had very short hair and wore boys' shirts, but I'd never been fooled like this.

"Looks can be very deceiving," said Jake, reaching for my bag. And smiling.

Dear Mom and Dad,

We went to the Haight today, and Jake thought it would be fun to take a picture of me in front of the very café where Mom stood for a picture when she was pregnant with me (it's been through three name changes since then, according to Jake, but it looks the same). I'm having a wonderful time. Will tell you more when I return. Love, Rachel

By my fourth day in San Francisco, I'd ridden the trolley five times, seen Chinatown by day and night, eaten fried shrimp for the first time, and befriended a part Irish setter–part origin unknown named Acid who lived in the Opium Emporium, a poster-souvenir-head shop in the Haight-Ashbury, where I bought a blue tie-dyed T-shirt for my father and a purple one for my mother.

"Here's one for you," said Jake, unfolding a white T-shirt that had "San Francisco" superimposed over a post-earthquake skyline. He also bought me a red bandanna, the very same red bandanna Acid wore around her neck, and when she saw him hand it to me, she put her paw on my arm.

"She wants a biscuit," said a raspy-voiced woman at the cash register, who had sparkles in her long, wavy blue-black hair and was wearing a black leather miniskirt with zebra tights. "She used to charge—kind of like a bull, if you know what I mean—whenever she saw someone holding a red bandanna. A charging dog is not very good for business, so my old man trained her to give a paw instead. Then she gets rewarded with a treat." The woman slipped me a biscuit. "Go on—give it to her. She won't bite you."

I opened my hand. Acid, who had been eyeing me from her bright yellow beanbag pillow, jumped up, slurped the biscuit from my palm, chomped it down, and positioned herself for another. Only this time she whimpered, and if I had closed my eyes for a few seconds, I might have mistaken her cries for the serenade of a hungry cat.

"When she was a puppy, she accidentally swallowed a tab of acid—that's how she got her name—and then she disappeared for two days." The woman at the cash register threw a biscuit in the air toward Acid, who leaped a foot off the ground and caught it in her mouth. "We were sure we'd never see her again, and I was—to put it mildly—quite distraught. Then, at about five o'clock in the afternoon of the second day she was missing—I remember the time because we have a clock in the foyer that chimes—some kid who lived down the street brought her home. His cat, it turned out, had given birth a couple of weeks earlier, and there were all these kittens running around his backyard, and Acid—remember now, she was tripping—apparently dug a hole under the fence and made her way into the backyard. Contrary to conventional wisdom, cats and dogs are not natural enemies if you bring them together when they're babies, and Acid must have thought she died and went to some sort of animal heaven. 'She was having a great time with the kittens,' said the boy, 'but my mom said this was not a case of finders keepers and I had to bring her back.'"

The woman, who also had sparkles on her fingernails, pulled her hair back in a barrette and looked me squarely in the eyes. "You look like a good kid. I bet you'd do the same thing. Anyway, the long and the short of it is that in less than two full days with a litter of kittens, Acid seemed to have gone through an identity crisis of some sort. She won't go near dog food, except for these Milk-Bones, and it took her the longest time—not to mention a broken leg—to realize she cannot climb trees. I know this sounds pretty weird, but I'm telling the truth, I swear."

Dear Jerry:

I know how much you "hate" postcards, but I'm writing to you anyway. San Francisco is very, very hilly, and the brakes on the cable cars have to be fixed all the time to keep them from wearing out, but they make getting around this city a lot of fun. Jake lives a few blocks from a cable car stop, and you can look down at the bay while you're waiting to board. The view is like the one in this postcard—in a word, awesome. Your friend, Rachel

Jake's apartment was oriented around a sunny bay window filled with plants, most of them the flowering kind. Nestled among the plants was Jake's drafting table, and on the adjacent wall was a bulletin board filled with business cards, postcards, and some of his cartoons. Jake used animals in his cartoons a lot (particularly cats) and troll-like creatures that wore suits and ties or Hawaiian shirts and shorts. Sometimes he drew people. I thought the drawings were funny, though the humor of the one-liners that went with them was mostly lost on me.

One morning while Jake showered, I sat at his drafting table, writing postcards. Glancing over at the bulletin board, I noticed the edge of a photograph sticking out from beneath a cartoon that showed three astronauts standing on the inside of a spacecraft. One of them, hands on hips, was saying, "This place could do with a little decorating, don't you think?"

"Curiosity killed the cat," Grandma would say whenever Grandpa lifted the cover of a pot or pan on the stove to get a better whiff of whatever she was cooking. The first time I heard the expression, there happened to be a pressure cooker on the stove, and while I didn't think Grandpa was foolish enough to lift *that* lid, I can recall a moment of uncertainty when I envisaged chunks of pot roast and potatoes shooting into my grandfather's face, even up to the ceiling. The vision did not make me laugh.

Curiosity killed the cat.

With the light touch of a cat burglar, I rotated the astronaut cartoon to find, underneath, a postcard-size photo of a man leaning against a porch railing. He was wearing jeans and no shirt, and he was holding a black-and-white kitten against his chest.

Through the bathroom door, which was slightly open, I could hear Jake singing along to the music on the radio. It was a song I liked, "Ready for the 80's."

To the left of the photo was a postcard I had sent Jake, which showed King Kong swatting airplanes from atop the Empire State Building, and to the right of it was a piece of paper with all my flight information.

Why is this photo hidden? I asked myself, looking for clues in the notes and phone numbers, business cards and cartoons that crammed the bulletin board. There were no other photos pinned to the board, except for two postcard photos of James Dean (one color, one black and white). Why was this photo hidden?

With the tip of my finger, I touched the pushpin that held the photo in place. It was a metallic silver pin, slim and cylindrical, and I rotated it slowly, first to the left, then to the right. There is an art to opening a combination lock, a deftness required to hit the numbers right on the first try, and I imagined that, by carefully turning the pushpin to the left, to the right, I would crack the secret of the photo. The pushpin loosened as I turned it. To the left. To the right. A few more turns, and the cartoon, along with the concealed photograph, would drop like flower petals.

The music suddenly seemed louder. Clearer.

My heartbeat quickened. Jake had finished showering, and any minute he would be out of the bathroom. The photo slipped to the drafting table, along with the cartoon. I picked up the photo, flipped it over to see if there was something written on the back—a name, a date, a message. It was blank.

Jake stopped singing. I quickly posted the photo and cartoon back in position, tried to unscramble the images jumping out at me. The restrained smile. The thick, sandy hair. The broad, square shoulders. The large fingers scratching the small cat's head. The cards and cartoons that started spinning before my eyes, scraps of paper with phone numbers arranged in no particular pattern on a crammed bulletin board. There seemed no order to it at all.

Except for one deliberately hidden photograph.

⌒

Dear Laura:

I drove across the Golden Gate Bridge this morning, and later in the day Jake took me to a small, quiet beach for a picnic dinner.

(He has a convertible!) The sun was the biggest and pinkest I've ever seen it. I felt like I was looking at a painting. When two girls came riding down the beach on horseback, I thought of you—coming here with you one day. I'm off on a "magical mystery tour" now. Jake won't tell me where he's taking me. Will tell all when I get home. Love, Rachel

"Close your eyes," said Jake, "and take a deep breath." We'd been heading south out of San Francisco, guided by a twilight pearl moon beckoning like the dot in a sing-along, playing a game of peekaboo with clouds as soft and flowing as the gauzy skirts I used to hide behind in my mother's closet.

I could smell the salt air as soon as we turned down the dirt road.

"When I was a boy, Arnold Pearl used to take me to the beach at night during the summertime. He hated going during the day. Sun and crowds and barbecued grease did not agree with him. But he loved the beach at night. Ocean air—especially at night, he said—was the most purifying smell in the world. The salt, he admitted, sometimes felt like Chinese mustard going through his nostrils, but he loved it anyway."

We parked the car, then headed to the beach. A large white dog with a stick in its mouth was weaving its way among clumps of people gathering along the shore. The moon shone like a spotlight on the wet sand. The only sound, other than the tide, was a roll of whispers—*Here they come! Here they come!*—and indeed, with the next incoming waves, they did come. Thousands of silver fish twinkling under the moon's light like earthbound stars. Grunions, Jake called them. Once a month between March and August, they rode the waves to the warm sand, where eggs were fertilized and buried until the new moon.

Another wave, another rush of incandescence, and it was over.

Like the best of magic, there was a shuffling of cause and effect, a moment of doubt—did I really see what I thought I saw?

Yes, I told myself, when the spectacle had passed and I stood staring at the bright spotlight that overpowered everything else in the sky, holding fast to the image of small, silvery fish settling like moon-dusted stars for a few brief moments on the beach.

Back in the car, the Village People on the radio, Jake singing along, with me this time, as we headed down Highway 1. *Is this what it means to be high*? Driving in a convertible, top down, wind against my face, along a cliff overlooking the ocean. Nothing but wide-open sky, and an aura of marble moon spreading a misty glow on the breakers a thousand feet below. The car hugged the road, Jake said, and it seemed a funny word to use about a car, but each time we slipped around a curve, I took comfort in the hug.

When I wasn't staring straight down, straight ahead, I was watching my uncle, noticing things about him I'd never paid much attention to. The way his mouth puckered when he was concentrating. The pointed arch of his eyebrows. The way his right hand dropped to his lap when we were on a straightaway and how he gripped the steering wheel with two hands when we rounded a curve. The occasional freckles hidden by the hair on his forearm.

A flush swept through me, a flash of heat that quickened my pulse. *Breathe in breathe out*, I told myself. Slowly. I leaned my head back against the headrest, breathing in the cool air against my face. Breathing out the feeling that had tightened my chest like a thousand tiny cactus thorns. I could not say it, would not say it. Could not would not contain it. Breathing out, breathing in, I saw cactus thorns blossom into cactus flowers. Felt a cool, rippling breeze turn my skin to gooseflesh. I hugged my knees to my chest, wrapped my arms around them.

"Cold?" he asked. I shook my head. He reached around to the backseat, grabbed his sweater, put it around me anyway. I drank it in, the smell of salt air and eucalyptus and lemon-lime aftershave. Could not would not say it. Could not would not contain the feeling that had swept through me like a thousand tiny ripples. Could only think it.

Is this what it means to be in love?

We spent the night in Big Sur, at an inn that served granola for breakfast and played music that mimicked the sound of the sea. And rain.

"Sounds more like static," I said to Jake (deliberately making loud sucking noises as I spooned up my granola and milk), though I had to admit the thunder was convincing.

The breakfast room was a mix of moods: country-blue gingham curtains; blue-and-white-checkered tablecloths; posters of Jimi Hendrix, the Grateful Dead, and Bob Dylan covering the walls. It was a small room, only eight tables, each with different-colored plates. The "mauve" table, where Jake and I sat, was near a window that looked out onto a garden shrouded in early-morning fog, light as chiffon, moving like the tail end of the fog I was running through in last night's dream, a fog so dense I could not see a foot in front of me. Laura was with me, running up ahead, and I was trying to catch up with her. *Slow down*, I heard a voice say, and I didn't know whose it was, but I slowed to a walk. The sound of thunder startled me from sleep, caught me, in the fog of a dream, at the edge of a cliff overlooking the ocean. And not feeling afraid.

When I opened my eyes, I half expected to see Laura, instead of Jake, in the other bed. He was in a dead sleep, and it was raining so hard, so steadily, I wanted to lie down next to him, feel the comfort of his strong arm against me. There was lightning, too, casting shadows on the walls, on the ceiling. Lighting Jake's face. I sat up, on the edge of my bed, just staring. Should I? Could I? Would I?

There'd be nothing wrong, he was my uncle, I could just cuddle with him, tell him how the thunder and lightning and unrelenting rain had scared me. I got up from my bed, took baby steps over to his. Was about to sit down, when a crash of thunder so loud it rattled the windows sent me scurrying back to my bed. I pulled the covers tightly around me and lay still, listening to the beat of a thousand small drums against the wooden roof. To the splashing of rain collecting in puddles. To the sharpness of raindrops against glass. Breathing in the smell of old pine, intensified by the rain.

Should I—would I—wake him, if for no other reason than to ask how he managed to sleep through this? Must be all those earthquakes and tremors they get here. You get so used to them, I figured, nothing scares you anymore.

I tossed and turned, kicked the blanket off, pulled it back over me.

"Get weightless," he whispered. It was the thing he always said when he babysat me. *Get weightless. Pretend you're on a cloud. Floating.*

He was sitting on the edge of my bed, holding my hand, gently massaging my palm. It was the thing he always did to help me get to sleep. I closed my eyes, pretended I was on a cloud. Jake kissed my forehead, went back to his bed. The rain finally slowed down to a steady lull. Weightless on a cloud, I fell asleep, drinking in the lingering smell of lemon-lime aftershave.

Jake and I finished breakfast and headed down the road, into the fog. Trees up ahead, mist covered, were woven together with rays of sunlight. No forest in any fairy tale I'd ever read could have been more enchanted. We came to a clearing where there was a tree stump shaped like a large heart and covered end to end with carvings: "John loves Lorraine," "Lucy loves Tim," "Vicki was here," "Give peace a chance," "Vicki loves Lucy." Some of the carvings were faint, they'd been there so long, and someone had drawn peace symbols around individual letters in what seemed to be a random pattern until Jake unscrambled the letters and read aloud the not-so-cryptic message: "God is dead." I was impressed with how quickly he figured it out.

"It's a skill you acquire living in California," he joked. "Kind of like a sixth sense."

"You don't believe in God, do you?" I fingered the Star of David around my neck, which Grandma had given me before I took off for California. It was the closest she could get to a guarantee that God might watch over me, and I had promised her I would not take it off. It was a small gold star, the first religious ornament I'd ever worn, and almost immediately after putting it on I began to pay closer attention to the way people call on God. Grandma, for instance, often punctuated stories of tribulation with "*Gottenyu!*" (i.e., "oh my God!") or "God should strike me down if I'm lying." My father, who tended to exhibit no faith in a power other than his own, let out an unrestrained "goddammit!" whenever something annoyed him. Minor annoyances (trying to open a jar of jelly) provoked the same cry of indignation as major ones (the Knicks losing a game in the final three seconds).

Then there was Jerry Goldberg, who was always putting a "God will get you for that" curse on anyone who called him Tubby or Fatso or Four Eyes, despite his professed conviction that God did not exist. "I see no evidence whatsoever of God's existence," Jerry insisted. To prove his point, he would rattle off some disturbing news story, like the one about Jack Smith, who spent fifty-four years in institutions because his mother (who appeared to be "not all there") died two days after giving birth to him and his father was an alcoholic. "Where was God?" Jerry asked. "The guy was treated like a total retard from the start, sent from institution to institution, because nobody took the time to see what was really going on inside his head. I'm not suggesting that the world is supposed to be a place where only good things happen, but if you read the newspapers—really read them—and take a look at history, you'll be left with the very distinct impression that God probably disappeared off the coast of some heavenly Pacific island during World War II. Not that I blame Him."

Jake squinted, looked up at the sky. He picked up a small rock. "If I throw this rock, we know it's going to land someplace, right? Depending on how hard I throw it, I could probably even tell you where it will land." He tossed the rock into the woods. "What I can't tell you is whether some small animal hiding in the woods will pick the wrong moment to come out and be hit by the rock. Which of course would make me feel terrible." He picked up another rock, rolled it around in his hand. "Cause and effect is what I'm talking about—the need to believe that everything in the universe happens for a reason. Or that there's an indisputable order to it all." Being a leap-year baby, he said, gave him a very skewed perspective.

"When I was eight years old, I was told, for that first time, that my birthday really wasn't February 28—it was February 29. I didn't understand this at all. How could there be one day that came only every four years? At first, I was upset. Did this mean I was really only two years old? Then George gave me a book on astronomy. 'No matter how precise the measurements are,' he said, pointing to pictures that showed the earth revolving around the sun, and the moon revolving around the earth, 'nature has her own way of telling us things.' 'Just like February,' I said. I didn't exactly know what George meant—or what I meant, for that matter—but it was the only way I could make sense of something that seemed so arbitrary to me.

"I soon began noticing things I'd never noticed before in February. A sudden whiff of early spring one day, followed by a snowstorm the next. A certain restlessness in the air. Vivian would parade around the house in her new spring clothes, counting the days she might finally wear them outside. Ruth would start collecting wool sweaters from everyone's drawers and send them to the cleaners before storing them away. Harry would start spending evenings in the basement, working on his golf swing. In the meantime, we'd still have frost in the morning.

"Then one year we had a major snowstorm on Valentine's Day. Ruth and Harry were stranded in Florida for an extra day. Two days later, when they were home, Harry had his first heart attack. Ruth blamed it on his shoveling snow after a week of relaxing in Miami. But he'd hardly done any shoveling, since George and I had cleaned up most of the sidewalk. That's when I really understood what George had told me a few years earlier, and what I somehow intuitively knew. There's an overpowering human need to make sense of things, to take bits of information, like letters in a game of Scrabble, and see how they fit together. That all works fine—until some new information comes along and changes the whole per-spective. And then there's randomness, pure chance, the letter that can't be used to create any more words on the board. My father's heart attack was not caused by the little bit of shoveling that he did. But nothing anyone said—not even the doctor—could convince Ruth of that. She swore they would never travel in February again. 'It's too unpredictable a month,' she said."

"What does this have to do with God?"

"Everything. My grandfather—Ruth's father—used to tell me God was a bird viewing the world from the top branch of a tree. Try to catch it, it flies away. Let it be, and it will sing songs sweeter . . ." He stopped midsentence, craned his neck. A figure was giv-ing shape to the mist. Jake stood up, moved toward it. Suddenly jumped back, like he'd seen a ghost. Which, in a way, he had.

"Hello, Jake." He kept his distance, despite the familiarity. Moved closer only when Jake introduced him. Gary was his name. He shook my hand, said he was glad to meet me. There was some-thing vaguely familiar about him.

"What brings you here?" Jake crossed his arms, uncrossed them, crossed them again. He reminded me of my mother when she was annoyed with my father.

"Business," said Gary. He'd been up in Santa Cruz yesterday. Thought he'd take the scenic route home. He sat down next to me on the tree stump, told me it had become like a Blarney Stone for lovers. "People who visit here think they'll be blessed in love." He glanced at Jake. "You know the story, don't you, Jake? About the lightning that cut the tree trunk in half, leaving only a heart-shaped stump?" Gary shaded his eyes with his hand. The sun was just breaking through the fog. Rays crisscrossed the trees. The air was heavy, redolent with something sticky-sweet. I lifted my nose, like a dog picking up a scent that had settled in this clearing of eucalyptus and love.

"Yes, I know the story well, only it wasn't lightning." Jake moved closer to us, knelt, started pulling at a clover.

He loves me. He loves me not.

"A woodsman chopped the tree, trying to release his lover, who'd been petrified by a witch."

"Oh, *pleeease*," said Gary. "You're being positively morbid." He turned to me, raised his eyebrow. "Bet you didn't know about this dark side of your uncle, did you?"

I shrugged, staring at the falling clover. *He loves me. He loves me not.* Smelling something sickly-sweet that brought an indefinable ache to the pit of my stomach. Feeling a charge—there was no other word for it. Bouncing, dancing, flying. Looking for a place to settle in this clearing of eucalyptus and love. Jake lost his balance, and Gary reached for his hand to help him up. It was then that it dawned on me.

The thick fingers, the restrained smile. The face in the hidden photograph. I almost blurted out that I recognized him but stopped myself. I would hate it, absolutely hate it, if Jake knew that I had uncovered something he wanted hidden. Of course, I could be making too big a deal about this. Maybe he just ran out of room on the bulletin board. Maybe whatever order there appeared to be in the patchwork of postcards and notes, pushpins and cartoons was a figment of my imagination.

There was nothing funny about Jake on his backside and Gary pulling him up, but it made them laugh. Shared secrets, I thought. The kind that made Laura and me giggle as if we were reading each other's minds.

I picked up a sharp rock, began digging it into the stump. Jake told Gary we were heading to Disneyland, and Gary said he'd love to join us. It was on his way home anyway.

Who invited you? I thought, watching him head toward his car. Or was that the shared secret? The meeting (coincidental?) in this place where love hovered in the mist above a tree turned to a stump through lightning or a witch's magic—what difference did it make? I watched him walk away, an animal out of hiding, thought about what might have happened if Jake had thrown the rock five minutes later. Maybe it would have hit Gary right in the head, no calculated act, just an accident. No cause, except for bad timing. Only an effect, an imprint on time and place, in a way like the tree stump, with its scramble of letters and words leaving impressions of luck in love, good and bad. There were carvings of animals, too, tiny ones reminiscent of the primitive figurines I'd seen at the museum. Two birds. A unicorn standing. A rabbit. A frog. One bird. A unicorn again, on its belly. A deer with a bird perched in his antlers. Had the same person come again and again, carving a cryptic story of love? Had a telephone game of sorts been played here, one person after another carving whatever it was that struck a fancy? Maybe it was daytime and a rabbit had darted out from the woods. Or maybe it was the night of the moon when small frogs sing. There were, oddly, no dates anywhere on the tree stump; the carvings themselves had become a puzzle of time, and timelessness. I wanted to stay here forever, take rubbings, spend my days doing nothing but figuring out where the stories began, where they ended.

Jake took the rock from me, carved my initials into the tree stump. As a blessing, he said. To one day make me lucky in love.

This is not about luck, I thought. It's about letters and pictures and making them tell the story you think they're supposed to tell. It's about animals in and out of hiding. It's about words formed and unformed, letters hanging loose, not a syllable to grab onto. It's about secrets inscribed in wood, whispered in raindrops. Secrets spinning in your head till the spinning becomes its own music, its own mystery. Like the song of the planets. Like the sky brimming with spring before a storm. In February.

postscript

"Would you like something to drink?" the stewardess asks.

"I'll have a Coke." I look at my watch, thinking, *If it's 11:00 a.m. in Los Angeles, what time is it in New York?* I move the hour hand to two o'clock. *If my mother doesn't like me to have soda before lunch but it's already two in the afternoon, am I doing anything wrong?* I smile, savoring every sip.

I take my new diary, handmade in China, out of my knapsack, rub my fingers over the silk threads woven into a pattern of flowers and pagodas. I like the turquoise cover and the way the corners are reinforced in small triangles of red leather. And I like the feeling of permanence. I open the diary to the first page.

August 28, 1979

    Jake's friend Gary was waiting for us at the entrance to Disneyland. He lives in Los Angeles and he writes screenplays, but he took the day off to be with us. Everyone needs to take a day off once in a while to go to Disneyland, he said.

    Space Mountain was one of the scariest experiences of my life, though it helped to have Gary sitting in front of me and Jake behind. Thankfully, it's a very short ride.

Late in the day we went to Gary's house, where Jake and I are spending the night. He lives in a little house a block from the beach. The guest room is tiny, though it's big enough for two beds, and you can see the ocean from the window. As soon as we arrived, I met the cat he was holding in the picture. The cat's name is Dylan, and he was curled in a corner of the couch and started purring when I went over to pet him. After dinner Jake and Gary said they had a surprise for me, but I had to go out on the back porch to wait for it. Then they brought out a cake with a sparkler in it and a beautiful diary from Gary and a small bouquet of zinnias from Jake. In the language of flowers, he said, "zinnia" stands for "thoughts of absent friends." When the petals start to fall, he said, I should crush them in my notebook.

The zinnias, which I've placed in the magazine slot of the seat in front of me, are starting to wilt. By tomorrow, the petals will be dropping like confetti. I riffle through the starchy pages of the journal, imagining them filled. How long will it take? What will I write?

August 29, 1979

I'm sitting in seat G3 of a 747, looking out the window at orange clouds. They seem to be making a circle of pollution in the sky over Los Angeles. A voice from the airplane radio tells me to pay attention to the stewardess, whose hands are doing a kind of dance. Her props are a seat belt and an oxygen mask, and her movements are graceful, synchronized to a very calm, very gentle voice that terrifies me with its talk of changes in cabin pressure and seats that can be used as flotation devices.

My vacation came to an end today. I cried when Jake left me at the gate. I probably won't see him until next spring or summer.

I told him I'm going to move to San Francisco when I get older, to be near him.

It feels like I've been away longer than two weeks. I don't know why. If my father asks whether I missed him, I'll have to lie. I didn't really miss anyone. I was too busy, having too much fun, seeing things I'd never seen before. Tree trunks larger than my room. Grunions shining in the moonlight. Minnie Mouse kissing my uncle at Disneyland. Goofy with his arms around Jake and Gary.

I love Jake. I love him so much, I can't stand knowing he's so far away. I would feel embarrassed if my mother or father read this. Of course, they have no business looking through my diary, but just to be safe I'll keep it hidden in my drawer. What a shame! It's so pretty.

I think I saw Gary kiss Jake. Maybe it was my imagination, but I was looking all around for Dylan this morning after breakfast and when I passed the kitchen I saw Jake at the sink cleaning some dishes and Gary's hands were around his waist and maybe it was my imagination but I could swear I saw him kiss Jake. I was going past the kitchen doorway, and it all happened so fast so I can't really be sure I saw what I thought I saw. And I'm certainly not about to ask Jake. Besides, what's the big deal? Isn't that the way they say hello and goodbye in France?

skeletons
in the closet

Through a large porthole window in the attic of my grandmother's house, I could see the moon. I discovered this one night after returning from San Francisco, when I went up there to put away Jake's duffel bag. The moon was full. Moonshadows danced on the walls. I lay down in front of the window, bathing in white light. If you slept in the moonlight, people used to believe, you went crazy, became a lunatic.

To get to this ringside view of the moon, I had to weave my way through an obstacle course: trunks filled with clothes, piles of old books and large cardboard boxes brimming over with photographs, shiny silver-plated trays, crystal bowls, ceramic ashtrays, glass vases, knickknacks of every kind (some of them still in their original packaging). These were, in Grandma's thinking, collectors' items of the future. To me, they were relics of the past, pieces of a puzzle that, the longer I sat, would tell me a story before it would be lost forever. At least, that's what I hoped. Sometimes I thought I was seeing things: I'd get a picture of Jake, a little boy, hiding behind a box, and my mother feigning surprise when she found him. Or I might see Vivian, cross-legged in front of the window, taking quick drags of her cigarette. It was either the attic or the bathroom, she'd told me. If you were on the sneak, where would you go?

I had no one to hide from, nothing to sneak. I just sat there, hoping it would all spill out on me.

"Come on down from the attic," my grandmother called to me. "Have a little soup. Or cookies and milk."

"Five more minutes," I answered her. "Give me five more minutes."

Five more minutes of must, sticky with the residue of forgotten moments that collected here, in this space that sat above the house, so apart from it. So a part of it. Or five more minutes of moonlight casting a beam on one of those moments, isolating it, giving it clarity. Without the must, without the moonlight, a family's tales might as well be fiction.

Once, I came across a map of the ocean: "Property of George Cohen. Do not touch." The subterranean uncle. The one I hardly knew. The one I could never picture in the attic. His world was the basement, where his fish tank, empty now, still sat on a table alongside the shelf that once housed his library of books about marine life. The map, old and crinkled, he left behind, rolled under the day bed where he slept, until one night, long after the visits home had become fewer and farther between, Grandma sat on his bed, looked around the room, saw only the dust of emptiness. *Time for a clean sweep*, I imagined her thinking. *Time to stop pretending.* She began with the bed, found a bright mosaic bedspread and matching bolsters to make it look like a couch, under which she discovered an old map of the ocean. *Did he leave it behind?* she wondered. *Or did he forget about it, thinking it was lost?* She rolled it up, slipped a rubber band around it, brought it up the attic. *One day*, she thought, *it may be useful, if for no reason other than memory.*

I spread the map open on the floor, weighted it down with books. "There are places so dark that light never penetrates, canyons that go deeper below the surface than Mt. Everest rises above it," wrote George in the corner of the map. I saw what looked like mountain ranges beneath the sea. The legend on the map pointed to volcanic clusters. The Mariana Trench, the deepest spot in the ocean, was the place he wanted to explore.

"Did you know there were undersea earthquakes and volcanoes heating up the ocean?" I asked my grandmother, showing her the map.

"What do you think's causing all those volcanoes and earthquakes? They'll never tell you it's all that drilling—too much of it, I might add. Of course, George thinks I'm crazy when I tell him things like this—the little I talk to him, that is. But if you ask me, they're gonna kill the ocean, just like they're killing our air."

Another night, I sifted through a box of old *Life* magazines. A reel of images rolled out: JFK and Jackie in the backseat of a limousine in Dallas, smiling. Jackie Kennedy in her bloodstained pink suit, dazed, standing next to LBJ. John-John saluting his father's casket. Neil Armstrong weightless on the moon. The Beatles. Marines in Vietnam. An antiwar protestor slipping a flower into the nose of a military officer's rifle. Elizabeth Taylor, in all her Cleopatra splendor. Stuffed sideways in the box was a manila envelope. I opened it, found an assortment of newspaper clippings.

"The Way to Judge Tuna Brands": "A good canned tuna should taste fresh and clean; a fishy aroma is a clue that the tuna is not freshly canned. The oil should not taste strong or rancid. Iodine flavor is a drawback."

"How Crystals Can Ease the Agony of Arthritis": "You can banish the agony of arthritis by wearing a crystal-powered T-shirt, top medical experts say. The key to all healing is energy. Crystals function as transformers and amplifiers of various subtle energies that can rebalance and reenergize the human biological system."

"Earthquake May Have Parted the Red Sea": "Archeologists have uncovered evidence that the biblical parting of the sea that saved the Israelites from the pursuing Egyptians may have resulted from an undersea earthquake caused by a volcano."

As I skimmed through this cache of undisputed truths—"Asparagus Tips," "Beauty Tips," "Incredible Powers of Common Gemstones"—it occurred to me that some people find comfort in psalms from the Bible or books that promise inspiration taken from the wisdom of ages. For my grandmother, comfort was sitting at the kitchen table, reading through newspapers in the hope of finding that one headline, that one new bit of scientific trivia, that would confirm, or at least shed light on, something she thought she knew. If I took this envelope, slipped it in a drawer under my sweaters or on the floor of my closet, pulled it out from time to time, would that wisdom trickle down its comfort? If nothing else, I knew it would make me smile.

One article, published in a high school newsletter, was in a protective plastic sheet.

Year of Confusion
by George Cohen

Unbeknownst to most people, the year 46 BC extended to a luxurious 445 days. Call it hubris. Call it the first of Western man's efforts to reconcile the cycles of the moon and the sun and put them into a coherent, calendric framework. Or call it simply the folly of a man in love. All would be correct. After a long-overdue return from Egypt, Julius Caesar was back in Rome. What he brought with him—a way of reckoning time by the sun, instead of the moon— more than made up for leaving behind (temporarily) his beloved (pregnant) Cleopatra. In any event, his newfound knowledge about the Egyptian solar calendar gave him the means to correct the Roman lunar calendar, which by this time had veered two months off the true solar year. To adjust this in a way that would also assure a vernal equinox occurring on March 25 (yes, March 25), intercalary months had to be added. Hence, 46 BC became known as the Year of Confusion.

Jump ahead a few centuries to 1582. Imagine going to sleep on October 4 and waking up October 14. No, you have not been on some psychedelic trip. You have simply lost ten days, owing to a papal bill signed by Pope Gregory XIII. Another year of confusion—all for the purpose of ordering our days?

If it's true that nature abhors a vacuum, maybe she also resists efforts at dissecting her into calibrated increments. Or have we become so arrogant, as a species, as to believe that everything—even time—is within our control?

"Come on down, Rachel. Have a little soup."

"Five more minutes, Grandma. Just give me five more minutes." In just another month, there would be no more moons or must, no more bartering for minutes. No more chance to piece the stories together.

"Your grandfather and I are moving to Tucson, Rachel." She just sprang it on me one night, no preparation, no advance warning, though I should have seen it coming. All the talk about desert colors and dry heat, so good for arthritis. And the golf—there was nothing like it. Grandpa could become a pro on the senior circuit.

I need a change, Rachel. Nothing is the way it used to be. Jake hardly visits. George never visits. This house is too big.

I should have seen it coming.

Sometimes I sat up in the attic and devised ways to bring Jake back or keep Grandma from leaving. Sickness always worked, at least in movies. I started seeing myself on a couch—no, a divan—wasting away, like Camille. I practiced coughing. Consumption, as an ailment, had such a nice ring. I was consumed. With love. With sadness. I lay on the floor, bathed in moonlight, coughing. I lifted up my hand to Jake, who had returned. He kissed my knuckles.

If I worked hard at getting sick, my grandmother would not, could not, possibly leave.

Or would she? Had something changed so fundamentally the night she had what I would always call her breakdown?

Nothing was the way it used to be.

The next day, she switched everything in the kitchen. The wax paper, always on the second shelf in one cabinet, was moved to a drawer. Newspaper clippings, which I'd taken so little note of in the kitchen drawer, were now in a manila envelope, neatly tucked away in the attic. She'd even changed the wallpaper and stopped talking so much about earthquakes.

I should have seen it coming. All the talk about sunsets like rainbows gone berserk. And the picture postcards of cactus blooming in the spring. Not a word about *alter kockers* with brown alligator skin. Even the summers, 110 degrees in the shade, she thought she could handle. Dry heat, so good for the bones, the swelling joints that seemed to stop hurting as soon as she got off the plane.

"You can't take *all* of this with you, Grandma." She had stalled in the packing, saved the attic for last, when she knew it should have been cleaned out first. We had two weeks to do it, and her approach, she thought, was simple: go through all the boxes—*one two three, no lingering*—separate the "must-saves" from the things that held no value, sentimental or otherwise. At this point, the mountain of must-saves far outbalanced what the Salvation Army would pick up.

"You don't just throw away an entire life when you move. There's history here—memories." She reached into a dusty trunk, pulled out a skirt made of pink felt. I had seen a picture of my mother wearing it. She was in her bedroom, one foot up on a chair, hand on her knee, in a pose intended to look as if she were petting the head of the large black-and-white poodle appliquéd on the skirt.

I took the skirt, held it up against my waist. Swirls of black stitching danced along the hemline.

"If I . . . tell . . . you," sang Grandma, watching me spin around, "things always come back into style. I've seen girls on TV wearing skirts just like this." I could see she was proud. Something had been saved for a reason.

I let go of the skirt, dug deeper into the trunk, found another skirt, almost identical. *Pay dirt*, I thought, imagining Laura and myself dressed as girls from the fifties for Freddy Becker's upcoming Halloween party. I had hit pay dirt.

"I bet you'll want this, too." She put Jake's old brown bomber jacket around my shoulders, mumbling something about a time when girls were girls and boys were boys and they didn't wear each other's clothes.

Sometimes I strayed off on my own treasure hunt while Grandma sorted. Like an archeologist on a dig, I picked and poked. A rectangular gray box with a plastic handle on the lid caught my eye. I opened it, found a collection of old 45s. A card at the front of the box listed all the records, which were clustered in groups of ten or fifteen separated by alphabetical tabs. Paul Anka. Little Anthony and the Imperials. The Duprees. Dion and the Belmonts. The Ronettes. The Shirelles. On the label of each record were my mother's initials written in black magic marker. A milk crate filled with LPs stood next to the little gray box. Jake had debated taking his LPs with him to San Francisco but at the last minute decided to leave behind all but a few of his favorites. Some of the albums I recognized, since my parents had them. *Blonde on Blonde. Beggars Banquet. Layla.* I knew the voices of Barbra Streisand, too, and Billie Holiday, since Jake had played their music a lot when he lived here. All told, there must have been more than a hundred albums crammed into the milk crate. Sarah Vaughan. Ray Charles. Betty

Carter. Ella Fitzgerald. Bette Midler. Smokey Robinson. I claimed each and every one for myself.

Boxes of photos slowed us down the most. The older photographs, the black-and-white ones with scalloped edges and the sepia-toned ones, were thrown together like a jumble of jigsaw puzzles. How would I ever piece them together? Without my grandmother to tell me, how would I ever know that the woman with the carved cameo face was my great-grandmother? Or that the boy in a large baby carriage, blond ringlets framing his face, was my great-great-uncle? The more recent ones were mostly in envelopes from Kodak, with negatives still in their thin paper sleeves. Once in a while, when Jake was still living here, my mother would bring a box down from the attic and sit at the kitchen table with him, passing the photos back and forth like playing cards: Jake's bar mitzvah, my mother's sweet sixteen, George's college graduation, Vivian's sweet sixteen. I would sit with them, asking questions—"Who's that?" "When was this?"—or offering my very astute observations: "You look stupid." "That can't be you." Sometimes memory caught them by surprise, like a shock of cold water from a hose. Other times they needed to work at distilling what they could from one image frozen in time. The fun for me was seeing how the game animated them, hearing my mother shriek, "I can't believe we ever looked like that!" when they came across a photograph of her teased high school hairdo or the one Jake took just before he joined the army, when his hair fell over his eyes. They laughed a lot at the photos that Jake said seemed to be from another life, like the one showing George, in a beach chair, covered with a towel and trying to read while Vivian sunbathed in a bikini on a blanket next to him, playing her radio too loud. Grandma was stretched out on a chaise longue right behind them, with tiny eyecups pinched across the bridge of her nose.

"When was this?" I asked, looking at a picture of men wearing yarmulkes and women wearing dark lipstick and children I imagined squirming in their seats. I knew, from the silver cup at the center of the table, that it was Passover.

Grandma sat down on a stool next to me and seemed to take a long time examining the photo. She shook her head. "I still can't believe he's gone. How long is it now? Almost twenty years?" She reached into the box, pulled out some more photographs, spread them on the floor, went over them one by one.

"There's Sidney," she said, pointing to Sophie's husband. I'd seen one picture of him before, sitting at a nightclub table with my grand-parents and Sophie, all of them squeezed together for the photo. Grandpa's arm was around Grandma, and Sidney's arm was around Sophie, and he had a broad grin on his face. In the photo Grandma was holding, the shiny dark hair had turned thick white and whatever bit of a smile he could muster was overshadowed by a complexion turned green from jaundice and cancer and whatever complications resulted from the botched stomach operation he'd had two weeks earlier. They cut him open, Grandma explained, cleaned out whatever cancer they could, told him he could live months. A week later he was back in the hospital, hemorrhaging, and when they opened him up again, they didn't have to fish around too much before finding a scalpel hidden like a prize in a Cracker Jack box.

In another photo, Jake was sitting next to Arnold, and Grandma and Sophie were behind them, serving, and everyone's eyes seemed to be on Sidney, who was at the head of the table, reclining on a pillow propped against the back of his chair.

"Nobody made seders like Sidney. He was a real showman—used to be in vaudeville. And what a voice! Like Mario Lanza."

The tradition of having seders the first two nights of Passover made it easy to accommodate Sidney's fans without overwhelming Sophie. It also kept apart the first cousins from Ohio and the second cousins from New Jersey, who generally could not be in the same room for long without finding some excuse for blowing up at each other. Sensing that this might be Sidney's last seder, knowing he would be too weak for two nights of visitors, Sophie orchestrated one large seder in the hope that sickness would make friends of enemies, for at least a few hours.

"His voice was so weak," said Grandma, "and hoarse. You wanted to cry, just hearing him try to talk." She sighed. "He died a week later." Grandma shook her head, told me to put the photos back in the box. As I collected them from the floor, an unsettling feeling took hold, the very same feeling I always had when I could not complete a puzzle because a piece was missing. Days or weeks later, it would turn up under my bed or mixed in with the pieces of another puzzle, but when I needed it—right then, right there—it was nowhere to be found.

"Can I keep this box?" I asked.

Grandma hesitated, stared down at the box, pursed her lips. "You don't know half the people in these photos. What do you want it for?"

I shrugged my shoulders, said I liked looking at old photographs.

"Well, you know, when you come visit me, we could look at the pictures together. Like we're doing now. You can come—with or without your parents—and I'll make sure Jake is there. He'll be so close now."

When I visit, I thought, *she'll make sure Jake is there. He'll be so close now.*

Why didn't I see it coming? No more talk about earthquakes, though I knew they still troubled her. No more jokes about overheated old-age communities. It was suddenly clear as moonlight. If she couldn't bring her baby, her favorite, back home, she would take baby steps to inch her way closer to him.

I heard footsteps, looked toward the attic door to see Grandpa entering, his faithful Polaroid camera in hand. He was wearing a Hawaiian shirt and his Yankee baseball cap, which he tipped to us. "I may be moving to Tucson," he said, "but I'll always be a Yankee fan."

"You've had that cap since the year of the flood," said Grandma, frowning. "I think it's time you got rid of it."

"Look who's talking." Grandpa scanned the attic with his camera. He took a picture of the must-saves, then zoomed in on the things that would go to the Salvation Army, and finally, catching us by surprise, he took a picture of Grandma and me hovering over a box filled to the brim with photographs.

October 7, 1981
Dear B:

How do you make three dimensions into two? My art teacher this year is teaching us about perspective, and I kind of understand the optical illusion part—how depth of color and shadow bring dimension to a flat piece of paper—but how do you really turn three dimensions into two? It's like memory. Yesterday I was sitting in Jake's room for the last time. The furniture was there—the people who bought the house wanted it—but the bed was stripped and there were faded spots on the wall where pictures used to hang and the room seemed cold, nothing at all like the room I really knew. This is the image I was left with, not the one I want to remember. It's the same thing with the rest of the house. I see the kitchen, cabinets open, empty. No plate of cookies on the table. No table. I found quarters and dusty pencils in corners of the living room that used to be hidden by speakers, gone now. The dimension I want most is the one mostly gone.

Grandma and Grandpa left today. We—my mother, my father, and I—took them to the airport. I was very quiet in the car. Everyone was trying to make it seem like this is just one big vacation for them. But something is already different.

I feel like I'm in the projector room of a movie theater, looking down at images running along, into one another. I can't focus on any in particular. They're moving too fast. One image, though, keeps popping up, like interference. I see my mother and me in Grandma's bathroom. And I see you, a tiny red blob, being put into a large white plastic bag.

On the way back from the airport, my parents (they would have been yours, too) started arguing (for a change!). My mother went on and on about how a couch is not the kind of thing you surprise someone with. It was supposed to be an anniversary present, a few weeks late. My father said she was overreacting, which is not the thing you say to my mother.

"You like this couch, don't you?" said my father. He sat down next to me, rubbed his hand along the smooth velvet pillow, felt around for the remote, which had fallen between the cushions. He turned on the TV. The Yankees were losing. "Bunch of bums," he said.

Did I like the couch? Did it matter? The old couch, a white Haitian cotton, had become shabby, spotted. My mother bought an afghan, gold and brown, to perk it up, hide the stains. She bought pillows, too, kept trying to plump them up with karate chops. *Good thing she's not trying to make a career as decorator*, I thought.

The new couch, burgundy velvet, came with large pillows you could sink into. My mother complained that they were too soft. My father said they were just right. I said it was just a couch. Which was not the thing to say. Would Goldilocks have negotiated any better?

"Can't talk. Maybe later. Gotta go."

I could hear my mother whispering on the phone in her bedroom. All the chanting, all the meditating, did not seem to relax her anymore. Something was on her mind all the time these days. Something secret. Clandestine. Putting her on edge.

"Gotta go get some milk." She whipped on her jacket, rushed out the door.

The Yankees had three men on base. A chance to tie the game. My father was at the edge of his seat. On his couch.

I went into the kitchen, hungry for something, I didn't know what.

Can't talk. Maybe later. Gotta go. It sounded like a code.

I opened the refrigerator, felt a rush of pure, cold contemplation. Yogurt (plain or vanilla)? Tofu salad? Brown-rice casserole? Soy milk? Juice? Beer?

The Yankees had three men on base.

I slammed the door shut, went over to the pantry. Granola? Crackers that looked like Styrofoam? Beans that looked like marbles?

On the counter was a photograph of the condominium my grandparents had bought.

How do you make two dimensions into three?

How do you make three people into one family?

The food I wanted most, the food I craved, was the food mostly gone. If I closed my eyes, I could almost smell the rugelach baking. If I licked my lips, I could almost taste the noodle pudding with roast chicken.

I went back to the refrigerator. *Eggs*, I thought. *If I can't have noodle pudding, I'll make an omelet.* I took out six eggs, a chunk of cheese, a tomato, leftover potatoes (cut into bite-size pieces), mixed it all together in a bowl. Added a little flour, a dash of salt and pepper. Sprinkled in some nutmeg. Poured the mixture into a cast-iron frying pan sizzling with butter.

I watched the cheese melt and pieces of tomato start to soften and spread.

Can't talk. Maybe later. Gotta go.

I let the mixture set, the way I'd seen Grandma do. When she made *matzo brei* or French toast, she always sprinkled sugar on it. I reached for the sugar canister. *Can't hurt*, I thought, throwing in a teaspoonful. Next to the sugar was some baking soda. *Can't hurt*, I thought. I sprinkled some in. The eggs sizzled, the cheese oozed, the juice from the tomatoes made the frying pan look like an experiment in watercolor mixing. Suddenly the whole thing puffed up like a volcano. The pan started smoking. *Chemistry*, I thought. *This is what my mother means by love.* It's chemistry, she'd told me more than once. Electrons and protons attracting and repelling one another.

My mother came running into the kitchen with my father, screaming at him.

"She could have burned the whole building down, and you'd still be engrossed in a ball game!" She removed the pan from the burner, took a spatula, and lifted the omelet onto a large plate.

"Smells good," said my father. The Yankees were winning now.

My mother hissed.

Chemistry? Electrons repelling one another?

My father cut himself a piece of the omelet and one for me. "Where'd you learn to cook like this?"

"Observation," I told him. "It's a skill you acquire."

My mother was still wearing her jacket.

Where's the milk? I thought. *The milk she went out to buy.*

My father offered her a piece of the omelet.

She thanked him, said she had to admit it did smell good.

Chemistry, I thought. Eggs and tomato and cheese in a pan. Turn up the flame. Watch it all melt together. Light as a soufflé.

Next time I'll add some milk, I thought. Staring at my mother.

Some people count sheep to fall asleep; others drink warm milk, take hot baths, listen to soft music. I made up stories. I was on a beach, early morning. A handsome man (about Jake's age) found me, took me to his house. If this were anything more than a lullaby narrative, he would ask who I was, how I got there. And I would claim an orphan's amnesia. More important, for sedative purposes, were the mood, the setting, the cozy fire inside a musty beach house. Details were all in the feelings.

Last night the story evolved into a dream. The setting was still a beach; the mood, though, grew more unsettling with each second of dream time. I had no clothes on, which didn't bother me at first, because no one on the beach seemed to notice, but the longer I walked, the more self-conscious I became. I headed toward the dunes, looking for a place to hide. Behind the dunes was a house with a large deck. I ran up to the house, grabbed a white towel I found thrown across the railing, wrapped it around me, knocked on the door. Jake emerged from inside the house. I reached out to wrap my arms around his neck.

"Who are you?" he asked.

"It's me," I kept saying, "Rachel. Don't you know me?"

I woke up just as he turned away from me to walk back into the house.

I called him the next day, told him about the dream, except the part about being naked. "You didn't know who I was."

"A*ha*," said Jake. He sounded just like Grandma. "You know what a psychiatrist friend once told me? He said that when you dream, every person in the dream is really a part of you."

I liked thinking that Jake was a part of me, though I still found the dream troubling and was sorry I had brought it up. "I spoke to Grandma the other day. She told me you helped set up the new house."

"That I did." Jake's voice, which normally had a warm ring to it, suddenly sounded like shattered glass. "Did I ever tell you about my friend Tom? The one who flew me to Tucson in his little plane?"

"No," I said.

"Well, he was supposed to come back for me the next day." Jake sighed. His voice sounded shaky. "He collapsed that night. Something wrong with his lungs."

"How is he now?" I asked.

"He's not very well at all, Rachel. I've been spending a lot of time with him—which is the reason you haven't heard much from me. He's got this infection and that infection, and the doctors don't really know what's wrong with him. He's going to Washington, DC, next week, where his family lives."

"Doctors can fix just about anything today. I'm sure he'll get better." There was a beep on the line. Jake took the incoming call, left me waiting. My mind wandered. I pictured my grandmother, the relief on her face when she learned that Jake would not be returning to San Francisco in a small plane. For the first time in my life, I truly understood irony.

"Rachel, I'm really sorry to hang up so abruptly, but I have to take this call. It's Tom, and he sounds pretty bad. How about if I call you later?"

Jake never called. A week later, I received a letter from him.

Dear Rachel:

I'm sorry I never called you back. One thing led to another, and before I turned around, days had passed. I hope you understand.

Anyway, I'm writing to let you know that I'm moving back East. With Gary. You can read between the lines. I began thinking about this some months ago, and it's hard for me to say why. Maybe too many sublime sunsets over the Pacific have jaded me. Or maybe it's just time for a change. I don't know. Sometimes we want a reason for something, but there isn't one. Or it's hidden so far below the surface of our thoughts, like a message in a bottle stuck between crags deep down in the ocean. One day a shark pulls at the bottle, frees it, sends it floating to the top, where it stays. Floating. I'd like to be able to tell you exactly why I want to come—I started to write "home," got as far as the "h," couldn't finish the word, turned the "h" into a "b"—back East. But I can't.

I had a dream about Ruth last night. She was in a Laundromat—it looked like the one I usually go to here—her back to me as she sorted and folded clothes on a large table. I was about to sneak up behind her and put my hands over her eyes, but I woke up.

I don't know if I ever told you this, but the only time she ever yelled at me was in a Laundromat. She'll deny it, but it's true. The old Maytag we had at home had broken down in the middle of a wash, and Ruth was not about to leave half-washed clothes in the machine for twenty-four hours, which is how long it would have taken for the repairman to come. So she squeezed as much water as she could out of them, put the load in a large plastic bag, and headed for the nearby Laundromat. With me. I was eight at the time and not particularly interested in going, but I had no choice. "Go buy some candy," she said when we got to the Laundromat, which was down the block from a candy store.

I decided to be helpful, as long as I was there, so I started pulling clothes out of the machine when the wash was done. A sock fell into a bed of dust between machines, and, after admonishing me in a harsh but not very loud voice, Ruth became energized. "You'd think they might sweep this place once in a while," she said, loudly enough for everyone in the Laundromat to hear. "After all, it is a place people come to clean *their clothes, not dirty them." Then she told me she had a good mind to call the Board of Health. She'd read some-where—she couldn't be sure—about some people who came down with a mysterious virus, and the only thing they had in common was that they'd all been to the same Laundromat on the same day.*

I've begun working on small watercolors. Call it a new hob-by—I don't flatter myself to think it will amount to much more. The last time I gave any thought at all to watercolors was the sum-mer I spent a few weekends with my friends Marsha and Jason in Sag Harbor. We were sitting on the deck of a restaurant overlooking the harbor. It was late afternoon, and the sky seemed to change from minute to minute. There were sailboats docked in the harbor and a small bridge spanning it, and I remember thinking I would paint my heart out if I lived here.

I don't want anyone to know quite yet—especially Ruth and

Harry. I'm afraid it would put a damper on their change of life. In any case, I won't make the move until springtime. I know I can trust you to keep my secret.

Love, Jake

October 15, 1981
Dear B:

If you sense something and pretend that you don't, are there consequences? Right now it feels as if some transcontinental shifting of the plates is taking place, Grandma moving in one direction while Jake moves in another. I can almost feel the earth shake.

If you know something and pretend that you don't, are you fooling yourself? Jake loves Gary. My mother doesn't love my father. Last night while he was at work, she sat on her bed, reading old love letters from him. She would read a letter, start to cry, then tear it up. I tried to stop her. She said I could not possibly understand what it meant to love someone the way she loved my father and be so disillusioned. It's amazing how little she knows about me. By tearing up the letters, she believes she can pretend she never got them. Is she fooling herself? Or is she simply reconstructing her life, the way you edit a story to make it better? Jake loves Gary. Gary loves Jake. My mother says she doesn't love my father. Is she fooling herself? My father says he loves my mother. Is he fooling himself? When they have sex—and I know they still do sometimes—are they making love to ghosts? Right now I wish I were you—the unformed life— instead of me. And I wish Gary would disappear. Maybe he'll get some horrible disease and die.

~

"I can't believe girls ever really dressed like this," said Laura. She twirled around on the sidewalk in front of my house. The poodle on the skirt seemed to fly. She'd found two cardigans—one white, one black—in her mother's armoire to complete our out-fits. My father called us the Doublemint twins.

Jerry came running down the street, apologized for being late. Said a bunch of Mouseketeers had ambushed him. He hated Hallow-een, didn't really want to go to Freddy Becker's party. Laura said he *had* to go, we needed a beatnik to complete our ensemble. She found a black beret for him. I pulled a copy of *On the Road* from my father's bookshelf, brought it along as a prop. Jerry slipped it into his book bag, where he carried the cassette player he was supposed to turn on when we made our grand entrance.

Jerry pushed the play button of the cassette player, held open the door as Laura and I danced our way into Freddy's basement, to "Runaround Sue." The sound from the cassette player was tinny, and nobody paid much attention, until Philip Kamin positioned himself next to us, holding a cup like it was a microphone. "Ladies and gentlemen," he said, "it's the homo and lez-be-friends show." He was dressed in a black turtleneck, black pants, and a black cape, which meant he was either a pirate or Batman—it was hard to tell.

Laura and I kept dancing, but I could feel her tense up, espe-cially when everyone started closing in on us. The girls clapped. The boys watched and drank Coke. Laura's palm started to feel clammy.

Philip played to his audience now, lip-synching to a song he didn't know and doing a bad imitation of Michael Jackson moon-walking. There was laughter, hesitant, like when you're not sure something is funny but the person who makes the joke is a regular wiseguy so you laugh at anything he says or does. I glanced around at smiles outlined with smudged whiskers and eyes peering through cut-out sheets and a skinny body in a skeleton suit. Philip inched his way closer to us, tried to cut in, to dance with me. Laura, usually unruffled, seemed glad for the chance to break away.

"I would sooner dance with a porcupine," I said when he reached for my hand. He grabbed my wrist, tried to hold me close. My knee went up reflexively, jabbing the air between us. Like a warning. Immediately, his hold on me softened and my leg dropped. I looked into his face. Something had changed, and it wasn't just the baby cheeks taking on a more defined shape. It was the mockery that was gone, as if someone had taken sandpaper to Philip's face and scraped away a layer.

"Apologize," I demanded.

"For what?"

The old face was back. The hard, night-blue eyes. The lips as pointed as a bird's beak. The irrepressible smirk. *Just like his brother*, I thought. It was easier to pull away now.

I went over to Jerry, took the cassette player from him. Turned it off. With near-perfect synchronization, someone turned up the music from Freddy's record player, which was playing "Stayin' Alive."

Laura was back on the dance floor. With Harold. Hair slicked back, jeans ultra-tight, he'd dressed himself to look like Elvis Presley. He slipped his hand around her waist, pulled her back in a dip. He had such control. She had such grace.

Jerry by now had situated himself in a corner near the snack table, pretending to read. "Quick—take a picture," he said. "This is how I want to be remembered."

I pointed my Instamatic at him. "Say 'cheese.'"

"If you really want a smile, the word is 'chocolate.'" I gave him a handful of Raisinets. He gave me a corny smile, asked how soon we could leave the masked ball. "Soon as I take a few pictures," I said. Just for the fun of it.

I walked around the basement, camera up against my eye. Laura and Harold stopped dancing to pose for me. Freddy, dressed in the striped shirt and black pants of a referee, held his whistle to his lips. Jane Roberts, in her black leotard and tights (with a tail attached), pretended to scratch at the skeleton face of Marc Friedman. I caught a whiff of something, thought it was cigarettes, traced the smell to the bathroom. There was giggling inside, the distinct squeak of

Ellen Marcus playing counterpoint to Tony Girardelli's coo and the raspy effect hormones were having on Philip Kamin's voice.

"Acapulco Gold," boasted Philip. "Straight from my father's humidor." I shuddered. He sounded so much like his brother, it felt like déjà vu. I could walk away, pretend I didn't notice anything. Who would care anyway? Or I could alert Freddy. It was his house, after all—haunted now, whether he liked it or not, by the specter of something totally out of his control. It wasn't the pot that bothered me; I'd been around it so much I almost liked the smell. It was the harsh, unsettling reality of Philip, twelve going on twenty, stealing from his father's stash. The oh-so-skewed reality of Philip, stoned now, going on and on about his brother's success in California. Managing a big restaurant, was what he said.

McDonald's, I said to myself.

Marc Friedman walked over to me. "Talking to yourself, Rachel?" I shook my head, asked Marc if he'd been to the new McDonald's down in the Village. It was all I could say to keep from saying that Philip Kamin was in the bathroom, smoking pot, telling lies about his brother, who lived in a halfway house in the city. And worked at McDonald's. Too much angel dust had done him in. His father sent him packing. His mother, who knew my mother was a social worker, discreetly called, asked if she could come over to talk. Her face was drawn, her eyes shadowed with worry. *Is it the pot calling the kettle black?* she asked. *We all smoked grass. We all survived. What's happening now? Why this out-of-control behavior?* My mother corrected her. *Most of us survived. Not all of us.* Peter's mother broke down and cried. In my kitchen. *Just tell me it's not my fault. Tell me you see it, too—this mutation. That is what it is, you know. A cultural mutation. A geometric progression of the worst kind. Nothing in moderation anymore.* My mother gave her the name of a social worker who ran the halfway house where Peter ended up. *It'll be our secret*, she said. *A mother-to-mother thing.*

Marc waved his hand in front of my face. "Earth to Rachel."

I stared at him in his Day-Glo skeleton shirt. A confirmed Deadhead, Marc was small and bony, and his shirt, glowing a greenish-white, had a hallucinatory effect on me. Wherever I looked, after looking at Marc, I saw skeletons. Dancing skeletons. Sitting skeletons. Skeletons eating potato chips and drinking Coke. I rubbed my eyes. The long whiskers drawn on Jane Roberts's cheeks became wrinkles, the subtle, splintery wrinkles of a fractured life: first comes love, then comes marriage (Jane, lean, sinewy, in a white satin wedding gown, the same one her mother wore), then come sleepless nights with baby one and baby two and a husband on call and will I ever sleep again. I turned away from Jane, looked at Freddy Becker wearing the striped shirt and black pants of a referee, holding a whistle to his lips, sucking out the music only he could hear. I saw his fingers, long and buttery, flying across the piano, fingers that cramped every time he used the adding machine set aside for him in his father's accounting practice.

I felt dizzy, needed a drink. My mouth was suddenly so dry.

Earth to Rachel. Earth to Rachel.

I hurried past Marc, toward the snack table. Almost tripped over Laura's leg, which was sticking out from the couch where she and Harold sat entwined, like they'd been bronzed into a moment of bliss. Behind the snack table hung a large mirror with beveled edges, the last vestige of a bar that once stood in the corner of the basement. It wasn't enough for Freddy's mother, anticipating the wild parties her son might one day have, just to remove all traces of liquor from the cabinet on the wall; the glass-top bar and the faux-leather stools had to go as well. Once the bar was removed, the edges of the shag carpeting, flattened and dulled beyond repair, stood like a boundary line between what was and what she hoped would never be: there were drugs now, and kids, too stupid to know better, were mixing them with booze, getting drunk, and stinking up carpets with their vomit. Take away the illusion, and maybe, just maybe, you take away the temptation, too.

I stared into the mirror, which, with the bar gone, bore no relation to anything else in the room, just seemed to suck in images without giving anything back. "The mirror never lies," Grandma often said when she was at her vanity, putting on makeup. Contorting her face, trying to stretch out a wrinkle or will away the crow's-feet that seemed to get deeper each year, she would tell me there's no point in trying to pretend you're anything other than what you are. *The mirror never lies. Except if you're in a department store, trying on clothes. There, the mirrors lie. No matter how many pounds you might have gained in a year, the mirrors in department stores will tell you that you look good.*

I continued staring into the mirror. Laura had put pink lipstick and dark eye shadow on me. My cheeks were lightly rouged.

Mirror, Mirror, on the wall—

With my hair pulled back into a ponytail, I looked more and more like my mother, who looked like Jake.

Ladies and gentlemen, it's the homo and lez-be-friends show . . .

This is not my face, I thought. *The eyes are too narrow, the lips too pouty, the forehead too prominent.*

Mirror, Mirror, on the wall—

The girl with the lightly rouged cheeks, not the prettiest of them all, stared back at me.

Jake loves me loves me not.

Behind my reflection, I saw skeletons dancing. Skeletons eating chips. Skeletons sitting on the plaid couch, making out.

Mirror, Mirror, on the wall . . .

This is not my face.

Who's the smartest of them all?

The girl with the lightly rouged cheeks, not the prettiest of them all, laughed at me. Around her neck was a scarf, light pink, translucent. She lifted the tip of the scarf to her nose.

My grandmother's scarf, infused with the scent of Estée Lauder bath oil.

"Light can play tricks on you," she had told me. "It can make your face look tired or worn one day, bright and smooth as silk the next."

I rubbed my hand across my lips. They felt dry, pasty, not at all like the moist pink lips of the girl in the mirror. Was it the light playing tricks on me? Or was it the mirror, full of lies on Halloween?

I poured myself some Coke, drank it down quickly, poured some more. I closed my eyes for a minute, relishing the cold soda scratching my throat. I suddenly felt a hand on my back, moving up my shirt.

"She's wearing an undershirt," the familiar, raspy voice said.

It's called a camisole, I wanted to say, should have said. Instead I jumped, mortified. Turned around, took a step back, aimed my Coke at Philip's face. Only he moved away. And my soda splashed all over Jerry. Philip thought this was very funny.

"I like this game," he said, filling a cup with soda and pouring it on Jerry. I could tell, under his beret, behind his dark glasses, that Jerry felt like crying. I went into the bathroom, got him a towel. He stood up, wiped his face, dabbed his sweater. Everyone laughed. Except Jerry. Except me.

———

October 31, 1981

Dear B:

If you think something and it happens, is it a coincidence? Or did I will the police into Freddy Becker's basement after Jerry and I left? I saw the patrol car turn the corner. I thought about getting back at Philip for what he did to me, and to Jerry. He was smoking pot, he shouldn't have been, wouldn't a bust be just what he deserved? He was the one with a joint in his shirt pocket when I left, with his hand conspicuously in his pocket when the police walked in, Laura told me. And he froze, just froze. He should have known better, should have thought to take his hand out of his pocket, but he froze. Just froze. No one admitted to smoking, so everyone was read the riot act. Except Jerry. Except me. What a coincidence, they all said in school on Monday. No sooner do the homo and the lezzie leave the party than the police come charging in. What a coincidence.

I do think you were the lucky one not to have been born. I don't feel particularly bad about Philip getting busted—he deserved it—but a lot of innocent people got in trouble just for being in the wrong place at the wrong time. Laura believed me when I told her we didn't call the police. But no one else did. If you think something and it happens, is it a coincidence?

"I couldn't make it all fit," said Grandma. She was talking about furniture. The olive-green club chair and the couch, reupholstered to match the chair. The oversize speakers. She'd spent a couple of hundred dollars to have it all moved across the country, only to find it all looking so cramped in the condominium.

"I just couldn't make it all fit." She was sitting on a cardboard shiva box, next to the couch. Staring at the empty club chair. She had to beg the Salvation Army to take the speakers, they were so old. Dinosaurs, said the very nice young man who sold her a new, compact sound system. And the couch, so perfect in size and color and texture for the house in Brooklyn, was all wrong for the desert. It was Grandpa's idea to ditch the old furniture, start fresh, bring desert colors into the condo.

Except for the club chair. No recliner, no La-Z-Boy, could take its place, give him the same sleepy comfort. It held his body like nothing else could. We'll work around it, he said to Grandma. We'll get a new couch, a new stereo, even a new kitchen table. But we'll keep the chair.

He didn't die in the chair, but he might as well have. That's how Grandma saw it.

"How does a man die on the golf course?" She closed her eyes, shook her head.

"It's not so strange, Ma. You hear about it all the time in Florida."

Vivian, sitting next to Grandma, was filing a chipped nail. Grandpa had been buried two hours earlier. "All it takes is one swing too hard."

"But he wasn't swinging," Grandma shrieked, "if I may be so bold as to remind you. He was telling jokes. Standing on the golf course in the rain, holding up his club. Telling jokes!"

Everyone became silent. We knew Grandma would tell the joke—again—trying to figure out what was so funny.

"It's thundering. It starts to rain hard. Unusual for this time of year. Instead of leaving the golf course, what does he do? He points his golf club to the sky. He must have thought he was being funny. Neil Hirsch tells me he stood there, looking up, letting the rain spill onto his face. 'Even God can't hit a two-iron,' he says. Neil admits that he laughed. Until he saw the lightning hit the golf club. Harry falls down, even then telling jokes. Something about Ben Franklin—Neil never got it all." She leaned her elbows on her knees, covered her face with her hands. "What a disaster this move has turned out to be. I come to a dry climate, only to have a husband struck down by lightning."

George walked into the living room, biting into a sandwich. "Did you know"—he chewed as he talked—"that the word 'disaster' is rooted in the Latin word for 'star': *astrum*, derived from the Greek *astron*."

"Didn't know you were the astrology type," said Vivian.

"I'm not—I don't even believe in God." He sat down on the couch.

Grandma reprimanded him. "You could at least honor your father's memory by sitting on a box. It's what we call sitting shiva, in case you forgot."

George didn't move, kept munching away. "What I'm trying to say"—he wiped the corner of his mouth with a napkin—"is that you'll replay Harry's death a thousand and one times in your head, and all you'll ever come away with is the emotional underpinning of disaster. And the illusion that you could have prevented, if not controlled, it."

Grandma burst into tears. My mother, sitting next to her, told George he was being harsh. "Save the philosophy, George." She put her arm around Grandma.

"Remember the time Harry burned a pot trying to make spaghetti for us when Ruth was sick?" said Vivian. Even Grandma laughed. He mistakenly put a cup instead of a quart of water into the pot. He didn't think it looked right, but he figured the spaghetti would soak up the water. Like rice.

"He was very good with a nail and a hammer—could fix anything." Grandma was smiling. "Except food." She was staring at the club chair again. "One day I may see the humor in this." She turned to George. "Are you trying to tell me your father's death was 'in the stars'? I mean, he did buy a cemetery plot. We're not here a month, sitting and having dinner one night, when he says, 'I bought a plot, Ruth.' He says it like he's giving me the weather report. Someone he plays cards with told him if you live in this retirement community, you get a good deal at the Jewish cemetery. So he buys a plot. Never asks me if I want to be buried here or back in Brooklyn. Just goes out and buys a plot."

"The beauty of the stars," said George, "is their distance. If you could get close—which is of course impossible—they would look nothing like diamonds twinkling in the sky. It's the illusion of what they are that makes them appealing. It's the patterns they *seem* to make that give them their power."

Twinkle, twinkle, little star. Jake, who'd been napping in Grandma's room, whistled as he came into the living room.

"Exhibit number one," he said, pointing to Grandpa's golf bag. He reached in, pulled out a golf club, held it in both hands, paced back and forth like a prosecutor. "Ladies and gentlemen of the jury, you've been told that an infamous two-iron invoking the name of God was responsible for the death of Harry Cohen. Well, Harry, as we would all agree, was a man known for corny jokes. In the case of his sudden, tragic, and *disastrous*"—he looked at George—"death, I have in my hands proof that the last laugh was on him." He lifted the golf club up toward the ceiling, pointed to a number on it. "This, my friends, is a two-iron."

My father, who'd been sitting quietly, reading the newspaper, let out a laugh. "This gets better by the minute." He got up from his chair, took the club from Jake to examine it. One by one, they took each club out of the bag. The putter was missing. Buried with my grandfather.

"Two-iron, putter—what difference does it make?" Grandma got up from the box, said she wanted to lie down. She walked slowly, weighted down by grief. I got up, too, went outside. The sun was setting. I leaned against a rock, soothed by the red and pink and orange spreading like finger paint across the sky. Soon the stars would be out. Coyotes would start yipping. My grandfather's body would settle, become part of the earth. With the putter that God had no trouble hitting.

My mother, Jake, and I stayed with Grandma for the full seven days of the shiva period. My father left the day after the funeral; George and Vivian stayed for three days. It was like one big campout, Grandma and I in her bed, George and Vivian in the twin beds of the guest room, Jake in a sleeping bag on the floor, my parents on the crimson sofa bed in the living room.

The night before Vivian and George left, I had trouble sleeping and got out of bed for a midnight snack of rugelach and milk. My mother, in the kitchen with Vivian and Jake, was whispering. I stood behind the main door leading to the kitchen. There was another door on the opposite end of the kitchen, which opened to the guest room.

"Glen," she said. "I told you about him. We had a little fling. Now he thinks he's in love with me."

I sat down on the floor, hugged my knees to my chest. How much more did I really want to know? Vivian asked if my mother wanted to stay married. She didn't answer, or if she did, I just didn't hear what she said. Jake was talking now, about his move back East. Vivian thought he should tell Grandma. It might help her decide whether to stay in Tucson or come back to New York. My mother thought he should wait. "She just got here. Give her a chance to see if she wants to stay or leave, without any added pressure." At the very least, she thought he owed it to Grandma to visit once or twice with Gary. Let her get used to the idea that her baby boy had an alternative lifestyle.

George, who'd been reading in bed, came into the kitchen, began talking about the songs of humpback whales. "With all that we know about them, we still can't determine exactly how they make their songs. What's so remarkable, though, is their tonal similarity to our music." Jake asked what it was like, being out in the ocean, hearing a humpback whale. "Mysterious," answered George. "You hear this sublime, strange sound. You can't really figure out where it's coming from, because you don't see the whale. In fact, you're receiving the sound—the vibration—right through the hull of your boat."

I stood up, peeked in, saw Vivian pour herself a drink. She shook the ice in the glass, drank it down quickly, started to giggle. "Tell me, George, have you ever been laid?" She was sucking on an ice cube, talking at the same time. George coughed.

"Once," he said. There was silence, dead silence, in the kitchen. Vivian prodded him.

"You can't just leave it at that."

"You're drunk, Vivian," said my mother. "Leave him alone. Time for us all to go to bed." But Vivian could not leave it alone.

"If I tell you the truth, you invent a perception of my life that is totally off-base," said George. "What I mean is that you would think the chicken came first, when it was really the egg."

"You're not talking to a prude, George. Air it. Let your sisters and baby brother in on the secrets of your life. Consider it therapy—right, Susie? I mean, how many times will we all be together like this?"

George hesitated, took a deep breath. "I was fifteen. Harry, who was very worried that I would turn out queer, took me to a prostitute."

Jake burst out laughing. "Say no more, big brother." Vivian wanted details.

"It was horrible," he said. "Well, not really horrible so much as embarrassing. I didn't care. I didn't want any part of it. I guess you could say I wasn't really there during, you know, the 'act.'"

"Good thing Harry stopped worrying about these things by the time I was fifteen," said Jake.

"It's quite a gene pool we have here," said Vivian. My mother made her apologize for putting George on the spot.

"Nothing to apologize for," he said. "Just don't go away thinking that my lifestyle—and my distance from each of you—is a direct result of my father's bad judgment. It's not the case at all. I simply have always found more pleasure—call it erotic, if you like—in a more ascetic existence. Though I know you probably think I'm queer anyway."

I felt two warm hands on my shoulders. "You shouldn't be listening in on other people's conversations," said Grandma. "Come with me." She led me back to her bedroom, sat down on the bed, pulled something from her night-table drawer.

"This was the first cartoon Jake ever did," she said. "Take a good look at it." She handed me the three-by-five drawing, which she'd laminated. It was an ink sketch of a cat curled under a blanket on a bed. Only its tail was sticking out. "Cat hiding," Jake had captioned it. "That's what children are often like. They think they're keeping something from you. Only their tails are out, in plain sight."

She leaned back against her pillow. "I'm tired," she said. "You must be tired, too—all this eavesdropping."

I kissed her forehead, sat up against the headboard, not ready for sleep just yet. The sheet over the dresser mirror was beginning to slip, already tired of the grief it was supposed to be covering. Four more days, I thought, and the sheets could come off the mirrors. "You're not supposed to see yourself in mourning," Grandma had told me when we returned from the cemetery and my father, with George's help, covered all the mirrors in the house. From what I'd learned this night alone, it seemed as if they had always been covered. What would happen if we exposed them now? Would the ghost of my grandfather come back, with a thirst for vengeance about queers? How soon before my grandmother noticed the deeper lines in the corners of her eyes, no illusion, just the desert light playing tricks on her? More than ever, I wanted her to come back to Brooklyn. I looked down at the cartoon in my lap. *She knows*, I thought. *She knows everything.* And because she knew everything, she would never come back to live in Brooklyn. She would forgive. She would love unconditionally. But she would not come back to live on streets that would never again be familiar.

The words of a song Grandpa had taught me started floating through my head. He would begin:

Once I went in swimmin'
Then I would sing a line.
Where there were no women
And every third line we'd sing together, his arm around me.
In the deep blue sea

Seeing no one there
I hid my underwear
Upon a willow tree

I dove into the water
Just like Pharaoh's daughter
Dove into the Nile

Someone saw me there
And stole my underwear
But left me with a smile.

When did we stop singing? I asked myself. *When did the song we sang so many times fade into a backdrop of memories running together like watery paint on a canvas?* I felt for the locket around my neck, a gift from Harry one spring day after we'd gone out for ice cream. An early birthday present, he said. My seventh birthday was three months away. Glued onto the small gold heart was a painted enamel rose, pearlized to make it look antique. It was the only thing he'd ever given me on his own (Grandma always bought the birthday presents, chose the cards), and I wore it day and night for months, until the chain made a green ring around my neck. Grandma berated Grandpa for the cheap chain and replaced it with a more expensive one, which I hid away. I never put on the necklace after that, until now, though I often took it out of its blue velvet box just to open the locket and admire the tiny image of Jake as a little boy that I'd cut from a larger photo. You could hardly recognize him, the face was so small, and maybe that's what I liked about it. If the locket, as Grandpa had told me, was to contain my secret love, then maybe the very notion of my love needed somehow to be obscured. When I'd finished looking at the secret inside, I would click the locket shut and let it settle in my hand. I liked the way the cheap chain tickled my palm.

womanhood

January 16, 1982

Dear B:

Rice paper is very delicate, almost powdery to the touch. You can't erase on it. I tried it once. The ink smudged. The word I wanted to erase faded, taking grains of paper with it. Everything I did to fix it made it look worse. It's like when you get chocolate on a new white shirt. Leave it alone, I finally told myself. Isn't that the point of a diary—to write without erasing?

Today would have been (is?) Grandpa's birthday. Grandma said she baked an apple kugel, his favorite. I never knew her to bake just for him when he was alive. It was like a new beginning for us when we moved here, she said. Who could have guessed there'd be such an ending?

When does one thing end and another begin? Night becomes day, the weeks fall into one another. Knowing I'll never see Grandpa again makes me want to see him more than ever. I want to sit on his lap and sing with him. I want to see Grandma roll her eyes when he tells stupid jokes or when he tries to put his arms around her. Why do people so often seem to want something more when it's gone?

There is no way I'm saving myself for marriage," insisted Laura. "I don't care what my mother says. I mean, I understand where she's coming from. Her older sister—my aunt—had an illegal abortion when she was seventeen and got really messed up. Can't have kids—ever. Of course, now that she's very seriously Catholic, God may stop punishing her—if you can believe my grandmother." Laura had a glass-topped vanity table with a large oval mirror in her bedroom, and I was sitting at it while she brushed my hair. My hair was wavy and thick, and Laura knew just how to brush through the knots without hurting me. She would take long, even strokes, talking or humming as she brushed, and my head would tingle. "I know my mother doesn't buy into the fire-and-brimstone part of religion; she's just afraid I'll be dumb enough to get pregnant. But I just can't see myself holding out. If I love someone, that is."

This was not an issue I thought about as much as Laura did. Every since the previous Halloween, she'd been spending more and more time with Harold, less and less time with Jerry and me. She'd outgrown the club, that much was clear, and maybe we all had. But nobody—not Laura, not Jerry, not I—wanted to be the one to say those words, "we can still be friends," and bear the burden of rejection. I like to think that something else was at play, too, something too precious to give up when you're on the fence, caught in that barbed-wire netherworld called growing up. The last time we were all together, Laura jumped the fence. It was after Jerry accused her of being a slave to social pressures and hormones. "At least I have them," she said. "At least I have full-fledged, working hormones."

I now spent my time with either Laura or Jerry, rarely the two together. One night, Jerry and I tried kissing. My parents had gone to the movies, and we were sitting on my living room couch, very close to each other, watching *The Hunchback of Notre Dame*. "Can I kiss you?" Jerry asked, putting his arm around me. "I won't hold it against you if you say no . . . but I would just like to . . . "

I didn't let him finish. Maybe I was as curious as he was. Maybe I just didn't want to hurt his feelings. Maybe there was a rational dimension to kissing that I needed to explore. Besides, what harm could there be in a little kiss? So I turned my body toward his and let the kiss happen. It was a tentative kiss, on the lips, cut short by a shock of static electricity. We laughed, with some relief. And we knew, without having to say it to each other, that we would never try it again.

"I don't know what I'll do," I said, indulging Laura. "I mean, if somebody I like comes along."

"You're so *picky*, Rachel. I don't mean to say that you should like a boy just because he likes you. But I can't really see anything so wrong with Philip. Okay, so he acted like a jerk at the Halloween party, but I happen to know he would do anything—I mean *any-thing*—if you would just give him the time of day."

I frowned. "Even if he didn't think I was a lesbian—"

"He doesn't really think that. He just said it. It's like an ego thing with guys—know what I mean? A girl doesn't like you, so you gotta find *some* reason . . ."

Laura's little sister Ricki came padding into the room. Her hair, falling into her eyes, reminded me of the inside of a corn husk.

"You're supposed to be sleeping," said Laura. Her parents had gone out to dinner, and we were babysitting.

"I can't thleep."

"Well, try harder."

"Come on, Ricki," I said, taking her hand. "I'll rub your back."

"Laura thez I was adopted," Ricki whispered when we were in her room.

"Laura's teasing."

"She thez I don't look like anyone in the family." Laura, like her parents, had the coloring of someone who tanned easily, and Ricki was fair.

"That doesn't mean you were adopted. Lots of people don't look like anyone in their family." I kissed her on the cheek, pulled her *Sesame Street* comforter over her. "Me want cookie," I grumbled. Ricki's laugh turned into a yawn as she rolled onto her stomach. I sat on the edge of her bed, rubbed her back. "Get weightless," I said, in the soft way Jake always said it to me when I was Ricki's age and had trouble falling asleep. He would lie down next to me, arms at his side. Relax your arms, he would say. And your legs. Imagine yourself on a cloud. Floating.

"Get weightless," I said again. "Imagine you're on a cloud. Floating." Ricki yawned again, tossed and turned a little more, finally fell asleep.

"Harold and I French-kissed," Laura confided. We were at the kitchen table, slurping up tomato soup with melted American cheese. Raiding the kitchen was one of the things I liked about spending the night at her house. There was not an ounce of granola or brown rice in Laura's kitchen. Her pantry was filled, instead, with items that my mother said took the joy out of cooking. Campbell's soup. Rice-A-Roni. Instant macaroni and cheese. There was always soda and candy, too, and Cool Whip to spread on top of chocolate pudding or Jell-O.

"Did you like it?" I could not imagine a boy's tongue in my mouth.

"It felt a little weird at first—like your tongue doesn't know what it should do."

The image of a lizard came to mind. I made a face. "I'm trying to eat, Laura."

"No, seriously—I know it sounds disgusting, but it really isn't. You kind of get into a motion." She moved her tongue across her lips. "Harold is a good kisser. He moves slowly. Know what I mean? Doesn't, like, try to ram his tongue into my mouth."

"I don't really need a blow-by-blow description."

Laura jumped up from her chair. "Hey, I gotta show you something." She led me to her parents' bedroom, a small room overwhelmed by an oak-veneer dresser and a matching armoire. A tray with bottles of perfumes sat on the dresser. There were also photos in a variety of wood and plastic frames: Laura's mother and father on their wedding day; Laura's grandparents; Laura and Ricki in a pose of sisterly bliss. Laura reached into one of the dresser drawers and pulled out a deck of cards with illustrations of men and women having sex. As she shuffled through the cards, the figures seemed to be in motion. Standing. Lying head to foot. Straddled in a chair. How could there be so many different ways to do one thing? I wondered. The card Laura seemed most intrigued by showed a woman kneeling on all fours. She was wearing black stockings and a garter belt. "That's the way Greeks do it," said Laura. "Up the butt."

We heard keys in the front door. Laura fumbled with the cards to get them back in the drawer, exactly where they'd been, and we dashed to the kitchen.

"Did Ricki go to sleep okay?" asked Laura's mother. Her mouth had a way of puckering, as if smiling were an effort, and, much as I tried, I had trouble connecting her with the woman who wore the G-string Laura had once exhibited to Jerry and me. There was a card, in the deck Laura had just shown me, of a woman in a G-string sitting on a man's face. Cunnilingus, she called it. I looked at Laura's mother, with her chin-length hair streaked silver in a pretty, premature way. And I looked at Laura's father, who made me think of pictures of men from the Klondike I'd seen in a magazine. Was it possible? I wondered. Did they really do things the way the cards showed them?

"Uh-huh," Laura answered her mother, slurping down the last bit of soup in her bowl.

"Jake's coming back," I said to Laura. We were propped against the headboard of her double bed, surrounded by the teddy bear and the panda and the fuzzy white cat she would not relinquish to Ricki. "For good, I think."

"I wish I had an uncle like him." Laura hugged her panda. "I have two uncles, one married, one not. Mike—the married one—scares me. He's very big, which may be why he's a good cop, or at least an intimidating one. Plus the fact that he always looks at you like he's expecting you to do something wrong. I sometimes think he'd arrest *me*, just because I know someone who sometimes smokes pot.

"Now, John—the other uncle—is kind of okay. He always brings me presents: bottles of perfume, and sweaters with bold floral prints that sit at the bottom of my drawer until they're too small for me and I give them away. He works at a bank—the same job for I don't know how many years—and, according to my mother, he still pines away for some girl who jilted him when he was twenty. They were engaged—he gave her a ring and all that. Makes you kind of feel sorry for him. Plus the fact that his face has these, like, potholes all over and when you look at him you can't help but pray to God you never get acne like he must have had it."

"I wonder why she changed her mind. About marrying him, I mean."

"You wouldn't have much to wonder about if you knew my grandmother, who, I might add, John still lives with, which seems a little weird to me since he's, like, thirty years old. My father almost didn't marry my mother because of her. Or so he says."

Laura rolled onto her side. "Want me to tickle your back?"

I rolled onto my stomach, lifted my pajama top. Laura's nails made swirls across my back, and long sweeping lines, and gentle pinpricks. We took turns. I traced letters on her back, made her guess what I was writing. "Harold loves Laura."

"A little harder," she said. I dug in a little harder, watched the faint imprint of my fingernails disappear with each breath. Laura's cheek was resting on the backs of her hands, and her eyes were closed, and she had the smile of a good dream on her face. She yawned and lifted her head, and together we climbed under the covers, tossing and turning, following each other's sleepy voices in the dark, tugging at opposite ends of the blanket until it encased us like a cocoon, and then, out of restlessness or curiosity or both, we held each other close, giggling and trying to get a sense of what it was that excited boys.

May 15, 1982
Dear B:

There are things you can't even tell your best friend. What would she think, I wonder, if she knew how I dream about Jake? Trekking all around the world, spending days picking through the rubble of ancient cities, staying in hotels with fancy names. Holding him in the dark of the night. There was a time, I think, when girls really could marry their uncles.

Sometimes I still tell myself stories to fall asleep. These days I'm on a time trip, back in the Middle Ages. My name is Eleanor. Eleanor of Aquitaine, Queen of the Troubadours. I surround myself with poets who write "chansons" of love and fill my court with tales of King Arthur and Queen Guinevere, Morgan le Fay and Merlin. Last night I played a recording of medieval music, as a mood setter. The sound of the lute made me cry. That, plus the news that Raymond, my handsome uncle, for a brief time my secret lover, had been killed in battle.

I think I blushed when I walked into the Upper West Side restaurant where my father worked and saw Jake sitting at the bar. He was alone, looking at a newspaper. I wanted to sneak up behind him, put my fingers over his eyes, play Guess Who? Only he turned around.

"Look at you!" he said, planting a kiss on my cheek. "You get more gorgeous every year." He let go of me to hug my mother. My father, who was at the other end of the bar, mixing drinks, glided over to us. He leaned over to kiss me. All this kissing was beginning to embarrass me.

"How about a Shirley Temple?" my father asked. I had not had a Shirley Temple in at least three years, but he still thought it was a favorite drink of mine.

"How about a Coke instead—with lemon?"

"One Coke with lemon coming up." I liked watching my father mix drinks. He seemed to have a particular flair for squeezing small pieces of lime or lemon into glasses.

"A margarita for me," said my mother. My father had practiced a lot at home making margaritas and martinis and testing them on my mother before he got this job. She didn't like martinis as much as margaritas, but she drank them to help him perfect his skills. Any decent bartender can make a martini, she said, but it takes a great bartender to make a good margarita. I had no reason to doubt her. She always got giddy in the middle of her second margarita.

"Where's Gary?" she asked.

Jake gestured toward the men's room. "Powdering his nose." My mother ignored Jake's remark, told him how good he looked, asked about Grandma.

"The desert agrees with her," he answered. "She has a year-round tan now." He raised his eyebrows. "And a boyfriend she's been keeping a secret."

A boyfriend? My grandmother has a boyfriend? I started to feel queasy, must have looked sick.

"Don't be so shocked, Rachel," said my mother. "Ruth is a very vibrant woman."

Vibrant? I thought. *Is this how we describe a sixty-two-year-old woman who lost her husband barely four months ago? Vibrant?* The queasiness was turning into a full-scale nausea. I downed my Coke, trying to tune out whatever it was that Jake was saying about Seymour and his crop of thick white hair. "Distinguished" was the word he used. So different from Harry.

"So, what do you think?" asked my father, refilling my glass.

"About what?"

"About me. About being here."

I shrugged my shoulders. "It's okay."

"Just okay?" In the past five years, my father had held a variety of jobs, each for a period of about six months. He'd worked as a dispatcher for a car service, a bookstore manager, an account executive in training for a public relations firm, and now he was a bartender. Between jobs, he did what he believed he had a natural gift for—namely, writing. Like skywriting that keeps your attention for only as long as you can read the words, his pronouncements—"I have so many stories to tell," "I can write better than this or that writer"—dissipated almost as quickly as they filled a room. That's not to say he didn't try. If he'd had a good day writing, I'd know it by the greeting I got from him when I came home from school. If he'd had a bad day, our apartment would reek of the smell of pot. Not that my father smoked only when he was down. He just smoked more.

"I'm sure you'll get lots . . ." I started to answer my father, but he was gone, in a flash, to the other end of the bar, where the waiters and waitresses put in their orders for drinks. *Of material.* That was what he told me he got from jobs. Material for his stories.

"Guess who?" Cold fingers that smelled of soap covered my eyes. I played along.

"Let me see—the voice is too deep to be my mother's."

"I think our table is ready," said Jake.

"You didn't give her a chance to guess," complained Gary.

"Bitchy, bitchy, bitchy."

Gary released his hold on me. A kiss followed. And a present.

Jake and Gary had stopped in Washington on the way home, to visit their sick friend Tom. The present—freeze-dried ice cream, the kind astronauts ate in space, and a hologram of the moon—was from the NASA space museum.

As we made our way to our table, I started noticing the tops of people's heads, mostly the men. So many bald spots, I thought. So many receding hairlines. One man, at a corner table, had shiny silver hair, thick and peppery. The woman he was with looked a lot younger. At least, I thought she did, until I got closer and noticed the wrinkles in her forehead and doughy texture of her skin. The man squeezed her hand, moved his lips close to her ear. I thought of my grandmother, in a restaurant with a man who had thick white hair, as he squeezed her hand, whispered some secret into her ear, some word or two hanging on the breath of a moment already shared or yet to come. She pushed him away. *Not now, Harry—I mean, Seymour. Not here.* He moved closer, planted a gentle kiss on her ear. I felt like throwing up.

"I don't know what to order," said my mother. A steak restaurant was not the place for a vegetarian. Gary suggested lobster.

The waiter was hovering nearby. "It's from Maine," he said. "It doesn't get much better."

My mother seemed hesitant. "I never quite acquired the knack of it—you know, cracking open the claw, using one of those tiny forks to scoop out the meat. It makes me feel very . . . what's the word I'm looking for? Gauche."

Jake turned to Gary. "My sister has been spending too much time in the trenches," he said. "It's dulling her taste for the finer things in life."

"What's so great about lobster?" I blurted out. I'd seen tanks of lobsters in Chinese restaurants. Tanks of cool water I knew they'd be taken from, then plunged whole into a pot of boiling water. How, I wondered, could that be a delicacy anyone wanted to eat?

Gary, who was sitting across from me, leaned forward and clasped his hands under his chin. He seemed older than when I'd met him. At first I thought it was because of the way he wore his hair now, short and off his face. A closer look made me notice a barely perceptible tic in his cheek that surfaced when he smiled. They were like opposing forces, the smile and the tic, and they made me think he was nervous about something. Or worried. Grandma always said worrying takes years from a person's life. At least, she said, that was what it did to hers.

"Imagine," Gary began, "something you love to eat, but not every day, necessarily. Something you get once in a while—something that just the thought of makes your mouth water."

Grandma's rugelach came to mind. She would roll out pieces of dough. I would fill them with cheese or chopped nuts and chocolate. Or raspberries.

"What are you thinking of?" my mother asked. I told her.

Jake reached into his knapsack, said I was psychic. "I was going to save this for later." He pulled out a box of rugelach. It was a bakery box. Whenever Grandma bought bread from a bakery, she asked for an extra box. For occasions just like this. "This is for you."

Gary winked. "Don't tell her how many we ate on the way."

"Ruth complained," said Jake.

"And complained and complained," added Gary.

"About her oven. 'Electric doesn't bake the same as gas,'" Jake said, in a voice that sounded almost like my grandmother's. "But I'll be damned if I can tell the difference." He passed the box to me. "Can you?"

I took one bite. It was as close to perfect as any cookie she'd ever made.

"This is supposed to make me appreciate lobster?" I said, putting on a face that was totally antithetical to the sweetness coating the inside of my mouth. "You cannot—in any way, shape, or form—compare my grandmother's rugelach to lobster." Out of the corner of my eye, I saw a lobster being delivered to the next table. It was cut in half, adorned with lemon wedges. It looked disgusting to me. "People die from eating lobster." I said it loudly enough for the man who was about to eat his lobster to hear me. He was just tying his bib around his neck, when he turned to me with a snarl.

My mother, who was normally unfazed by anything I said or did, looked alarmed. "Are you sure you're not confusing lobster with sushi?"

"I'm not stupid, you know—I know the difference between cooked fish and raw fish. But go ahead—you want to eat lobster and poison yourself? Go right ahead." There was a dead silence at the table. Three seemingly mature adults not knowing how to contend with a twelve-year-old whose emotional circuitry was hitting its peak overload. The current was running like crazy, in me, outside of me. And all the wrong buttons were being pushed.

The introductory chord to a song, played by a man sitting at the piano, which stood in a corner of the restaurant, cut through the silence. One of the waitresses came twirling around the piano, singing a song from *My Fair Lady*. Her voice trembled, like she was gargling. She wore her hair in a dancer's bun.

"The waiters and waitresses take turns singing here," my mother explained to Jake and Gary. "Kind of like a showcase for budding Broadway stars, though you have to admit it makes conversation a little challenging."

Gary bent his ear toward my mother. "What did you say?" He thought he was being funny. So did my mother.

Jake, who was sitting next to me, leaned closer. "You and I have to go to a *real* Broadway show—not this amateur-night stuff."

I liked the idea. Just Jake and me. But he turned away before I could tell him that I'd never been to a real Broadway show and how much I wanted to go.

Jake and Gary were smiling—no, laughing quietly—and my mother was giddy, and my father was in his very own world, singing along with the waitress while he mixed drinks. I, on the other hand, was seething. Nothing seemed genuine to me. Nothing anyone said. Nothing anyone did. I excused myself, went to the ladies' room, sat on the toilet, thinking. Between the kitchen and the restrooms was a poster on the wall with instructions on what to do if someone choked. What if I choked? I smiled at the thought, not so much of choking as of how it would put a dead stop to the singing. I scanned the pink metal door of the stall. There wasn't much in the way of graffiti: a phone number for a good time, another saying the good time was a wrong number. I pulled out the marker in my purse, started to write, hesitated, then went full force.

"He loves me. He loves me not," I scrawled.

"I hate him. I hate him not."

I put the marker back in my purse, started to pull up my panties. How could I not have noticed the warmth between my legs, the blood?

Oh, shit!

I sat down again, dabbed the blood, started to cry. How could this be happening? To me. For the first time. In a restaurant. All the talk with my mother—*When did it happen to you? What does it feel like? Does it hurt?*—the endless search for the right mini-pads to keep under the bathroom sink, just in case, had not prepared me for this moment.

How could this be happening? To me. In a restaurant.

I started to get up, felt shaky, sat down again. I could not go back to the table. Not like this.

I stared at the small stain of bright red blood, almost the shape of a leaf, on my underwear. *Everyone will know*, I thought. *All I have to do is stand up. And everyone will know.*

I needed to talk to someone. There was a phone booth outside the bathroom. I stuffed toilet paper into my underwear and went to call Laura. She wasn't home. Afraid someone would see me, I went back into the bathroom.

Grandma, I thought. *I'll call my grandmother. Collect.*

I dialed her phone number. A man answered. He knew my name.

"I've heard a lot about you, Rachel," he said. His voice was thin, tinny.

I gulped.

"Can't hear you," he said. "Maybe I should turn up my Miracle Ear."

My words came out in a squeak. "Can I please talk to my grandmother?"

She seemed to take forever getting to the phone. Didn't even ask where I was, why I called. It was Seymour this, Seymour that.

"I was standing in line at the bank, looking over the latest issue of *Earthquake Watch*. Seymour was right behind me, practically reading over my shoulder. 'You can only do so much to prepare yourself,' he said. 'After that, it's in God's hands.' He sounded like a man who knew what he was talking about, so I listened. 'I had a very good antiques business in Los Angeles—survived a few minor quakes without much damage.' What he couldn't survive was the death of his wife six months ago—being in the same house they shared for twenty-five years. Oh, you shouldn't know from these things, Rachel. So anyway, he goes on and on about how he needed a change of scenery and all that—are you still there, Rachel?"

"Yes, Grandma."

"We seemed to have so much in common. And he was rather a gentleman from the start. Handsome, too. Remember how Grandpa used to make fun of my reading about earthquakes? Not Seymour. He's a man who really understands." She sighed. Almost like Laura when she talked about Harold. "You're very quiet, Rachel. What's wrong?"

"Nothing."

"You're not mad at me or anything like that—for not telling you, I mean?"

"No, Grandma." My face was becoming hot, tears rolling down like lava. If I didn't hang up soon, I was afraid I would explode.

"It's not as if I didn't *want* to tell you. But I was afraid. So soon after Grandpa's death—you can forgive me, can't you? For not telling you, I mean. I just needed to be sure this wasn't a fling."

A fling? I thought. *How does a sixty-two-year-old woman who recently buried a husband have a fling?*

"Are you there, Rachel? You're so quiet. Is something wrong?"

"No, Grandma."

"I can hardly hear you. What's all that racket? Where are you?"

I left the receiver hanging like the end of a noose. And walked away.

I sat back down at the table, didn't say a word. Just stared at the lobster on my mother's plate. Splayed open. So exposed. So red. *How fitting*, I thought, watching my mother tackle it. For the first time.

"It's because of you that I'm ordering this," she said to Jake and Gary," so you'd better help me."

"Do the claw first," advised Gary, who had also ordered lobster.

She squeezed the nutcracker, could not make any headway with the claw.

"It's all in the angle," said Jake, taking over for my mother. With one snap, the shell split open.

"Did you know," said Gary, turning his attention to me, "that if you put a pencil in a lobster's claw, he'll write his name?"

Jake winked. "He ate too much lobster as a child." Gary had grown up in New Hampshire. "Affected his mind." He leaned forward, pretended to be telling me a secret. "Next thing you know, he'll be telling you about lobster races."

"How did you guess?" Gary dabbed his mouth with his napkin. "Whenever my father brought home lobster, before cooking them, he'd set them on the floor. My brother Daniel and I loved watching them try to scramble across the room. They weren't very fast. The slowest one went into the pot first."

I imagined lobsters, disoriented, on a cold tile floor, thought about the funny cartoon Jake could create from the scene. *After you*, one lobster might gesture to the other, looking up at the pot of boiling water on the stove.

"All this for one little piece of meat?" said my mother, digging into the claw with her tiny fork. She looked funny with a bib wrapped around her neck.

"Now dip it in the butter," said Jake, in a singsong voice.

"Do I have to?" My mother preferred her lobster, like her corn, unbuttered. She turned to me. "Why don't you try some? It's really good."

"Nah—I'll pass." I had my doubts about lobster, or, for that matter, any of the various foods and drinks I was told I would one day acquire a taste for. Beer. Fish of any kind. Pesto. Coffee. Snails. I scrutinized the lobster, cut in half, thought about the frogs we would be dissecting in school next year. Jerry Goldberg said he would absolutely refuse to do it. I wasn't sure what I would do.

My mother tackled her second claw with ease, but when she tried to pull the meat from the shell, it went flying across the table, onto Gary's plate.

"Why, it's . . . Superlobster," said Gary.

My mother frowned. She was embarrassed.

"This is a very common phenomenon among first-time lobster eaters," Gary reassured her, retrieving the meat for her with her fork.

Her luck with the tail wasn't much better. I don't know if she squeezed the nutcracker too hard, but bits of shell went flying. I started to laugh, caught myself by once again thinking about dead frogs, pinned down, ready to be eviscerated. My mother dug in. She pulled. Pieces of lobster landed on Jake's plate.

"Why, thank you," he said. "Don't mind if I do have a taste." Jake used his fingers, instead of a fork. The lobster, dripping with butter, seemed to slide between his lips, into his mouth. I needed something else, immediately, to fixate on, and turned my attention to my mother. "Remember that story you told me about the time you had to dissect a frog?"

She screwed up her nose. "Rachel, we're eating. That's not exactly dinnertime conversation."

"Why not?" I asked. "Don't people eat frog's legs?"

"That's not the same thing. First of all, you're talking about entirely different kinds of frogs. Second of all"—my mother was starting to get the hang of eating lobster—"you don't eat the whole frog. Just the thought of it turns my stomach."

I smiled. "But it's such a good story—you know, the way you put the heart in a little bag and carried it home."

"Rachel, enough!"

"Remember how warm your hand felt? And how you hid the heart under Vivian's pillow to kind of freak her out? Only Jake went snooping around after you—"

Gary perked up. "I never heard *this* story."

"And I did what any four-year-old who was excited about finding a red blob would do," Jake continued. "I hid it, though of course everyone thought I ate it."

My mother pushed away her plate. The singing started up again. A waiter this time. Liza Minnelli in *Cabaret*.

"I think we have a contender for Miss America," said Gary, shifting his eyes toward the singing waiter.

"He *is* cute." Jake's smile, directed at Gary, was noticeably restrained. I excused myself from the table, went over to the bar, studied my father as he mixed drinks and sang along, told him he had a much better voice than the skinny waiter in the white shirt and bow tie who flung his arms wide as he sang.

"Thank you," he said. It was a busy night at the restaurant, and he couldn't really talk, which was fine with me. All I wanted was a close-up of him: the strong jaw, the piercing blue eyes, the way he held the shaker to mix a drink—some detail about him unnoticed by me before. Something that would explain, by comparison, the way Jake smiled at Gary.

I stayed at the bar until the waiter finished singing, returned to the table with another margarita for my mother. Her appetite dulled by the forced memory of a dead frog, she drank it down quickly, got giddy again, ordered another margarita, held up her glass, and toasted Jake's return.

"Now, don't go saying anything that will embarrass me." Jake held his napkin to his face, pretending to be shy. I looked for details unnoticed before. Something that would explain.

"Don't be silly. I'm just happy to have my baby brother back. Of course, it won't exactly be the same, now that Ruth has settled somewhere else. With a boyfriend, I might add."

A fling, I thought. *My grandmother is having a fling. Stuffed in my panties is a wad of crumpled white toilet paper getting redder by the minute.*

Everyone was talking about Seymour this and Seymour that, and even if it was "just a fling," so what? She'd been so depressed after Grandpa died, afraid to make any more moves. And then along came Seymour. Talk about timing, said my mother. She couldn't wait to meet him.

The queasiness, not really abated, was growing intense again. *Talk about timing.* I'd hardly touched anything on my plate, though no one seemed to notice. It was Seymour this, Seymour that. I slipped my hands under the table, between my thighs, tensing up now. The blood, probably just dribbling, felt like it was flowing in buckets. I would never get out of this seat, I thought. When it came time to leave the restaurant, I would continue to sit here, pretend I was having a cataleptic fit. Like Eppie in *Silas Marner*.

"Are you feeling okay, Rachel?" my mother suddenly (finally?) asked. "You look a little pale." I nodded, said I just wasn't very hungry. Too much Coke.

My father, taking advantage of a brief lull in tending bar, came over to the table. "Everything okay?" He put his hands on the back of my mother's chair.

"Perfecto," said Jake. I looked at my uncle. At Gary. At my father, who could stay only a minute. Nothing surfaced in the way he stood, or the way Gary shifted in his seat, or the way Jake lifted his glass, that would explain.

My mother, a little tipsy, suddenly became exuberant. "I have a great idea," she said, just after my father left. She could hardly contain herself. "Next year I'm going to make a seder. At our place."

"A *seder*?" I said. "When did you ever make a seder? When did you ever want to make a seder?"

"Well, I never had to, because my mother was around. But now that she's so far away . . . well, I'm thinking about it."

She's drunk, I thought. *Really drunk.*

"It's not that I'm going 'religious' or anything like that," she went on. "I just realized, since we didn't have a seder this year, that I like the rituals associated with Passover. Besides, it will be a great reason to get Ruth—and Seymour—here. Vivian will definitely come; flying up to New York just isn't the same, she told me, without spending at least one night with Ruth. And I'm going to call George way ahead of time, so he won't have any excuse for not showing up."

"I hope you're not planning on serving lobster," said Gary, teasing my mother.

"Only if it's kosher."

Though I had doubts about my mother's ability to pull together a seder, I liked the idea.

"Maybe Grandma will come out a few days early and help cook." I closed my eyes, took a deep breath, imagined our apartment redolent with the smell of onions frying for chopped liver. Gefilte fish. Chicken roasted with potatoes.

"Sentimentality suits you," Jake said to my mother.

"You think that's what it is?" She'd eaten all the lobster meat by now, was down to sucking the tiny legs. "I'm not so sure. Although you may be right, to some degree, since there is a connection between sentimentality and ritual. Which I've been thinking about a lot lately. Call it my fieldwork, if you will, but I've been carefully taking note of something that all the dysfunctional families I work with—and I work with a lot of them—seem to share. Now, this is not something I can say conclusively, mind you—it's more of an observation—but the ones that are the most far-gone seem to be the ones in which there is not an ounce of ritual. No birthday celebrations. No Chinese dinners on Sunday night. No bedtime stories. Do you see what I'm getting at? Ritual is like a glue."

I thought about my father glued to the TV during football season and how it annoyed my mother. A male ritual, she called it. I don't think that was what she was talking about now.

"Of course, there's a lot about ritual that's awful—stultifying—especially in the area of religion. Makes it next to impossible to formulate your own judgments."

I yawned. Everybody, including me, laughed.

"Need oxygen?" my mother asked. It was a private joke between us. Yawning, a biology teacher had taught me and I had informed my mother, is the body's response to a need for oxygen. My mother explained the joke to Gary and Jake, put aside, for the time being, her thesis on ritual.

The yawning became contagious. Gary, yawning, said he

wanted to drive out to Sag Harbor that night. Jake, yawning, preferred spending the night in the city, in the apartment of a friend. They argued. Gary hated the idea of sleeping on a bumpy sofa bed. Their last stretch of driving had been ten hours, without stopping, and his back, he said, was crying out for a real bed. Jake wanted to go to a club, dance off the stiffness, have breakfast in SoHo. To me, Jake's idea was a lot more appealing. But Gary argued more forcefully and got his way. Like my father, I thought. So much like my father.

I flew out of the car when we got home, ran into my room, peeled off my jeans and panties, got a fresh pair of underwear and took it to the bathroom. Under the sink were the pads: maxis, minis, ultras with wings—I'd sampled them all. Maxis felt too bulky, too big. Minis felt flimsy. Ultras with wings were the ones that felt right, with their diaper-like security. I sat on the toilet, attached the pad to my underwear. *How brilliant technology is*, I thought. *No pins, just peel and stick. Like a Band-Aid.* I pulled up my underpants, padded now, stood over the sink, and splashed some water on my face. The queasiness was gone, replaced by a feeling that something foreign had invaded my body. Something warm, like a trickle of pudding. Something cold, like a pile of wet autumn leaves. Something totally out of my control. I pulled down my panties again, saw a stripe of blood, changed the pad. *I'm not moving from here*, I thought. *They'll find me asleep in the bathtub before the night is over.* I leaned my forehead on the vanity, not queasy, just overcome. *My grandmother is having a fling. My uncle is in love with a man. My mother is convinced that her brief affair with Glen had an affirming effect on her marriage. That's what she told my father. How forgiving he was. Or so he seemed.*

"Congratulations," my mother said through the door.

How could she know?

The underwear, I thought—stained, lying on the floor of my room like bread crumbs leading her right to me. I opened the door, almost collapsed in her arms. Crying.

"Your grandmother's on the phone. She wants to talk to you."

"Does she know?"

My mother nodded. Grandma had just called. She'd been worried since I'd telephoned earlier, wanted to know what was wrong with me. My mother had gone into my room, found the underpants on the floor. I told her I wanted to throw them away.

She wiped the tears from my face, walked me to her bedroom, handed me the phone. "Just tell her I slapped you, if she asks. It's an old Jewish custom. Some sort of superstitious protection. If nothing else, it brings the bloom back to your face—for a minute."

"Hi, Grandma."

"I hope you know that you had me worried half to death," she said. "Did your mother give you a little slap on the cheek?"

"Sort of."

"Well, thank God nothing's wrong, but you should have told me."

"I tried," I said. If she had seen me, cramped in the phone booth, catching snippets of song with one ear, echoes of newfound love with the other, maybe she would have understood.

"Never mind. The important thing now is that you have to be careful—with the boys, I mean."

"Grandma, you're embarrassing me."

"Never you mind. This is important. You're a woman now. Boys—men—are going to start looking at you in a different way. If they haven't already. There's an old expression: 'Why should a man buy the cow if he gets the milk for free?'"

I burst out laughing. "Grandma!"

"I told it to your mother—and I was almost right in her case. And I told it to Vivian. And I'm telling it to you. Because I think—no, I know—you have a good head on your shoulders. Don't make the same mistakes they made."

Before hanging up, she told me how glad she was that Jake had moved back East. Earthquake watching was getting a little nerve-racking, she said. It was Seymour who helped her see that, even if there were some pattern she could detect (and she was sure she could), some rhyme or reason to the swell and shifting of the plates, the big ones happen so fast, there isn't much anyone can do. "I just thank God," she said, "that Jake had the good sense to move back East."

"What does Miss America do?" I asked Laura. We were at her house, watching grown girls parade around in bathing suits, with shoes dyed to match.

"She gets to meet the president—and the First Lady. I think she has lunch with her. She also gets a whole new wardrobe. Travels a lot."

"But what does she *do*?"

"I think they give her a scholarship for college—and a car." Laura got up from the couch, stood near the TV facing me, pivoted her body from side to side. "If I become Miss America," she said in a nasal drawl, "I promise to make the world—the country, I mean—a safer place for virgins."

I applauded. She took a bow, came back to sit down. "My mother has a second cousin who was a runner-up for Miss New York State. Everyone in the family kept hoping Miss New York State would break her leg or something like that. No such luck for this cousin." Laura turned her attention to the TV. "Now, that one, you have to admit, is a real dog. I mean, doesn't she ever look in the mirror? How does she think she can be Miss America?"

"She managed to get this far."

Laura shook her head. "Maybe we should try to enter when we're old enough. I mean, if *she* can get this far, it's got to be a cinch for us."

I wasn't as confident about my looks as Laura was. "You try," I said. "I'll be your talent coach."

Laura pulled her knees to her chest. "I wasn't serious. Not that I wouldn't love all the attention. But I met this cousin of my mother's—I wouldn't say she's gorgeous, but she's certainly prettier than half the girls in this contest. Anyway, you know what she told me? She said Miss America is not allowed to drink or smoke in public. And during Pageant Week, when all the contestants are arriving, they're chaperoned practically every minute of the day. If any of them is so much as caught alone with a guy, it's all over for her. That doesn't sound like a lot of fun to me. I mean, you get that far—you enter all these local contests—and you're finally there, a contestant in *the* Miss America Contest, and you can't even be alone with a man? Doesn't make a bit of sense to me."

"What doesn't make sense to me is how you hardly hear a thing about Miss America *after* the contest. I mean, don't you think it's weird that there's all this fuss about becoming Miss America, but once the contest is over, you never see her in the newspapers—except if she does something wrong?"

Laura, half listening, disappeared. When she returned, she was wearing a gold lamé bathing suit and her mother's silver slingbacks. Laura was proud of the fact that she and her mother wore the same size shoe and almost the same size brassiere. She paraded around the living room, angling her body to the left, to the right, lifting and lowering the baton she held in her hand, the same baton her mother had used when she was a high school majorette. Laura's movements, even when they took on an air of parody, were as effortless as ripples on a lake. The more easily she moved, the more awkward I felt. The more her body blossomed, the less comfortable I became with my own boyish shape.

When it came time for the talent segment of the contest, Laura lifted the baton, sang along with Miss Arkansas, a waxy blonde with a voice that could destroy crystal.

"You win—hands down," I said, crowning her with my sun visor. I took one of the silk flowers her mother kept in a vase on the end table and handed it to Laura. She pretended to cry, said what a wonderful moment this was in her life.

In the meantime, the drama taking place on TV intensified. Miss Arizona strummed on a guitar, Miss Texas pounded on a piano, and Miss Georgia, who both of us were sure would capture the title (unless the contest was fixed), did a dramatic reading from a play neither of us had heard of.

The tension grew, the finalists came out for their interviews, and when the winner was announced—it wasn't Miss Georgia— Laura was upset.

"It's never who you think it's going to be," she complained, turning off the TV.

"I can't go with you next weekend," Laura whispered. We were in bed, ready for sleep.

"What do you mean you can't go? Jake is expecting us."

"Don't ask me any questions, Rachel. Please! I can't go. That's all there is to it."

I turned on the light on Laura's nightstand and looked at her. She looked away. "What's going on?"

"Not so loud. You'll wake Ricki."

"I don't care who I wake. You can't just spring something like this on me. I want to know what happened to make you suddenly change your mind."

"Just forget it, Rachel. Go. Have a good time. But forget about me coming with you." Laura got out of bed, went to the window. I followed her.

"There has to be a reason," I pressed her. "I have a right to know why you can't go."

Laura sighed. "It's my mother. She won't let me."

"But why? Didn't she say it was okay?" I shook her arm. "Well, didn't she?"

Laura pulled away. "I really don't want to talk about it."

Angry, and getting nowhere, I put on my jeans, tucked my nightshirt into them.

"Where are you going?" Laura demanded. "It's practically midnight."

"I'm not staying here, that's for sure—not if you won't talk to me."

"Okay, okay. Just calm down. This isn't easy, Rachel. My mother . . ." Laura paused, licked her lips, which were dry with nervousness, began again. "My mother doesn't want me to go. She says Jake is, you know . . . strange."

"What are you talking about?"

"She says he's strange." Laura shifted from side to side, avoided looking at me. "A homo, Rachel. I mean, it's not as if this should surprise you. It's right there"—she pointed to my knapsack—"in your diary."

I don't know if it was her tone of voice or just her words or the fact that she had been poking through my diary, but I slapped Laura hard across the face. Then I tore out of her house to mine, five blocks away. It was near midnight, a sticky summer night, and I ran fast, past my house, until I become breathless, until I came to the playground where Laura and I took Ricki, the same playground Jake used to take me to. I sat on a bench to catch my breath, to think, but quickly got up when I saw, or thought I saw, a boy, a stranger, heading toward me. I ran out of the playground, kept running until I was once again breathless, until I was on my doorstep, ringing the bell of my own home, forgetting for a moment that my parents were not home. I fumbled for my keys, dashed to my room, threw my knapsack on the bed.

A homo, Rachel . . .

My knapsack, tottering on the edge of my bed, fell to the floor. The diary Jake and Gary had given me two years earlier, the diary almost filled now, no place else to go, spilled out. I started riffling through the pages.

I saw Jake at the sink, cleaning some dishes, and Gary's hands were around his waist.

My mother doesn't love my father.

I wish Gary would disappear.

No sooner do the homo and the lezzie leave the party than the police come charging in.

If you think something and it happens, is it a coincidence?

There are things you can't even tell your best friend. What would she think if she knew how I dream about Jake? Holding him in the dark of the night.

A homo, Rachel . . .

I went into the kitchen, pulled a candle from the shelf over the sink, lit it. Words rumbled in my hand, trembling now. *Don't do it*, I tried to tell myself. *Don't be rash. It's just a diary, a compilation of sporadic adolescent musings, nothing to get so worked up about. One day you may want to recall what you were thinking, feeling.*

I slapped my hand to stop the trembling, but it was beyond my control. More than just a diary, this thing in my hand seemed to have taken on a life of its own. The point of beginning was oh so clear, so neatly defined. The end was becoming clearer by the second.

I held the diary open, over the flame. I could have tossed it into the trash; no one would have known, and by the end of the next day the pages would have turned soggy, smelling of banana peel and peppermint tea. But the very act of watching my words go up in smoke gave me the one thing I needed more than anything else—namely, a sense of control. Laura—my best friend—had betrayed my trust. Now, I knew, I had to let go. Of Laura, who brought an ugly tempo to words. And of my own musings, violated beyond repair.

The pages, handmade, burned quickly. Large pieces of ash dropped to the sink. Like tears.

endings

On the first New Year's Eve I was allowed to stay up until midnight, my mother and father gave me a noisemaker and some sparkling cider, which I sipped as we sat on the couch in front of the TV, waiting for a large neon ball to make its ten-second slide down into the new year. My father popped the cork of the champagne bottle just as the ball descended to the roof of the building in Times Square. My mother and I blew our noisemakers.

I was seven at the time, and my memory is of noise that hurt my ears and kisses that exploded on my cheek and the feeling that something more was supposed to happen. I remember glancing at the imposing grandfather clock that stood against the wall at the entrance to our living room. It was the only piece of furniture my father had taken from his mother's house when she died, and it seemed to me to have a life of its own. The chimes had long stopped working, and the hour hand was a little shorter than it should have been because a piece of its tip had broken off, but the clock, over fifty years old, ran as smoothly as if it were brand new. When midnight approached and I glanced at the clock, I thought maybe I would see the minute hand move past the Roman twelve. Just being up at midnight was a thrill. But if I could see, finally, the tiny shift of time I'd tried so many times to observe by staring at the clock, that, for me, would be the real celebration. Seeing time move.

In the years that followed, my parents carted me off to my grandparents for New Year's Eve so that they could spend the night alone or with friends, which was just as well with me. Grandma made sugar cookies in the shape of stars for the occasion, and we always got a call from Jake at midnight.

This New Year's Eve, my parents were going out and I was staying home. Alone. It's no big deal, I said to them. Really. They tried to talk me into inviting a friend over or going to the party Laura was having. But I told them, like I told her, that I would not set foot inside her house anymore. The only person I would even consider asking over was Jerry, and he was in Florida with his mother.

It's no big deal, I said when they pressed the issue. Really. My father was speeding around the house, singing "White Christmas," my mother was yelling at him for leaving a tiny bottle of white powder on the kitchen table, and I was determined to treat this as just another night. If I were Celtic, I explained, the new year would begin November 1, which would make Halloween New Year's Eve. Of course, if I had lived in Roman times, my year would have begun March 1, unless I was Jewish, in which case, according to Jerry Goldberg, the barley harvest of spring would signal the new year.

"What are you, writing a paper or something?" asked my father, sniffling and speeding around the room. He reminded me of a steam engine.

"Actually . . ." I said. He stopped paying attention, darted into the kitchen. I could hear my mother's voice, the high strain of futility turning an angry whisper into a hoarse cry. "You want to do this shit, do it when she's asleep or when she's out of the house. Or when you're out." I knew "this shit" was cocaine, which my father indulged in on special occasions like his birthday and my mother's birthday and New Year's Eve. He made a point of telling me once, when my mother was out, that I shouldn't worry, he was not a drug addict, cocaine was something he used "recreationally," though he did claim to have written a novel in a week under the influence. It was so bad he ripped it up and swore off cocaine, except for special occasions. Like New Year's Eve.

"Actually," I yelled into the kitchen, "I'm thinking of becoming an astrologer." My voice diminished with each word, like a balloon losing its air. I jumped up from the couch, went to my room, picked up the little brass perpetual calendar sitting on my desk, a present Grandma had gotten from Seymour's antique shop. Small brass rings, held in place by pegs protruding from the calendar, denoted the days of the month, and there was a groove at the top for changeable tabs engraved with the names of the months. January, I learned from the booklet that came with the calendar, was named after Janus, god of endings and beginnings. Februus, rooted in the Latin word for cleansing and purification, gave February its name; it was the month of scouring and sacrifice, a primitive kind of spring cleaning, before the new year began. Mars, as the Roman god of war and agriculture, embodied, like his namesake month, both the lion and the lamb.

I slipped out the December tab, replaced it with January, began reconfiguring the rings to the new month.

"We're leaving now," my mother called out to me. It was nine o'clock. My plan was to read a little, maybe watch an old movie on TV. Just like any other weekend night I spent alone.

I opened my bedroom door. My father, still chugging around like a steam engine, left a trail of Old Spice in his wake. He placed his hands on my shoulder, kissed my cheek.

"Next time I kiss you, it will be 1983," he said. Even without the influence of cocaine, my father loved New Year's Eve. For years when he was a boy, he and his father and mother took the subway from their Lower East Side apartment to Times Square on New Year's Eve. You can't imagine what it was like, he told me, to be in the thick of things on New Year's Eve, ticker tape raining down on you, settling in your hair, on your eyelashes, like an offering from heaven. My father was not a particularly spiritual man, but sometimes when he watched the crowds on the TV screen, he'd single out two faces that reminded him of his mother and father, and he'd imagine a child sandwiched between them, layers of clothing making him feel like a little Doughboy. Looking at the sky.

"I can't find my purse," my mother muttered, as she hurried past us. She was wearing an ankle-length, midnight-blue velvet dress with Victorian boots and a batik scarf, almost as long as her dress, that seemed to swirl around her as she moved. If my father was a steam engine, she was pure percussion. Boots on the downbeat, softened by the brush of nylon stockings, a sound I loved.

The missing purse surfaced in the kitchen, under a magazine on the table, and, after more hugs and kisses and reassurances that yes, yes, yes, I really would be okay, my parents finally left. I felt relieved. Two days earlier, my mother had threatened to back out of their New Year's plans after my father had a jealous fit over a phone call from Glen. He'd moved back to Chicago to take a job as head of legal aid for a city agency. Just called to say hello, wish my mother a happy new year. That's what she told my father. "Read between the lines," he hissed. "Just read between the lines." He saw subtext in the phone call. She saw a windy city 1,100 miles away. "No one can be that delusional," she said.

Immediately after they were gone, I stretched out on the couch, sank back with my book, began reading.

My father's family name being Pirrip, and my Christian name Philip, my infant tongue could make of both names nothing longer or more explicit than Pip. So, I called myself Pip, and came to be called Pip.

The phone rang.

"Hello?"

"Hi, sweetie pie." It was my aunt Vivian. The lady of the per-fumed ankles. The last time I'd seen her had been during the summer, when she'd come up for a weekend visit. With Tony. They stayed at some hotel in the city, and my mother and I met her for dinner one night at the restaurant I'd come to call my father's. With-out Tony. Vivian talked a lot. About how well the car-wash business was doing, and how she really loved living in Boca, and how the idea of marriage had lost its luster. Irony, she said, is what life's all about. "You see this?" She flashed her new, one-and-a-half-carat, pear-shaped diamond ring. "To the rest of the world, it's an engage-ment ring. To me, it's nothing more than an emblem of irony." Her fingers, perfectly manicured, carried the diamond well, as though all the years of being soaked and filed and polished and buffed had been for the sole purpose of showcasing a stone.

The irony, as I understood it, had something to do with Tony's midlife longing for a son. He'd finally divorced his wife a year ago, at Vivian's insistence. Two months later, the ex-wife had remarried and was now the proud mother of a new baby. A boy. For Tony and Vivian, on the other hand, things were not falling into place so smoothly. "He wants another chance at fatherhood," explained Vivian. "Not that his daughters don't fill him with pride—the little he sees them, that is. But they're *girls*. And he can't stand the idea of going through life without pitching a ball to his son. So what does he do? He tells me to stop taking the pill; then he buys me a dia-mond. And just like that, he thinks it will happen. Only it doesn't just happen." Vivian blamed herself. "Maybe subconsciously I don't really want a kid," she said. "So I go through the motions, but my heart isn't in it. Know what I mean?" She glanced at me, raised her eyebrows. "Not that I don't think kids are great, but if I have a child now—at thirty-nine—I'll be over fifty when he—if it is a *he*—is only eleven. And Tony will be fifty-six. Seems a little old to be dealing with an adolescent." She held up her left hand, admired the stone. "Irony," she said. "Know what I mean?"

My mother reminded her it could be Tony's fault; it wasn't always the woman. Vivian frowned, popped her martini olive into her mouth. "Yeah, *right*," she said. "Try telling that to him."

"Too much sun," my mother said to me when we left her. "You can see it in her face."

Vivian asked me, like she always did when she called, questions that required simple answers: How's school? Good. Was I enjoying my vacation? Yes. Today she was more brusque than usual.

"Is your mother home, cookie?" Her voice, which normally had a slight rasp to it, seemed to quiver.

"She went out with my father. To a party."

"They left you alone? On New Year's Eve?"

"It's no big deal." I was getting tired of saying that.

"You should never be alone on New Year's Eve."

"Why?"

"Because . . . be-be-cause," Vivian stammered.

"I told him we're through," she said. She sounded nasal. Like she'd been crying a lot. "I don't care about getting married, I don't care about having a kid, I just want *out*." She let out a deep sigh. I imagined her hand around the receiver, clutching it tightly, her long nails digging into her palm. "You know what it's like, day in and day out, hearing a man pine away about not having a son? As if it's my fault. But that isn't even the point. I say, life is what it is. You roll with it. Know what I mean?"

"Sort of." I felt like I was a tape recorder and Vivian was talking into me. "But not Tony," she went on. "He says, there's no rolling, except when you're on the ground, cradling a football that's knocked the wind out of you. It's all about strategy, he says—kind of like a football game—and playing hard. Sometimes you win and sometimes you lose. But you plan your strategy and you play hard."

Vivian was sobbing again. "What is that supposed to mean—that I'm a loser?" I didn't know what to say, which, fortunately, was not a problem. My mother sometimes said, after being on the phone for a half hour or so with Vivian, that she was great at having conversations with herself.

"I hate to say this," Vivian went on, more composed now, "but maybe my mother was right—I should have married Stuart Eldridge, my high school sweetheart. He tracked me down, you know, ten years after graduating. Took me to lunch at a very expensive restaurant. 'I'm an attorney,' he said to me. 'I can give you a very good life.' But I'd been dating Tony two months already, and it was like the Fourth of July every time I saw him. So Stuart never really had a chance." Vivian got quiet for a moment, and I thought she was finally going to hang up. I was wrong.

"You know what the purpose of New Year's Eve is?" she said. I didn't bother trying to answer. "To make you think about your life—where it's going. And I think I just came up with my first resolution of the year: no more men in my life. They're not worth the aggravation. They make you feel old too soon. Tony. Stuart. I can give you other names, too, but it just doesn't matter. What it boils down to is aggravation. Who knows? Maybe the thing to do is to get involved with a woman. They're more understanding, that's for sure." Vivian let out a laugh. "That would be a hoot. I leave Tony to become a lesbian. The idea would probably excite him." Like someone awakening from a dream of deep disorientation, she suddenly changed her tone.

"Ignore what I just said," she told me. "There are *some* nice men in the world. Tony was once one of them."

My mother was right, I thought. *Too much sun.*

"Are you still there, sweetie pie? Did you fall asleep on me?"

"Yes," I said. "I'm still here."

"Well, I'm gonna go now. Open a bottle of Dom. Drink it myself. I mean, there's no law that says you have to drink champagne with someone else, is there?"

After Vivian hung up, I went back to my reading. The phone rang again. It was my grandmother this time.

"Happy New Year," she said.

"It isn't really New Year's."

"What are you talking about?"

I told her what I'd told my father. About the Jewish new year being in the spring. And the Celtic new year in November. And the Roman new year in March.

"Where's your mother?" she asked. "She's not letting you drink champagne, is she?"

I told her my mother and father had gone to a party, and no, I wasn't drinking, and yes, I was perfectly content to be by myself. "It's not as if they've never left me alone before. I *am* thirteen, you know."

"I don't care if you're thirty," she said. "New Year's Eve is not a night you should spend by yourself."

"What's the big deal?"

"The big deal, Miss Big Shot, is that it's a night for celebration. And you can't really celebrate by yourself—it's just not supposed to be that way."

"Vivian is."

"Vivian is what?"

"Celebrating by herself." I gave my grandmother the abbreviated version of my call from Vivian.

"She's always telling him to leave." Grandma sounded more sympathetic than annoyed. "And she always lets him come back."

"That doesn't make sense."

"Your aunt is not the first—and she won't be the last—woman to do things that don't make sense when it comes to a man," said Grandma. She had every hope that I would be smarter.

"Not to change the subject," she went on, "but have you heard from Jake lately?" I told her he'd called last week.

"Is he okay?"

"I think so. Why?"

"I don't know—he's just not calling as much as he used to. And when he does, he sounds jittery. Like he's keeping something from me."

"I think you're imagining things."

"Mothers don't imagine things like that."

"As far as I know, there's nothing wrong." I told her I'd seen him two weeks ago, when my mother and I took a drive out to visit him. All the work on the house he and Gary had bought was finally finished, and they had a small dinner party. Gary made lobster. For my mother, he said. And their friends Marsha and Jason brought a vegetable pie, plus three different desserts. Pumpkin bread. An apple tart. A petite madeleine. Marsha was a part-time caterer, part-time actress, and she always had her chef make extra desserts for her weekends out on the island. The pumpkin bread was Jake's favorite, the apple tart was Gary's, and the petite madeleine she packed for me. Marsha and my mother hit it off very well, though from appearances they were as different as night and day. If my mother was earthy, everything about Marsha was exotic. Her shiny hair, jet black, softly sculpted against the nape of her neck. The bracelets from Mexico and India and Egypt that clinked every time she moved her arm. The resonance in her voice that made me think of waves washing over a rock. Smooth and soothing. She wore stylish, offbeat clothes that made her seem much younger than Jason, in his plaid flannel shirt, with the pipe he carried in his breast pocket. Jason, a psychiatrist, was less talkative than Marsha, though he was the one who told me about their son, Bruce, who was spending the weekend with a friend. On some visit soon, he hoped, I'd meet him.

"Well, I hope you're right." My grandmother did not sound convinced.

"He's been working a lot, you know," I said. "And fixing up the house took a lot of his time. He and Gary planned to finish it over the Thanksgiving weekend, but they went to Washington instead, to visit a friend who's sick."

"He did? Wonder why he didn't mention that to me."

"Probably skipped his mind."

"He told me he was going to Washington," said Grandma. "But he didn't mention anything about a sick friend." Grandma began probing. "How sick is he?"

I knew Tom was dying. Why hadn't Jake told Grandma?

"Pretty sick," I answered.

"Do you know what's wrong with him?"

"I think he has pneumonia or something like that."

"Pneumonia? You sure it's not TB?"

"I'm pretty sure."

"That's not too bad, then. You know, I had pneumonia once, when I was fifteen. My mother—may she rest in peace—hears me coughing and sees that I'm having some trouble breathing, so she immediately calls Rosenberg—now, *that* was a doctor. We didn't have to go running to specialists in those days. We had doctors, *real* doctors, who didn't have to send you for X-rays to know there was something wrong with you.

"So Rosenberg comes over. He examines me, tells my mother I have pneumonia, but from my symptoms he can tell it isn't the kind that you give antibiotics for. Rest is what I need. 'No pills?' my mother says to him. 'You want pills, Rose,' he says, 'I'll give you pills.' My mother looks at me—and I can say this from experience: it is not easy looking at a child of yours lying in bed, so weak and pale—and she looks at the doctor. 'There must be *something* you can give her,' she says. He takes her hand in his. 'Believe me, Rose,' he says, 'this is not the kind of pneumonia you die from without medication. I know it looks bad to you—and I'm not saying it isn't serious—but if you give her lots of chicken soup, put a vaporizer near her bed, and let her rest, she'll pull through. If I give her pills, it will just be for your head.' My mother gets indignant. 'I don't need pills for my head,' she says. The doctor lets out a little laugh. 'I don't mean that,' he says. 'What I mean is that you'll feel better knowing your daughter is taking some medicine. But the truth is, it would all be in your head.'

"No sooner does the doctor leave than my mother goes to the bathroom and comes back with this awful paste that she spreads across my chest. Mustard, I think it was. It was a remedy *her* mother used on her whenever she had a cold."

"Sounds disgusting."

"It was. But my mother was convinced it cured me."

After extracting a promise from me that I would not open the door for anyone and that I would hang up immediately if I got any crazy phone calls—she'd read a newspaper article about the high rate of crazy (her word for "obscene") phone calls on New Year's Eve—Grandma reluctantly said goodbye. She had dinner plans with Seymour. Next year, she said, she was going to send me a ticket to Tucson for my holiday break from school. That way, there would be no chance of my being alone.

I went back to my reading, started to feel drowsy, and soon fell asleep. It was midnight when the phone rang again, waking me.

"Happy New Year!" I did not at first recognize Jake's voice, almost thought it was one of those crazy phone calls Grandma tried to warn me about.

"Happy New Year," I said drowsily.

"I can't hear you." There was a lot of noise in the background, drowning Jake's voice. Then a loud blast of music. I pictured everyone up and dancing, arms in the air spelling out the song "YMCA."

"I just did something really weird," said Jake. His words rolled together, almost slurred. "I dialed Ruth's old number in Brooklyn. A husky voice answered. Didn't sound anything at all like Ruth. Told me I dialed a wrong number. No, I said, I had the right number—did you know they recycle old phone numbers?—but the wrong person. Then I called you, though I didn't really expect to get you. Thought you'd be out partying. Figured I'd try anyway."

I heard something tap against the receiver on Jake's end—"Let's make a toast," I think he said, "to the New Year"—then a chorus of voices singing along with the music.

"Where are you?" I asked.

"Can you speak a little louder?"

"*Where are you?*" I shouted.

"Home."

"Sounds like you're at a club or something."

"She says it sounds like a club, Gary."

Gary got on the phone. "It *is* a club, Rachel. Chez Gary and Jake." He wished me a happy New Year, hoped he would see me soon, handed the phone back to Jake.

Jake kept talking, though it was hard to make out what he was saying. Something about a turtle he almost ran over the other day. "I stopped the car just in time," he said.

"What did you do with the turtle?"

"I'm staring at him right now." *Hallucinating*, I thought. *My uncle is hallucinating.*

"Right now?"

"Right now—right here. I picked up a glass tank for him at the pet shop and put it on a shelf near the telephone table, next to the picture of you in Big Sur. Did you know there's an Indian legend about the world being formed from a turtle's back? And each of the thirteen scales on its back represents the thirteen moons of the year? There's the Moon of the Popping Trees in January. And the Moon When Baby Bears Are Born in February, though it's also called the Snow Moon . . ."

Another phone was ringing. "I bet that's Ruth," said Jake. "She always calls on New Year's Eve—if I don't call first." He excused himself, asked me to hold on. I imagined my grandmother trying to conduct a conversation over the din. *At least you're not alone*, she would say to Jake.

When he got back to me, the drunkenness in his voice was gone, the slurred words replaced by hard, sober ones.

"That was definitely not Ruth," he said, his voice shaking. It was Tom's brother—my friend in Washington."

"Turn it down!" I heard him yell into the room, as "YMCA" kept playing. "Turn the fucking music down!" He was crying. "Tom is dead," he whispered, leaving me with a silent phone against my ear.

Tom is dead.

I hung up, stared into space. Empty, hard space. Fuzzy images stared back. My father's plants, glistening green. My mother's afghan. A small black bowl on the mantel, something Grandma had gotten at the Santa Clara pueblo. The old clock, ticking with song, too tall for the shelf, keeping alive the spirit of someone's grandfather. It was three minutes past midnight. Through the walls, through the windows, I could hear people spitting into noisemakers, making toasts, bringing strained harmonies to good old times. Drinking cups of kindness. Cups half-filled with promise, emptied of regret.

There was a knock on my door. Someone drunk, very drunk, going on and on like a broken record.

We'll drink a cup of kindness yet
We'll drink a cup of kindness yet

He kept stumbling on the *yet*. The crossroads. The point where the old rings itself out, the new struggles to ring itself in.

I held my breath, didn't move, until another voice, a woman's, took the cup of kindness away from my door. It was ten minutes past midnight. The noisemakers had dwindled down, the toasts fizzled out, till all I could hear, all I could feel, was a hush, more haunting with each passing second.

February 2, 1983

Dear Rachel:

> *I'm on the train now, on my way home from Washington. It was not what I would call a happy trip. Tom's brother got together as many friends from DC and San Francisco as he could for a memorial service. It was good to see some familiar faces from San Francisco. But there were a lot of tears.*

> *You get to see a lot through the window of a train. The landscape right now is still very wintry and bleak—and I have this terrible feeling that the groundhog is not going to give us that early spring we hope for—but sitting back, lulled by the movement, I watch for things. I just saw a snowman in the middle of nowhere, and a small child in a Big Bird stocking cap waved at me when the train slowed down, and there are hills in the distance that look like they're touching the clouds. The sunset today is going to be spectacular.*

> *I used to do a lot of my postcard writing on trains. Did you know that? I got so in the habit of writing to you, I didn't want to give it up, even when I moved to San Francisco and we could talk by phone. Writing, for me, is like a slow, sustained breath. Conversation, in comparison, can seem like rapid-fire breathing.*

> *Something terrible is going on now in the world, and on the surface it's about disease and death. But I'm afraid it's much more, which is why I'm writing to you. It's always easier to rewrite history—to look back on some crisis after it's passed—and try to make sense of it. But what do you tell yourself when you're right in*

the middle of it? Maybe, I say to myself, there is no sense to be made of it. Maybe—just maybe—any sense we try to make of tragedy boils down to rationalization, or re-creating who we think we are. Did you know that the word "tragedy" is derived from a Greek word that means "song of the goat"? The actors in old Greek tragedies wore goatskins when they performed, and it's got me thinking that life often seems more like a goat's kick than his song. Why did Tom have to die? I ask myself. He was in the prime of life. Are other friends of mine who are coming down with some very bizarre illnesses going to die, too?

Sometimes I wake up from a dead sleep and feel as if there's a rumbling—an earth tremor—and I'm still in San Francisco. Only I'm not there, and I still feel the rumbling. So I get out of bed to steady myself, to walk on firm ground, and tell myself there's nothing to be afraid of. Except . . .

Maybe what I want now is just to feel giddy, for a moment. Giddy with the kind of love you feel when you're young enough not to expect that love to encompass anything more than a moment in time. Innocent enough to forget, for a moment, that people will define you by the way you die. I hope I haven't depressed you terribly. It's just that writing to you somehow gives me hope. For the future.

Love and a hug, Jake

The Jewish holiday known as Passover begins the night of the first full moon after the spring equinox. To synchronize the observance of holidays in ancient times, the high court in Jerusalem, on the word of two eyewitnesses, gave the go-ahead for messengers to light torches or otherwise alert the Jewish community that a new month had arrived. With that knowledge, they could count the days to the holiday. Or they could look at the sky. For my grandmother, there was no better signal than *The Ten Commandments*. "Who needs a calendar," she would say, "when you have *TV Guide*?"

"I still remember the first time I saw that movie," she said to me, as the opening credits rolled down the TV screen. She had arrived earlier in the day, prepared to start cooking. Immediately. Gefilte fish takes time, she argued with my mother (who'd bought all the ingredients), and she was not about to do the short-cut, Cuisinart version of chopped liver. The seder was still a day away, so my mother acquiesced, let Grandma have her way in the kitchen. Until she wrinkled her nose at the spinach muffins just out of the oven. Certifiably kosher for Passover, insisted my mother. Much too nouveau, said Grandma. Not to mention tasteless.

Banished (temporarily) from the kitchen, Grandma settled into a corner of the couch, turned on the TV. At first, she couldn't seem to get comfortable, kept shifting position, blamed it on the softness of the couch. Visiting children is not as easy as one would think, she'd said. You have your habits, they have theirs. Seymour's daughter, living in San Diego, had a guest room with a small TV and a dresser where she always kept a pair of pajamas for him. Didn't make him feel any more at home. Sure, they want you, he'd told Grandma. They just don't want you in the way.

"It was in one of those luxurious old-fashioned movie theaters that don't exist anymore. Even the ladies' room was plush. There was a big sitting room with all these cushioned chairs before you even got to the toilets." She tapped a cigarette against the palm of her hand, lit it. That first inhalation, always the deepest, calmed her. "You could sit and relax, have a cigarette, talk about the movie. Take a break from the dark and the world it was drawing you into. There was a kind of pacing to the whole experience—know what I mean? It wasn't just about *seeing* a movie."

Watching the movie on TV brought a whole different pacing to the experience. For the first half hour, no commercial interruptions, she was mesmerized. By the second commercial, she was growing restless. By the third, she was sniffling. She pulled me close, said it just a case of pent-up emotion. The lingering image of a baby in a basket of reeds on a riverbank did it to her every time.

"All I want is a hint—some sign—that Moses's mother knew crocodiles were not going to snatch up her baby. This is such an important detail, yet it's totally passed over—no pun intended."

My mother came out from the kitchen, remnants of baking on her sweatshirt, in her hair. "God works in mysterious ways—isn't that what you always say?"

"Your mother's making fun of me, but the point is, she put her child in a river—"

"To save him."

"And you think that's an easy thing to do?"

My mother glanced at me. "No, Ma, I don't think it's easy. But if I were living thousands of years ago and I were a much more devout person, I might not analyze it quite like this."

"Doesn't matter what century you live in. A mother is a mother." My grandmother lifted her head, sniffed hard. "That *thing* you're making—cauliflower kugel?—is burning."

My mother darted back to the kitchen, left Grandma and me to blood and locusts. Frogs and boils. Water rolling up and backward, like hair being blown dry. Thousands upon thousands of people walking across the floor of the sea. "Hurry!" I found myself whispering. Like a sheepdog nipping at the heels of a flock, I nudged them along. It was the power of the film, drawing me in with its biblical pace. It was the power of God, taking the shape of Moses's staff. It was the power of my grandmother, extracting the human drama from an epic story.

"What a foolish man." She was talking about Ramses II, the pharaoh of the hardened heart cracked apart at the sight of his dead son.

"What a handsome man." She was talking about Moses, returned from Sinai, hair streaked white and gray. "My God," she said, "I never realized how much Seymour looks like him."

Not exactly, I thought, as he lifted up his glass of wine for kiddush."Baruch atah Adonai, Eloheinu melech ha'olam borei p'ri hagafen."

Sure, his hair was thick and white (distinguished?), but didn't anybody notice those ears? Like caverns. It was a miracle that his tiny hearing aid didn't get sucked down his auditory canal every time he cleared his throat. Which he did a lot.

He read the translation of the prayer, too, something he said he'd started doing when his grandchildren were young. Kept them more involved, he said.

"We praise You, Adonai our God, ruler of the universe, Who creates the fruit of the vine."

I laughed out loud, half listening, thought he'd said "fruit of the loom." Harry would have appreciated that. Harry, who should have been, would have been, at the head of the table instead of Seymour. Grandma, seated next to Seymour, lifted her glass of wine, took a sip. I noticed a new ring, blue sapphire, on her right hand. On her left hand, she still wore her wedding band.

Tony, seated between Grandma and Vivian, puckered his lips at the sweetness of the wine. "Gotta talk to the boys about coming up with a good kosher Chianti—*classico*." He was wearing a tie, silkscreened with horses. I figured Vivian had bought it for him. *Wear a tie for me*, I pictured her saying. *For once in your life.* He smoothed his hair with his hands, almost knocked Grandma in the eye with his elbow. It was a gesture of impatience. "I hope we get through this quickly," he said to Vivian, thinking no one else was listening.

"What's your hurry?" asked Seymour. "Gotta see a man about a horse?"

"You got it." Tony winked. Clicked his tongue. Vivian elbowed him in the ribs, making his stomach, paunchy enough, billow even more. "It's his daughters," she defended him. "This is the only night he can see them."

Seymour cleared his throat, picked up the Haggadah, began reading again. "Seder," he reminded us, means nothing more than "order." Not in the sense of "order in the court." More in the sense of ritual. He was beginning to interest me. "It isn't about reciting," he said, "although that's what *Haggadah* means—'recitation.' It's about doing things a certain way to remind ourselves of continuity. The past flows into the present. The present gives rise to the future. All in the act of recalling."

We dipped parsley in salt water, Seymour broke the middle matzo, I asked the ritual questions. Then everything fell apart.

I could blame it on Tony's impatience, the way he kept smoothing his shiny, flat-as-stone hair. Or I could blame it on George, launching into his dissertation on the parting of the sea just as we finished recalling the plagues that would test the heart, break the spirit of the foolish man.

Dahm (blood). *Tz' fardaya* (frogs). *Kinim* (lice). *Arov* (beasts). *Dever* (cattle disease).

It was a game to me, dipping my pinky in my glass of grape juice (wine, in the case of everyone else), seeing how long I could keep a drop of it suspended on the tip of my finger. Flicking it onto a napkin.

Sh'chin (boils). *Barad* (hail). *Arbeh* (locusts). *Choshech* (darkness). *Makat b'chorot* (plague of the firstborn).

"You know," said George, "there's been some research into the question of what caused the sea to part during the Exodus." He dabbed his mouth with his napkin, adjusted his wire-rimmed glasses on his nose, lowered his eyes. "One theory, for example, holds that tremendous waves caused by a volcanic eruption were responsible. Another theory I read about attributes the drop in the sea level to heavy winds, in which case the Israelites would have walked across rather shallow waters—which makes this not such a miraculous occurrence at all."

"That's an interesting point you bring up, George," said Seymour, nodding his head and squinting. "When my father—may he rest in peace—conducted a seder, he welcomed discussion. The four questions, *mah nishtanah*, that Rachel so beautifully recited"— he threw a smile my way—"are simply a starting point. We're not supposed to just tell the story of how we once were slaves, et cetera, et cetera, as if it were something in the distant past—something we don't feel connected to—he used to say. We're supposed to make the seder a meaningful—dynamic—experience. 'Ask questions,' he would say. But nobody ever did.

"So let me say this, George. Maybe it was a volcano that parted the sea. Or maybe, if you take a look at the Torah, you'll see that it was a wind. But let me ask you something: What do you suppose caused the wind to come at just that time?

"Which brings to mind something that often gets overlooked at today's *hurried* seders." Seymour growled. Everyone paid attention. "Did you know—did anyone here know—that when the Jews got to the edge of the sea and the soldiers were closing in on them, they didn't just stand there, waiting for the sea to part? They headed in, believing that God was with them. Don't misunderstand me— there was some hesitation. But they did it—'took a leap of faith' is what my father used to say—"

"And the women danced," I whispered. Exodus 15:21. *Then Miriam the prophetess, Aaron's sister, took a timbrel in her hand, and all the women went out after her in dance.* Not the men, just the women. I'd been sitting at the table alone with Grandpa. Everyone else had been in the kitchen, cleaning up. In front of him had sat a Haggadah and a tattered copy of *The Five Books of Moses*. He'd opened to *Shirah*, "Song at the Sea." "Nobody wants to sing anymore," he'd said. Then he'd pointed to the verses about Miriam.

"Rationalization," countered George. I looked around the table.

Vivian was rolling her eyes and humming. Tony was alternately looking at his watch and the big clock in our living room. My father was tapping his spoon lightly against the table. "Pure rationalization." Rising out of George's shirt collar, almost straining, it seemed to me, was a prominent Adam's apple. I'd once heard Vivian say to my mother that he lived life from the neck up, except, of course, when he was underwater. When I pressed my mother to explain what Vivian meant, she said that George was never one to show his emotions. Except once. He had just arrived home for winter break, was feeling very proud of the "brilliant" his professor had scrawled in red ink across the title page of a paper he had written. Only he made the mistake of placing the paper on the kitchen table, where Vivian was drinking soda and reading a magazine. That was the only time Jake said he'd ever seen George cry.

"The fact is, this whole Exodus thing is nothing more than an aggrandizement of a springtime ritual that had already been in existence." George paused, took a sip of water. If it's true that people, after years of living together, can begin to resemble one another, then the opposite, I think, had happened to George. He looked like no one—not my mother or Vivian or Jake—but in fact seemed to have acquired the same elusiveness that characterized some of the mysterious sea creatures he studied. "It was a grain-harvest celebration that, over time, melded with the biblical story. Beyond that, you're dealing with bits of lore pieced together to give some meaningful dimension to the story—the desired story, that is. I mean, think about it for a minute. If—and there's a big if—the parting of the sea really did occur, what do you suppose there is in Egyptian history to explain it? You can't possibly imagine some Egyptologist suggesting that the God of the Hebrews brought all these plagues on the Egyptians, killed their firstborn sons, and then parted the sea and swallowed up their soldiers. Can you?"

"Why not?" suggested Seymour. "Doesn't mean they have to

believe in this God. It just means they have to accept that, for at least one moment in history, His power reigned supreme."

"God works in mysterious ways," mumbled Arnold. He'd been sitting slumped back in his chair, playing with his tie, a mosaic of three-dimensional images. He wore a vest, too, the same deep green as his baseball cap, and a freshly starched shirt. "He's like a new person," Sophie had said to Grandma in the kitchen. "Doesn't get sick from smells the way he used to." Sophie coaxed Grandma into sniffing her neck, said it was about time they found a drug for Arnold's condition. "I can finally wear perfume." She even had a new hairdo, more styled and lacquered than I recalled.

Everyone looked at Arnold, who tugged at his baseball cap, like he was trying to pull it down over his eyes. Or his nose. He had a closet full of them now, the capstone of his newfound sartorial sensibility. The touchstone in his game of release and retreat.

"So what else is new?" said Sophie.

Arnold shook his head, looked around. He seemed momentarily unsure of where he was.

"You know," he began hesitantly, "after my father's last seder, he was lying in bed and he called me to sit with him." Still tugging at his cap, he spoke in a halting manner, his voice slippery. "He could hardly talk. I think he might even have been a little delirious from the drugs he was taking."

Tony tilted his chair back, stretched his arms behind him, again looked at the clock. "Could we, like, uh, move this along a little?" Vivian sneered at him. Arnold acted as if he didn't even notice.

"Then he took my hand—something he never did before—and laid it on his heart. 'Motion,' he said. 'It's all about motion. Ticking. Running. Playing the same records over and over again, until one day you get a scratch across it and it starts to skip.' He started singing—'You're nobody till. Nobody till. Nobody till.' Do you understand what I'm saying?"

"Not exactly," said my father.

Tony let out a laugh.

Sophie started to look worried.

Arnold went right on talking about Sidney.

"I was sure he was losing his mind. Then he said, 'All these years—all these seders—I tell the story, I sing, I have a good time. But I look around the table and I think to myself, *Is anybody listening—I mean really listening?*'"

Grandma sighed. "Nobody made a seder like Sidney."

Seymour pretended to be annoyed. "What am I, chopped liver?"

"Speaking of which," said my father, "if we don't want to be here all night—"

Arnold was not finished. "The last thing he said before going to sleep that night . . ." He stopped, cleared his throat. "Now, I realize this may sound a little melodramatic, like an opera where someone says something important, then drops dead—"

"Arnold!" exclaimed Sophie. "You're talking about your father!"

"But what he said before falling asleep that night was, 'God works in mysterious ways. That's all there is to it. So don't be like me. Don't wait until you're dying to accept that. Don't waste your life trying to figure out what you cannot—and I repeat, *cannot*—understand.'" Arnold looked at George. "It's that simple, George. Either you have faith in something that's beyond sight and sound, or you don't."

George looked like he was about to respond, but my father cut him off with a ghostly sound. "Why don't we tell some tales from the great beyond?" he said.

Tony seemed to think that was a good point to excuse himself. "Hate to eat and run—"

"We haven't even begun to eat," said my mother. She was livid, as much about my father's rudeness as about Tony's.

"It was a joke, Susie," Tony apologized. But he had to go. *One down*, I thought. Seymour sighed, complained that nobody *gets it*, finished the prayers that brought us to the beginning of the meal. Sophie's matzo ball soup.

I could blame my father, too, for his rudeness and his extreme insensitivity.

"It's kind of ironic," he said, "this talk of plagues." He slurped his soup, cast a sidelong glance at Jake. "Two waiters at the restaurant—one with pneumonia, the other won't say *what's* wrong with him. But everybody kind of knows what's going on."

"What *is* going on?" said Gary, more dignified than defensive.

My mother glowered at my father, tried to steer the conversation onto a different course. "Good soup, Sophie."

"Ruth insists it needs salt." Sophie had a triumphant smile on her face. "But thank you."

"Don't get me wrong," continued my father. "I'm not, like, worried—personally, I mean. Naturally, I'm a *little* concerned. I mean, if this thing is something that's contagious—"

Jake, almost shaking with anger that ran in little pulses from his temples to his jaw, started to say something, turned to me, stopped himself. Sadness shadowing his eyes settled like tiny thorns in the corners of his mouth. He leaned toward me, kissed my cheek, whispered, "I love you." Reached past me, to the plate at the center of the table holding the matzo, accidentally knocked over the cup of wine for Elijah. There was a gasp from Sophie. Grandma blanched, looked over at George. Her firstborn. Jake apologized. "I'm sorry," he said, over and over. My mother got a towel to wipe up the wine, Seymour tried to be reassuring. "It was an accident—let's forget about it." But the spilled wine blotting the center of the tablecloth became, like abstract art, imbued with presence. Everyone stared at it. Tried not to stare.

Finally George spoke. "We're acting as if someone died," he

said. "But it's just a cup of wine. Spilled."

"He's supposed to drink from that cup," said Grandma, staring at the silver goblet.

"Maybe that was Him," said my father. "A little thirstier than usual." He was the only one who laughed.

"Can't we just fill up the cup again?" I asked. The seder was not complete for me without that moment of suspended reality. I would hurry to the door, open it, feel the outside air carry in the prophet of Passover, then hurry back to the table to see if the level of wine in the cup had dropped. A sure sign that Elijah had taken a sip, blessed us. And the angel of death had passed over.

"What a good idea!" said Gary.

Jake shook his head. "What's done is done."

"Why don't we just get on with the meal and forget about it?" said Seymour.

"Good idea," Grandma agreed, with one solid tap of her palm against the edge of the table. She got up, disappeared into the kitchen with Sophie and my mother. Vivian started to get up, too, muttered something about too many cooks spoiling the broth, and decided instead to stay put. She began humming softly. Her eyes were closed, and her fingernails, as perfect as ever, tapped on the table in a steady rhythm that seemed to intensify when George began telling Arnold about his research project at Woods Hole. Migration patterns of dolphins was his area of specialization.

"I got a job with a law firm," Arnold said, when George asked him what kind of work he was doing.

George seemed impressed. "I always knew you were smart."

"I work in the mail room," Arnold went on. "When it's not busy, I sneak-read. I'm halfway through *Crime and Punishment* now."

Jake, uncharacteristically somber, gazed at my father, who was engrossed in a conversation with Seymour about the coming baseball season. The clatter of plates, the smell of roast chicken, seemed a welcome distraction, and he turned his head toward the kitchen.

"I take no responsibility for this cauliflower concoction," said Grandma, placing my mother's kugel on the table. The roast chicken and the string beans and Sophie's scalloped potatoes followed. Grandma positioned the largest serving plate, the one with the chicken, over the stain in the tablecloth. Uncalculated as it seemed, it was an act of deliberation intended to stamp out the curse of the spilled wine.

But the curse would not go away.

"I think we should skip the opening of the door tonight," said Grandma, afraid of the uninvited guest, biting her lips when, despite her protest, the door was opened. Shutting her eyes. Afraid.

beginnings

July 1, 1985
Dear Rachel:

I fell in love. I know that's the last thing you expected to be hearing from me, and it's not what you think. I never knew a city could be so beautiful. Forget Paris—though my mother, sappy romantic that she is, thinks there's no place like Gay Paree. For me it's Firenze. The city just glows. I now know, unequivocally, what I'm going to be doing with my life. Art history. See you in September.

Sincerely, Jerry

PS: I hope your uncle isn't too sick.

Déjà vu. The illusion that one has had a particular experience before. A feeling more palpable than impression, it weaves itself into the corners of memory, confuses the mind. *Have I ever really been here before? In this life?*

My father sat two feet from me, no illusion, his fingers tapping against the steering wheel of his recently acquired used Chevy. The silence between us was like a worn piece of fragile tapestry. *Have I been here before?*

His jaw, quivering with restraint, jutted forward. For an instant, he turned to look at me, his eyes telling me over and over again, *It's not my fault. Your mother and I just can't live together anymore.* Anything I said would just be a rehashing of what he knew to be true: *You were the one who walked out. You're the one shacked up with a girlfriend.*

What does it matter? he'd say, after reminding me that my mother broke the rules first. *The marriage just fell apart.*

Déjà vu. Rooted in sight, it confuses every sense. A vaguely familiar smell. The timbre of a long-forgotten sound. The gentle brush of air pushing thought into a pocket of time so real it could only have happened before.

How long before? Three months, by my calculation. Three months since I took this same drive, no illusion, with my father, to the same hospital to visit Jake. Last time, not yet living with Donna, my father came up with me. Tried to talk my mother into leaving the hospital. For a little while. She'd lost seven pounds in three weeks, running to the hospital three times a day, shuttling between Jake and Paco on opposite ends of the thin-man unit. That's what Gary called it. He was trying to be funny, said he had an idea for a screenplay, a remake of *The Thin Man*. A classic whodunit, updated to encompass the scope of mystery in the eighties. This was a mystery, wasn't it? Ailments with names as bizarre, as baffling, as their symptoms. Ailments too hard, too unbelievable, to pronounce, reduced to acronyms—Jake with PCP, Paco with KS. A classic whodunit, said Gary. Trying hard, oh so hard, to be funny. Paco, much worse off, lesions in a connect-the-dots map of his body, gave up even trying to laugh. His mother, living upstate, visited once. His father, never. As soon as he was released from the hospital, he left for San Francisco. Renata went with him.

Restraint gives way to something more urgent. On the surface it has the smell, the feel, of paternal love. Beneath the surface, where my father treaded so lightly, was a fear he had never known.

"You're sure you want to do this."

I nodded. How many times did we have to go over this? How many fights did he have to start with my mother about letting me spend the summer with Jake? Separated, not yet fully divorced, he threatened to fight for custody, argued on grounds of endangering my health. Which he believed to be true. This insult to her judgment made my mother livid. Time for the Great Defuser. I started to cry, pleaded with my father to let things be. He kissed me, said he would not upset my plans. He'd call to check up on things, maybe take a drive out to visit one weekend. Made me promise to think about spending some time with him on Fire Island, where he'd rented a house for the month of August with his Donna. "You might want a break," he said. "I know you don't think so now. But you just might want a break."

I found Gary at the pay phone near the waiting room on Jake's floor. Before saying hello, I stood back, eavesdropping.

"I feel the way a new mother must feel when she brings her baby home from the hospital," he said softly into the phone. "I'm not sure I can handle it, Jim. How do I take care of him? How do I know I *can* take care of him? These past months have been a living hell. I've had too much time alone, too much time to think. Do you know what too much thinking does to you when your best friend—your lover—has . . . Never mind." He took a deep breath. "I'll pull myself together. What else can I do? I'll just have to pull myself together. Thank God Brian offered to send a limo. I'd be an absolute wreck driving in the city."

He hung up, turned around, saw me. His face brightened.

"Couldn't get Indy to come up to say hello?" Indy was Gary's nickname for my father. Short for Indiana Jones. He had the same mock-tough face, said Gary.

"Uh-uh," I said, wishing my father really was Indiana Jones. Indiana Jones would not complain to my mother all the time about not having enough money to give her. He would not have a girlfriend so soon after breaking up with my mother. And he would not act like he had to rescue me from Jake. He would do something to help.

We headed toward Jake's room, and I was stopped, the way I always was, by the sign on the door telling visitors to wear a surgical mask and gloves. Jake said I had to do that only if I had a cold or something, that the sign was really for the orderlies, who handled food and bedsheets and things like that. Only one of them ever wore a mask, though they all wore gloves. The orderly who always wore a mask gave Jake the creeps. One time when I was visiting, he came in and Jake tried to joke. "Hey, masked man, who don't you let me see that pretty smile of yours?" The orderly, a tall, lanky man, emptied the wastebasket, cleared the lunch tray, whistled a few notes. Acted as if nobody was in the room.

Jake was sitting sideways on the bed, dressed, waiting for the doctor to release him. His smile was weak, almost forced. He was wearing the cream-colored sweater I had bought him for his last birthday. It hung on his shoulders. Would I lie to my grandmother when she called later and tell her how much better he looked? She'd been in for a visit when Jake was hospitalized in April, ended up staying three weeks, would have stayed longer, but Jake told her it was time to go home. "Make sure he eats," she'd said the night before she left. "He's much too thin." She'd made chicken soup, jars of it, and cookies to fatten him. But he was still too thin. "Pneumonia does not do this to a person," she'd said, her eyelids lowered. Fluttering. Overflowing with the fatigue that comes with sadness. Would she try her mother's mustard-plaster magic? I wondered. What wouldn't she try? She kissed me goodbye, brusquely, it seemed. Afraid, I think, of holding on too tightly. "Make sure he eats," she told me again, before closing the taxi door. Looking straight ahead through the front windshield. Never looking back.

Jake was insistent about her not coming to New York so soon after she'd left. Would I tell her his face was pasty, like the milk shakes my mother brought him every day? Hospital food will kill you, he'd tried to joke when he'd been there a few days and was feeling very nauseated from the new medication he was getting. He wanted milk shakes that tasted good, not the chalky ones they served in the hospital. So my mother found an ice cream store a few streets down from the hospital and brought him what he wanted—vanilla milk shakes one day, coffee another—hoping they would make him feel better. He barely touched them.

The doctor finally came, put his stethoscope to Jake's chest, signed the papers to release him. Wished him well.

Brian's limousine was waiting in front of the hospital when we got downstairs. The driver opened the door. I climbed in first; then Gary helped Jake get in.

"That's one place I won't miss," said Jake, once we were moving. He kept twisting his body around, trying to get comfortable. They'd given him a spinal tap that morning, so it was painful for him to sit. Finally, he put his head in my lap and his feet on Gary, who rubbed them, joked about how it was impossible not to love someone who wore aqua socks. Then he kissed Jake's foot.

I kept my hand on Jake's forehead, stroked it gently, thought about the only other time I'd been in a limousine. I was four years old, and when the shiny big black car came to pick up my father and mother and me, to take us to Grandma Lilly's funeral, I remember feeling scared. My father, hit hard by the sudden death of his mother from a heart attack, stared out the window, one hand on my mother's knee. "How are they going to get Grandma Lilly's coffin in here?" I blurted out, making them both laugh. When I saw the hearse in front of the funeral parlor, I was relieved.

WELCOME HOME, JAKE.

The banner, shaped from pieces of origami, hung from the kitchen ceiling.

"Only one person I know could have made that," said Jake. "Where's he hiding?"

Marsha hugged Jake, gave him a kiss on the cheek, poked her head into the dining room. Cooed her son's name. "Oh, *Bru-u-ce*."

"Doesn't anybody kiss on the lips anymore?" Jake meant it as a joke. Marsha took it as a challenge.

"There." She kissed him again, a quick kiss on the lips. "Is that better?"

"If I open my eye and you're still here"—Jake squeezed his eyes shut, like someone wishing, or praying—"I'll know I wasn't dreaming."

"How about something to eat?" I said.

"Not hungry." Bent like an old man, he moved slowly to a chair. It was scary to think that his body had deteriorated so much in so short a time. Even knowing how sick he was, I could not—would not—allow myself to think he might die.

"Gorgeous tomatoes!" exclaimed Gary, peeking into one of the bags Marsha had placed on the butcher-block island in the center of the kitchen. Besides her specialty desserts, she brought bags of fruits and vegetables. Top-of-the-line organic.

Gary pulled three tomatoes from the bag. Dylan, who had jumped up on the island, poked his nose in. "Did you know I used to be a juggler?"

"Never mind," said Marsha. She had a presence about her, like she was onstage all the time.

"Seriously." Gary winked at me, started flinging the tomatoes in the air. "I once worked in a restaurant—in the kitchen. And this is how we tested the tomatoes. The ones that were still whole when they landed in your hand were for salad." He twisted his body, caught a tomato behind his back. Marsha grabbed the tomato from his hand. I started laughing. "On the other hand," he continued, "if the skin of the tomato split, that one went for sauce or soup."

"You won't find tomatoes like these anywhere." Marsha ordered her fruits and vegetables from a supplier in California.

"Oh, *Bru-u-ce*," she cooed again. "Where are you? There's someone here I'd like you to meet."

I must have blushed, was sure I turned beet red when he gusted into the kitchen, nodded at me.

"Hello, Rachel."

He wore bleached jeans and a white T-shirt silk-screened with the figure of Bruce Springsteen holding a guitar. Memorabilia, I figured, from his most recent tour. He handed Jake a small present wrapped in blue-and-white marbleized paper, tied with a shiny green ribbon. His hair, light brown, hung down to his neck. He kept pushing it away from his face as he watched Jake tear open the wrapping.

It was a small book with a gold silk cover. Jake flipped through the pages, read some lines aloud.

Knowing others is intelligence;
knowing yourself is true wisdom.
Mastering others is strength;
mastering yourself is true power.

"Sounds like a 'Jason-ism.'" Marsha's lips, a perfect cherry red, stiffened in a scowl. It was the first time she'd ever looked unattractive to me.

Bruce flashed her a dirty look, told Jake that his father had, in fact, given him a copy. "'Even if you don't understand it,' he told me, 'just read it for the poetry. One day you'll get it.'" I glanced at the title. *Tao Te Ching: The Classic Book of Integrity and the Way.* I glanced at Bruce, who said he'd come across this deluxe edition in a bookstore that specialized in rare books.

Gary pinched Bruce's cheek. "Oh, the sophistication—and sentimentality—of these young, virile architecture students."

Jake thanked Bruce for the book, flipped through it some more.

I noticed his hand shaking. It had started in the hospital, the shaking when he held something, when he tried to write or draw. It seemed worse now. Jake, suddenly self-conscious, slammed the book shut, said he wanted to go upstairs, lie down in his own bed.

He clutched my arm, for leverage, to get up from the stool where he'd been sitting. Tried to make walking not seem like the effort it was. On his way out of the kitchen, he grabbed his car keys from a hook on the wall, threw them to Bruce. "It's a beautiful day." He winked. "Why don't you take Rachel for a drive?"

Have I been here before?

A smell, a sound, a shaft of afternoon light angling through the trees. Something vaguely reminiscent of another time, another place. The same convertible, top down, a different wind splashing my face, fooling me into believing there was no other time. No other place.

Silence, awkward, uncertain, permeated the air between us.

Why am I here?

Bruce leaned forward, turned on the radio. His arm brushed against mine. The silence, no longer awkward, was charged.

I found myself staring at his arm, time stilled by the illusion of movement. Just like in early films, when cars stood still while scenery moved. We were making our way down a winding back road out of Sag Harbor, potato farms passing us by. Grazing horses punctuating the stillness, so out of time. Out of place. And all I could seem to focus on was Bruce's arm.

His voice cut through "Sandy," the radio Bruce's song of love. "My father told me about some experimental drugs they're using in France. Some people seem to be doing okay with them."

I nodded. He didn't ask me to talk, seemed to understand the safe harbor of silence.

"Close your eyes," he said. He drove up a hill. The air became stickier, infused with honeysuckle. He stopped the car, told me to open my eyes. In the distance was the ocean, clear, sparkling.

Have I been here before?

"Happy birthday, Rachel." It was my mother, waking me. I yawned, opened my eyes. It was still dark out. I yawned again. "Did I really agree to this?" *Birthday cake on the beach. At sunrise.* It was Jake's idea.

By the time we got to the beach, the stars were beginning to fade from the sky. *Night becomes day*, I thought. *Day becomes night.* Jake walked toward the shore. He looked as spindly as the seagulls lined up next to him. I followed closely behind. "The sky at dawn is the hardest color to capture," he said to me. "Not really blue, not really gray. I like to imagine it's the first color newborns see." It looked to me like the stars had melded together into a wash of soft silvery-blue. A streak of orange spread across the horizon.

My mother had baked a small carrot cake with vanilla icing, and we had a hard time lighting the candles because of the sea breeze. Huddling together, we finally got them lit, and Jake and Gary and my mother sang "Happy Birthday" to me. Then they gave me presents. A pair of earrings shaped like hearts from my mother. A faded denim jacket and an oversize pink sweatshirt that said SORBONNE on it, from Jake and Gary, along with a birthday card with a picture of Paris. Inside it read: *Happy birthday—better bone up on your French.* Jake wanted to go to France, the only place you could get that experimental treatment. I said I'd go with him. *PS: Subtlety is the gift of sunrise. Don't dwell too long in the drama of sunsets. Yours forever, Jake*

We stayed an hour at the beach before Jake started feeling tired. When we got back to the house, he went right upstairs. "Need to stretch out," he said. I felt bad that he had gotten up so early just because of me.

The phone rang. I thought it would be my father, wishing me a happy birthday. It was my grandmother.

"Happy birthday," she said.

"Thank you." I looked at the clock on the kitchen wall. It was 9:00 a.m. here, six in the morning for her. "What are you doing up so early?"

"When you get to be my age, you don't sleep much." She asked if I'd gotten her card, whether I had any special plans that day. I told her about having birthday cake for breakfast on the beach.

"How's Jake doing?"

My mother always answered her by saying his color was good. I said the same thing, thinking it would reassure her. I was not convincing.

"Your mother has you trained well, doesn't she?" There was a hardness in her voice, which I'd come to notice more and more in recent conversations. "He's getting the best care, I'm sure," she had said the last time we'd spoken. "What more can I do?" I knew she'd been crying.

"Talk to him, if you don't believe me." He was, in fact, looking better after a few days home. "I'll go tell him to pick up the phone."

I ran upstairs. Jake's bedroom door was closed. I was about to knock.

"It's just from the medication," Gary's voice was agitated. "It will get better."

"Until something else goes wrong." Jake threw something, a pen or a pencil, on the floor. "What's left for me if I can't even draw a cartoon?"

"When you finish the medication, the shaking will stop. That's what the doctor said. Then you'll be able to draw all the cartoons you want."

It got very quiet for a minute, and I was about to knock. Then I heard crying. Deep, muffled crying. "I can't take it anymore." Jake's voice quivered. "I just can't take it anymore." I went back downstairs. My mother was talking to my grandmother.

"Tell her he's sleeping," I said, running out the door.

I grabbed a bicycle from the shed behind the house, went back the beach, to be alone.

Motion, I thought, walking aimlessly along the shore. *It's all about motion.* No thinking, just moving. No talking. No stopping. Following patterns in the sand. Bird prints. Footprints. Looking for messages in bottles washed ashore. Anything to keep moving. To avoid the jagged pain that cuts to that deep, still place.

Constant motion. No thinking. Just images moving along, carrying me from day to day. Like in a dream. Last night I dreamed that my father snuck into Jake's house, into my room. "Be quiet, baby," he said. "Everything's going to be okay." He lifted me from the bed, carried me down the stairs. I wanted to scream, but nothing came out.

In the next part of the dream, I was someplace in Brooklyn. A street vaguely familiar, near the street where my grandparents used to live. I was alone, scared, looking for a phone to call someone. The only phone I could find was broken. I started running, afraid of the unfamiliar streets. I was supposed to be going to a funeral. I was wearing a wedding dress.

Keep moving, I thought. *To avoid the deep, jagged pain. The unsweetness of sixteen. A little more than half Jake's age.*

The sun slipped behind a cloud; the air suddenly turned cold. I kept walking, aimlessly, my feet sinking with each step. The air seemed to get chillier by the minute, making me think of all the times Grandma had said I'd catch my death of cold if I wasn't dressed warmly enough on a cold winter day. It wasn't something I ever took literally. Until now.

The sun came out again, and I sat down on a piece of driftwood, staring into the ocean. Waves rolled in, rolled out, no beginning, no end, the tide inching closer and closer. Whispering secrets. *Jake has AIDS.* I shook my head, dug my toes into the warm sand. Waves rolled in, rolled out, no words, just sounds. *Jake has AIDS.* I looked up at the sky, into the blinding sun. My head felt heavy, like a low gray cloud had settled on top of it. No beginning, no end.

I heard the giggle first. She thought she was sneaking up on me, but I heard the giggle. "Blow," she said, handing me a jar of bubbles and her wand. Her mother watched closely from a blanket nearby. I dipped the wand in the bubble jar. And I blew. A cluster of small bubbles first that made her shriek with laughter. Then a large one, the size of her rosy face. She put her nose up to the bubble, giggled when it burst.

"Time to go, Claire," her mother called out. I gave her back the jar and the wand, watched her toddle away.

I stood up, started walking again, my head a little lighter now. From a distance I saw a large sand sculpture, almost like a mirage. I headed toward it, kept repeating the girl's name.

Claire. Claire Claire.

I was running now, toward the sculpture. A three-foot-high pyramid. Sculpted with perfection. By Bruce.

It's all about motion, I said to Bruce. Rambling on and on. About a little girl named Claire. And Clarence. Sent down to bring Jimmy Stewart to his senses.

You see, George, you really had a wonderful life.

"I don't really believe in angels, but you have to admit it's an odd coincidence that just when I'm feeling that life really sucks and things are almost hopeless, this little girl comes over and brings me a dose of magic; then, like a magnet, something pulls me in this direction. And I see this pyramid, which gets me thinking about an article I read in one of the weird health magazines my mother gets. Something about an energy in pyramids that gives them special powers."

Bruce was carving lines in the pyramid, to create the illusion of stone. The sleeves of his T-shirt, cut off, gave more definition to his biceps.

"This is all I know," he said to me. "There are over two million blocks of stone in the Great Pyramid at Giza. They weigh an average of two and a half tons. And the way the whole structure is aligned to the night sky is pretty amazing." He shaded his eye, looked up at the sky. "There are these two air shafts in the pyramid from the King's Chamber. One is pointing to Orion, which the Egyptians believed represented the cycle of birth, life, death, and resurrection. The dead king's soul would go up to the sky and—so the mythology goes—regulate the seasons and the calendar and stuff like that. The other shaft points to the north star of the Old Kingdom."

"*All* you know?" I teased him, said I was humbled. "All *I* know is that Gloria Swanson slept with one under a bed. She said it gave her energy."

He hesitated. "Well, not *all*." He stood staring at his work, nodding and smiling at everyone who came by to compliment him. One woman took pictures, told him he should put out a bucket for coins. "It's a labor of love," he told her. "Here today, gone tomorrow."

Bruce finished smoothing the capstone, said if I wanted to know about pyramids, his father was the one to talk to.

Jason was cleaning the deck of his boat when we got to the harbor.

"Rachel, I give you Jason, psychiatrist-turned-potter who gave up his land legs and his marriage at about the same time."

He took my hand, helped me onto the boat, said it was nice to see me again.

"Blame me all you want," he said to Bruce, "but it was your mother who could not accept the change in me. My 'midlife crisis'—isn't that what she called it? She couldn't handle someone who wanted to spend his days kicking a wheel, spinning wet clay in his hands. I'm not driven enough—isn't that what she said?"

"Never mind," said Bruce. "Rachel's on a quest for a pyramid."

Before Jason could say a word, Bruce led me belowdecks. On a shelf in the cabin were half a dozen pyramids in a variety of colors and sizes. One of them was shaped like steps. I picked it up.

"That's the one I made," said Jason, who had followed us downstairs. "The others were models I picked up, to study."

Bruce corrected him. "You mean *one* of the ones you made." In his studio, a block from the harbor, there were at least a dozen more. "Picasso had his blue phase," said Bruce. "Jason had his pyramid phase."

"For me, it's mostly about form—the perfection of it," said Jason. "The one you're holding is the closest I got to replicating a step pyramid. That's how the first pyramids were made, in layers of steps." He took a book from the shelf, opened it to a photo of the pyramids of Giza. "Science still can't fathom the advanced technological knowledge needed to build pyramids—or what it was about the pyramid structure that made it a central part of cultures that had nothing to do with one another."

I told him what I'd read about the energy in pyramids. He looked skeptical.

"It's not that I don't believe in 'energy.' All you have to do is mold a piece of clay to know that nothing in the universe is really static. But I am primarily a man of science. And I do worry about false hope, which is always acute in times of crisis. Like now. I know five men—five *young* men—who are frighteningly sick with AIDS." He shook his head. "I worry about false hope, grasping at straws."

I put down the step pyramid, picked up a smooth one four inches high, bluish-gray, cool to the touch. "Hope is a feeling," I said to Jason, "which makes 'false hope' a bit of an oxymoron. Besides, it's my birthday."

Jason took the pyramid from me, held it up to the light. If you look long enough, he said, the colors seem to diffuse. That's what he loved about this pyramid. The illusion of color diffusing. He hoped that's what I would love about it, too.

Bruce and I left the boat, drove back to Jake's house. Before I got out of the car, I reached for Bruce's hand. To thank him. He leaned toward me, kissed me lightly on the lips.

"Happy birthday, Rachel."

My heartbeat quickened. He moved closer, put his arm around me, pulled my hair back gently, kissed me again. My heart was pounding, the pyramid was in my palm, my skin was tingling. His tongue, like a butterfly, fluttered in my mouth, open now. Tingling.

"Earthquake," said Jake, sitting on the edge of my bed. "Got to evacuate this place *très vite*. No time to waste."

I rubbed my eyes. "What time is it?"

"Time is of the essence." Jake shook the bed. "Come on, kid. We're going on an expedition today."

"Where to?"

"To a place where we can sip piña coladas on the beach and loll about, listening to reggae, mon, in the shade of a palm tree."

"In other words you're not telling me."

"You are quick, girl." This was the old Jake talking. I glanced at the pyramid, glinting in the early-morning sun. I had placed it under Jake's bed, without his knowing it, hoping that the magic might take effect while he slept. But Dylan kept swatting it like a hockey puck across the room. I decided, then, to keep it on the table next to my bed, and each night before I went to sleep, I held it and whispered a chant to make Jake better.

If you think something and it happens, is it a coincidence? If you will something with all your heart, can you make it happen? The previous night, a whiff of something reminiscent of eucalyptus had drifted through the window as I lay in bed. For a brief moment, I had been back in Big Sur, walking through a forest of redwoods, driving down the coast with Jake. Today, for the first time in weeks, Jake was feeling good enough to get behind the wheel. Gary sat in the front seat next to him, whistling all the way to the harbor.

"All I said was that I felt like going to Shelter Island. And then, like Flash Gordon, Gary is out of bed, scrambling around, making mysterious phone calls. Then this guy"—Jake pointed to Bruce, who was standing on the deck of his father's boat—"just happens to call. 'It's a perfect day for sailing,' he says. 'Meet me at the dock in an hour—with Rachel, of course.'"

I sat against the side of the boat, looking up, looking out. Wisps of clouds drifted by, seagulls squawked, swooped down on lobster pots. Gary helped Bruce with the sail, and Jake stood at the front of the boat, still as a statue. Staring ahead. A chill ran through me, a thought carried on a sudden gust: *We may never do this again, all of us together.*

We sailed to the far end of Shelter Island, where Jake owned some property set back on a hill, with a view of the water. There was a house in front of it closer to the shore. Gary worried that we'd be trespassing if we docked there.

"What are they going to do, shoot us?" asked Jake. Bruce docked the boat.

The property was farther than it seemed from the boat, and Jake's walking was labored. "Look! Over there!" He pointed to a deer coming from the bushes. It was a buck.

"You don't often see bucks like that, even out here," said Bruce. Its antlers were enormous, didn't seem real to me. The buck darted up the hill ahead of us. Poised himself like he'd been summoned to stand guard.

"Ruth would say it's a good sign when a deer visits your property," remarked Jake. "Wouldn't she?"

I smiled. Maybe things were finally looking up. Maybe.

July 10, 1985
Dear Rachel:

Hope you had a happy birthday.

I still can't help but wish you came with me, though I'm at least glad that you finally forgave me for what happened. Seems like a lifetime ago. I really did try to make my mother change her mind, but you know how she is. She gets these ideas in her head, and that's that. Or, as she would put it, "The conversation is over." I think maybe the best thing about being away is that I won't have to hear her voice for eight weeks. I'm still surprised she let me go. I think she figured it was safer than having me hang around with Harold all summer. Boy, was she wrong! I'll get to that soon.

There was a girl in my bunk—Shelly Michaels—and she was here for all of two weeks when she got sick and was rushed to the hospital. She's not coming back to camp, and everyone is saying she has AIDS. It's very scary, Rachel.

What if she has AIDS, Rachel? What am I going to do? I smoked pot with her. She had a boyfriend here. His name's Dave, and he's best friends with my boyfriend, Richie. Richie tells me that Dave is acting cool but he's really freaking out because he had sex with Shelly.

Which brings me to Richie. I did it, Rachel. There's an old casino about a half mile from the campground. It's not used anymore, and three times now we've managed to sneak out of our bunks at night without getting caught. We all leave the bunkhouse at different times, and we don't put on any lights in the casino except a flashlight to keep us from tripping over one another.

I don't want you to get the idea the smoking pot was what made me give up my virginity. Richie is the handsomest—and the sexiest—guy I ever went out with. He did things to me that no one ever did. I feel funny saying this, but if I can't tell you, who can I tell?

All the time I spent with Harold, kissing and making out, was baby stuff in comparison.

Richie says he wants to marry me but first we have to finish college. He's going to be a doctor, and I told him I'll work as a teacher while he goes to med school. He isn't convinced that Shelly has AIDS. She could have hepatitis or mono or something like that, but Dave is still very worried. And I'm scared. We had sex in the same room. Dave and Shelly were at one end, and we were at the other. How do I know the germs can't spread across the room? I'd ask Richie, but I'm afraid he'll laugh at me.

Gotta go now. It's dinnertime. Please write soon.

Love and kisses, Laura

July 20, 1985
Dear Rachel:

Why haven't you written to me?

My period is five days late, and I'm a wreck. An absolute wreck. Richie told me I wouldn't get pregnant the first time we had sex (some doctor!), and I believed him. I can only hope he's right. I was a little uncomfortable about not using protection and I made him promise we would always use it after that first time. He claims it doesn't feel the same with a condom. That's tough shit, I told him. He doesn't have to worry about anything, because he can't get pregnant. Right? I'm going to get a diaphragm after the summer—Ellen Marcus knows a doctor—assuming I don't need an abortion first.

Dave got a letter from Shelly (she's the one everybody thinks has AIDS), and she says she's going to be okay—it's only mono—but Dave is still having a hard time. He believes her, but nobody believes him. (I do, and so does Richie.) None of the girls will go near him, and I think it's pretty sad the way they're acting, though

I don't know if I can really afford to talk, since I have a boyfriend. I might act the same as the other girls, if not for Richie and his being friends with Dave and all that.

Sorry to write such a short letter, but it's so hot today that I spend almost every free minute in the pool. PLEASE WRITE!

Love and kisses, Laura

July 30, 1985
Dear Laura:

I'm sitting in Jake's kitchen, staring at a piece of paper posted on the refrigerator that tells how you're supposed to care for someone with AIDS. It's okay to use the same utensils, the paper says, though you should wash them thoroughly. And you should hug the person, kiss him, make him feel loved. I want to rip up the paper, throw it in the garbage. Some things are just too obvious.

Do you know what the word "opportunistic" means? It's usually a word you think of in terms of people. Richie, I suppose, might be considered opportunistic in the way he's using you. But now when I hear the word, all I think of is Kaposi's sarcoma and pneumocystis carinii pneumonia and a host of horrific ailments I never in my wildest imagination thought people would suffer with. Sometimes it feels like a bad science fiction movie. "Opportunistic"—that's the word they use for these infections. As if the virus were endowed with will.

My mother's friend Paco died this morning. Jake is very very sick. I couldn't tell you before you left, didn't want to. Maybe I was afraid—you can't imagine what it's like watching someone you love get so frail so quickly from something so frighteningly mysterious. Or maybe I just didn't feel you deserved to know the saddest secret of my life. I don't need to make these kinds of judgments anymore. Jake has AIDS. He doesn't want to go out of the house much anymore.

Restaurants or movies, something he always loved, are totally out of the question because he's afraid someone will cough or sneeze on him. He's even avoiding the beach, though I don't believe it's because he's afraid of catching a chill. I think he just doesn't want to be around people he's not close to. They might ask too many questions. Or they might tell him something he doesn't want to hear.

I sincerely hope you're not pregnant. If you are, I'll do whatever I can to help you. Just promise me this—that you'll spend more time taking care of yourself and less time being afraid of the wrong things.

Your best friend, Rachel

The guest room where I slept used to have two small windows, facing east. When Jake and Gary bought the house, they turned the room into a studio for Jake. The windows were transformed into French doors opening out onto a deck. During his first year in the house, Jake did a series of sunrise paintings from the deck, which afforded a bird's-eye view of the harbor. Each season, the light took on a different cast. Jake would get up before dawn to capture the almost imperceptible shift from night to day. The gift of sunrise. By eight in the morning, light flooded the room and the gift lost its subtlety. Some mornings, a pillow on my head blocked it out, gave me another hour of sleep. Which I needed right now. Desperately.

Jake screamed so loud last night I felt like I was in a nightmare, being stabbed. Cancer had crept into him, taking his bowels, bit by bit. After the scream came tears. Muffled. I tossed and turned most of the night. Listening for any sound at all. Looking toward the doors. At daybreak, after falling asleep for maybe an hour, I woke to the unmuffled sound of Jake crying. I reached for the pyramid, always comforting to the touch. Bluish-gray agate, the color of sunrise. The color of hope, I used to think.

I dug a corner of the pyramid into my palm, at first unconsciously, then harder and harder, praying for pain, deep physical pain that might release me from this feeling of being paralyzed. All I got was a red mark in my palm, not even a cut. I could hear Jake crying—"Why me? Why me?"—and Gary whispering, "It's okay, I'm here. It's okay, I'm here." The doctor had wanted to increase the radiation treatments for the cancer, which seemed to be getting worse by the day. My mother said they should stop making Jake a guinea pig. The more radiation he got, the weaker he became. "Ease his pain," she said. "Just ease his pain." The phone rang. I ran downstairs to answer it. It was my father. I knew why he was calling. I had promised to think about staying with Donna and him for a few weeks. He figured it was time for an answer.

"I could have insisted on the whole summer," he said, reminding me that he had custody for the summer, technically. But he knew how much Jake meant to me. He asked me to understand, said it was not a healthy environment for me to be in. He'd be out on Saturday to pick me up.

"I've had a rough couple of weeks, baby," he said. "Donna and I are through. She's going to Fire Island with a friend. I'm staying in the city to sort things out. Don't make it any harder than it has to be."

So that's it, I thought. *He breaks up with Donna, and I become the most important thing to him. Someone to have around at night, watch TV with, walk on his back when he needs it cracked.* I was still light enough, he said, to walk on his back the way the Japanese do. Too much tension in his spine. He needed a light foot like mine to break through it. I imagined myself stomping. *Enough*, he would say. *That's enough.* And I would keep stomping.

"This may the cruelest, most selfish thing you've ever done," I said, hanging up on him. I was about to call my mother to complain, when I noticed the book Bruce had given Jake lying on the kitchen table. I picked it up, browsed through it. Much of it didn't make sense, but one chapter stopped me.

Everything under heaven has a beginning
which may be thought of as the mother
of all under heaven.
Having realized the mother,
you thereby know her children.

Immediately I called Grandma, told her how bad I was feeling, how bad things were. She already knew, said she'd booked a flight. Then I called my mother, who said she was sorry, really sorry, but she couldn't fight my father. She'd spoken with Glen, who told her there was probably not a judge around who wouldn't side with him.

I called Bruce next, to tell him I'd be leaving. "The whole situation sucks, really sucks," he said, "so why don't we just go to the beach?"

"I'll hide you in my room," he said, as we walked along the shore. "There's a cot you can sleep on." I liked the idea. "Who knows—maybe your father and Donna will get back together by the end of the week and he won't be so concerned about having you around."

"Wishful thinking," I said, reaching for his hand. *The tide rolls in, rolls out, no beginning, no end. The waves wash over me. Stinging my face.*

A streak of lightning flashed in the distance. The rain was sudden. Heavy. Bruce wrapped a large towel around us. His body, wet with fresh rain, felt good against mine as we dashed to the car. I stopped, turned to him. "Kiss me," I said. I wanted to feel the rush of rain down our faces as we kissed.

"What a romantic," said Bruce, kissing my cheek, my eyes, my lips. Whispering that I must have watched the same movies he did.

We kissed more in the car. I let Bruce pull down my bathing suit and kiss my breasts. It felt so good to feel his wet lips on my rain-wet body. He slipped his fingers between my legs, inside my bathing suit, and it felt so good I never felt so good. "Don't stop," I whispered. Fluttering, quivering inside and out. Letting out a moan, a cry. Clutching him until he stopped.

Then I began to cry in his arms. Tears, a flood of joy mixed with pain. "I want to . . ." I couldn't say the words. He held me tighter, said his father was in the city that day, let's go to the boat.

The boat rocked as he kissed me slowly, very slowly, said I was beautiful. Slowly, very slowly, he kissed my neck, my shoulders, my whole body—every inch, it seemed. He knelt, kissed my belly, opened my legs, kissed me more.

Please never stop, I wanted to say, didn't have to say. We lay down on a towel, and he eased his way into me. I was so wet and he felt so wet and warm. "Am I hurting you?" he asked, and I said a little, only please don't stop. Don't ever stop.

"So," Bruce teased me as we lay arm in arm, the boat rocking us, "does this mean we're going steady?"

I kissed his shoulder, reminded him I would be leaving in three days.

He kissed my cheek, said he'd come to the city to spend time with me. "It would get a little boring out here without you." I rolled on top of him, kissed him on the lips and on his shoulders and on his belly. Every inch of him. Bruce sighed, pulled me up, said he wanted to be in me again. I told him I loved the way he felt, so warm and wet, said it hurt just a little, would it always hurt? He pulled out quickly, afraid of coming, put on a condom, slowing down, slowing down so it wouldn't hurt, slowing down so he wouldn't come, not yet, slowing down and playing with me till I was ready, was ready, I said I was ready, no more slowing down I was ready I was ready I was . . . What was that? A siren, Bruce, an ambulance, what was it, oh no oh no it was a siren, Bruce, I know it was an ambulance oh no oh no would it always hurt just a little just a little?

August 6, 1985
Dear Rachel:

I cried when I read your letter. I'm sooo sorry about Jake—I know how much he means to you.

What's going on in the world? I'm sure you've heard about Rock Hudson. It's all anybody talks about here. Somebody started spreading this crazy idea that you can get AIDS from mosquitoes, so half the kids won't go out at night anymore, they're so afraid of getting bitten. Some of the girls in my bunk won't share their lipstick anymore, and one girl keeps all her cosmetics, even her brush and comb, under her pillow during the day. Is that sick?

Now I guess I should tell you that Richie and I broke up for the third time in two weeks, though this time I think it's for good. He says I'm too serious and he can't handle it. Too serious? I argued. I don't understand it, Rachel. You give everything to a guy—your heart, your body—and he doesn't complain about it, just cruises along and makes you believe it's important to him. Then suddenly he says it's "too much." He says he doesn't think it's really a good idea to be serious with someone before he finishes college and med school. It's quite a different tune from the one he was singing at the beginning of the summer.

Anyway, I don't care anymore. I just want the summer to end already. I can't wait to get home. There's another guy here who likes me, but I don't think I can handle it. Imagine that.

Tomorrow Dave and I are sneaking a bus ride to the Bronx to visit Shelly. She's home from the hospital, and it turns out that all she had was mono. (I think I told you that.) He's asked Richie to go a couple of times, but Richie always has an excuse. Tomorrow he's too busy with a tennis match. How could I ever have liked someone who's too busy to be a good friend?

I'm not pregnant, by the way, though don't think I didn't rack my brains over it. Why did I listen to Richie? I couldn't talk to any of the other girls about it, they're such nitwits. Just like they turned on Shelly, they'd turn on me. I know it. But why, I kept thinking, why did I put myself through the agony of worrying whether I was pregnant? Then I got your letter—the same day I finally got my period—and you know what you said? You said you think I'm afraid of the wrong things. And I believe you're right, Rachel. I've been afraid of the wrong things.

Hope Jake starts feeling better. I really miss you.

Love, Laura

One week. The doctors said Jake wouldn't live more than another week. What does it mean to be a week from death? Jake lay in a hospital bed, drifting in and out of sleep. He didn't want to see many people now. Did he know he was dying? The doctors said they knew because the cancer had spread and his kidneys weren't functioning. Every day I visited him, hoping to hear that today, yes, today, he finally peed. Bruce said his testicles were the size of grapefruits. He had never seen anything like it. The doctors said that unless his kidneys started to work, he would die within a week. They knew he was dying, they were so sure of it, because they had the graphs and the test results to prove it. I knew he was dying because he didn't smile anymore. Sometimes he was alert and we could talk and there was a little brightness in his eyes, a faint glimmer of life that made me forget the sour smell his body exuded. Sometimes I could still tell him not to give up, we'd go to France, and I almost believed it.

One week. I had trouble sitting still. I jumped whenever the phone rang. Sleep escaped me. I kept hearing the ambulance, seeing Bruce and myself dress quickly, drive to Jake's house, find no one there. "I should have been there," I said to Bruce as we drove to the hospital.

"Stop beating yourself up," he said to me, and so did Gary, as the three of us sat in the waiting room, waiting waiting waiting until they put Jake in a room. Two days later, he was off to New York City, to a bigger hospital, the one he'd been in and out of during the past six months.

My father tried to comfort me. It was difficult for him; he didn't really know what to say. "Things have a funny way of working out," he said. Staying with him in his Chelsea apartment made it easier for me to visit Jake. I could walk straight across town to the hospital. Bruce went there with me a lot, and we took different streets all the time. I didn't feel much like rushing to the hospital, but once I was there I couldn't leave unless Jake was asleep. Even when he fell asleep while I was sitting with him, I felt funny leaving. *What if he wakes soon?* I'd think, looking at his swollen face. *How will he feel if he wakes and finds me gone?*

We all took turns at the hospital. Grandma and Seymour came in a week earlier, George was coming from San Diego tomorrow, Vivian came yesterday. My grandmother stayed most of the day, took a break for dinner, then came back. We hardly talked; there wasn't much to say. She smoked less than usual, which surprised me. It was as if something in her had stopped. I was at the hospital, in Jake's room, the day she arrived from Tucson. She walked in, took one look at him, and all the color in her face was gone. I was glad he was asleep. Seymour walked closer to the bed than she did, touched Jake's hand, the one that didn't have the IV in it. I left the room with my grandmother, we walked down the corridor to the waiting room, she pulled me close. And she burst into tears. "I've lived too long," she said.

Gary was staying with Marsha and Bruce at their apartment on Hudson Street. When we weren't with Jake, we walked around like zombies. In limbo. In shock. Trying to take some pleasure from the harsh streets. Yesterday I was on the subway, going downtown to meet Bruce and Jason for dinner. It was rush hour, the car was packed, there was one empty seat, scribbled with graffiti. *Someone with AIDS sat here.* It was hot and sticky in the subway car, people were crushed against one another, cramming themselves in, holding on, reading newspapers, and no one would sit in the empty seat. No one, that is, but me.

The tide rolls in rolls out no beginning no end. Ashes to ashes dust to dust. A body lies in a fresh pine box, shrouded, smaller than it seemed in life.

I stared at the coffin, past it, into the space that has no beginning, no end. My grandmother sat next to me, sobbing quietly. If there is a dignity to sorrow, she had it. I hooked my arm in hers, pressed it against me, understanding for the first time her steely distance these past months. She was bracing herself against the thing that was not supposed to happen to a son. Or an uncle in the prime of his life.

I held her tightly, trying to listen to what the rabbi was saying about tragedy and God and the mysteries we cannot fathom, much as we want to. This was not, could not be, Jake in that small wooden box. Any minute the lid would open and up he would rise, beaming, looking nothing at all like the close-lipped putty face I had taken one last glimpse of before the casket was closed. My grandmother did not think I should be allowed to look at the body. My mother did.

Time moves on, no beginning no end. A life becomes memories, stories to share at Thanksgiving or Rosh Hashanah or Passover or late at night over a drink.

To mummify a person, the Egyptians removed the brain through the nose and the rest of his insides through a slit on the side of the body. Only the heart was left.

School opened today, and I felt like walking, instead of taking the bus. I passed my grade school, PS 117, and saw a mess of people—parents, mostly mothers, and children—picketing, boycotting the opening of school. One boy, seven or so, flashed a sign in front of me. No Kids with AIDS in Our Grades. The sign was bigger than he was.

At my school there was a hemophiliac boy, Rob Tyler, who contracted AIDS when he had a transfusion. He had sandy hair and milky-white skin that showed bruises easily. During recess he sometimes sat with Jerry, reading. The lines of protest against Rob's admission were already formed when I got there. I waited for Jerry and Laura before going in.

"Look at this!" Jerry was shaking his newspaper. He opened it to an article about these sheriff's deputies who put on surgical gloves when they escorted a man charged with murder, a man who had AIDS, to and from the courtroom. "Fourteen prospective jurors," he read, "asked to be dismissed from the case." He shook his head, disgusted. "That's really pathetic."

Laura came rushing toward us. "My mother tried to keep me home. I had to lie and tell her I was going to protest."

"You *are* protesting," said Jerry. "You're protesting small-mindedness. And stupidity. And a delusional sense of control. That's what I think it's about. We've lost so much control over our lives. The threat of nuclear war hangs over us, the environment is saturated with pollutants, and then this devastating illness comes along and people think, *Aha! Here's something I can control. Keep "it" away. Lock up the queers, quarantine them.*"

A police car pulled up, a red van behind it. Rob Tyler got out of the van, walked toward the school building, flanked by two policemen. There were jeers.

"Homo!" Philip Kamin's unmistakable voice cried out.

"Asshole!" said Jerry, who was standing near him. Then, locking arms, Laura, Jerry, and I walked through the crowd, into the building.

epilogue

January 28, 1986

Have I been here before?

All day, all night, it's the same image over and over again. At 11:39:13 a.m., the Challenger *is off the ground, gone in a puff of smoke four seconds later. Disintegrated. Burnished in our minds, burned from the screen more quickly than a skywritten word. I keep thinking about Christa McAuliffe, her students, her children, watching her go into the capsule, feeling so proud, so excited. Then what? Numb? Unable to believe, to understand how this could happen?*

Gone in a puff of smoke. I think about Jake, too, up there, the astronaut he once wanted to be. And if he had been up there, he would have died, it would have been fast, he would be a hero.

Jerry and I went to Laura's house after school. We were all so depressed. We kept the TV on, watched the shuttle go up in flames again and again. Jerry wasn't surprised it happened. "Things were going too well," he said. "There was bound to be a disaster sometime." Laura's little sister, Ricki, watched with us. "They're with E.T. now," she said. "E.T. has them."

Laura frowned at her. I smiled, pulled Ricki onto my lap.

Thought about what Jake would say. He would say it's just like February. The wild card. The springlike weather in winter. The snowstorm in April. The death that catches you by surprise.

Have I been here before?

Jake is dead five months, the astronauts less than a day. Bruce will call tonight, and we'll talk about what he did where he was what I did where I was. Today. While we talk, I'll take a gorgeous blue pyramid from my dresser, hold it up to the light. If I watch carefully, pay close attention, I'll see the colors diffuse, blue to gray, gray to smoky marble-white. The trick is to pay attention, not be deceived by the shift in light.

Or language. Once, a long time ago, there was an Old English word, caru, *meaning "sorrow." In the subtle way in which language changes,* caru *became "care," sorrow became a worried state requiring close attention.*

My mother says, "Take care" when I'm out with Bruce.

My father says, "Be careful."

Jake would say, "Pay careful attention." To the subtle shift in morning light. To a late-afternoon breeze carrying a long-forgotten scent.

about the author

A native New Yorker, Deborah Batterman is the author *of Shoes Hair Nails*, a short story collection framed around everyday symbols in our world and their resonance in our lives. She is a Pushcart nominee and her award-winning fiction appears in the Women's National Book Association centennial anthology. Her stories and essays have appeared in anthologies as well as various print and online journals, including *Dr. T. J. Eckleburg Review*, Akashic Books' *Terrible Twosdays*, *Every Mother Has a Story, Vol. 2*, *Open to Interpretation: Fading Light*, and *Mom Egg Review, Vol. 14*. Learn more about her at http://deborahbatterman.com.

SELECTED TITLES FROM SPARKPRESS

SparkPress is an independent boutique publisher delivering high-quality, entertaining, and engaging content that enhances readers' lives, with a special focus on female-driven work.
Visit us at www.gosparkpress.com

The Opposite of Never, Kathy Mehuron, $16.95, 978-1-943006-50-2. Devastated by the loss of their spouses, Georgia and Kenny think that the best times of their lives are long over until they find each other; meanwhile Kenny's teenage stepdaughter, Zelda, and Georgia's friend's son, Spencer, fall in love at first sight—only to fall prey to and suffer opiate addiction together

Trouble the Water, Jackie Friedland, $16.95, 978-1-943006-54-0. When a young woman travels from a British factory town to South Carolina in the 1840s, she becomes involved with a vigilante abolitionist and the Underground Railroad while trying to navigate the complexities of Charleston high society and falling in love.

The Absence of Evelyn, Jackie Townsend, $16.95, 978-1-63152-244-4. Nineteen-year-old Olivia's life takes a turn when she receives an overseas call from a man she doesn't know is her father; her mother Rhonda, meanwhile, haunted by her sister's ghost, must face long-buried truths. Four lives in all, spanning three continents, are now bound together and tell a powerful story about love in all its incarnations, filial and amorous, healing and destructive.

The Half-Life of Remorse, Grant Jarrett, $16.95, 978-1-943006-14-4. Three life-scarred people are brought together to confront each other thirty years after the brutal crime that shattered their lives, and as the puzzle of the past gradually falls together, the truth commands a high price.

The Rules of Half, Jenna Patrick, $16.95, 978-1-943006-18-2. When an orphaned teen claims he's her biological father, Will Fletcher—a manic-depressant who's sworn to never be a parent again—must come to terms with his illness and his tragic past if he is to save her from the streets. This explores what it is to be an atypical family in a small town and to be mentally ill in the wake of a tragedy—and who has the right to determine both.

ABOUT SPARKPRESS

SparkPress is an independent, hybrid imprint focused on merging the best of the traditional publishing model with new and innovative strategies. We deliver high-quality, entertaining, and engaging content that enhances readers' lives. We are proud to bring to market a list of *New York Times* best-selling, award-winning, and debut authors who represent a wide array of genres, as well as our established, industry-wide reputation for creative, results-driven success in working with authors. SparkPress, a BookSparks imprint, is a division of SparkPoint Studio LLC.

Learn more at GoSparkPress.com